A.J. Maguire

DEAD MAGIC

DOUBLE DRAGON

A DOUBLE DRAGON PAPERBACK

ISBN 978-1-78695-492-3

Double Dragon
is an imprint of
Fiction4All

This Edtion Published 2020
Fiction4All
www.fiction4all.com

Cover art by Deron Douglas
www.derondouglas.ca

CHAPTER ONE

For six copper bits and two brass coins, he should have been afforded a window seat. Winslow hid a scowl behind his fist and tried desperately to ignore the whining child just behind him. He thought it might be better if the kid cried or wailed. That would be preferable to the whimpering pitch of the little girl trying to get her mother's attention; but it would not have drowned out the chatter of the woman sitting beside him.

Fates help him, Winslow doubted he would ever forget the sound of Cosata Divenhurst-Lorlain, the newest—and if she dared say so herself, brightest—recruit to the Tormey University of Engineering. Given the tight confines of the train car, the proximity of his barely cushioned seat to hers, and the fact that there were only three other patrons nearby, he understood why she'd chosen him. The three other people included the simpering girl and her mother, and one blissfully snoring older gentleman two seat rows in front of them.

Winslow's strictly polite upbringing barred him from making any unkind remarks about his general disinterest with all things technology. He was a Witch-Born and therefore more prone toward the natural order of things. And, truth be told, Winslow didn't give a damn how water came through a pump, just as long as it was hot enough to fill his bath.

Fates alive! he thought and closed his eyes, *what I wouldn't give for a hot bath and five minutes of quiet.*

"Am I boring you, sir?" Cosata's phlegmy voice penetrated his thoughts again.

It would serve the girl right if he introduced himself now, after three quarters of an hour listening to her prattle. She didn't seem to care or notice that she had to call him "sir" because she hadn't bothered to ask his name. Even if she had, he wouldn't have told her the truth. It was better that no one know that he was Witch-Born, at least until he had checked all of the Warding Pillars in Magnellum. None of the individual House Witches whose lands he inspected would like his trespass, and the Council would most assuredly take offense.

Aside from bringing dishonor and becoming a general headache to his own family, Winslow didn't think there was much the Council could do about it, but Elsie had been adamant about the discretion. And with almost a full year of travel behind him, Winslow could understand why. She wasn't afraid of the Council, she was afraid of the Untalented. There was a low and ominous growl amongst the Untalented people, a discord and a distrust, and all of their blame was shifting toward the Houses.

"It would seem that I must be boring you, since you have the gall to fall asleep."

Winslow felt his left eye twitch and battled down a few snide remarks. Opening his eyes, he looked at her again. She was pretty when she was quiet; pert nose and puckered mouth, but her brown eyes glared at him.

"No, not at all. I find the internal workings of pistons quite fascinating."

The glare turned hard, "I spoke of pistons more than forty minutes ago. You've not paid attention to a word I've said!"

Winslow turned in his seat so that he could face her more directly. To hell with his genteel breeding, he'd had quite enough. "Have you always been socially inept?"

She gasped.

"Or is it simply a custom of your family to presume that whoever is nearest to you must hear your life's story?"

"How dare you!"

"Well, I have to assume that your preoccupation with yourself is either something you were born into, or a matter of your upbringing."

Cosata's chin lifted and she made a half-snorting, half-wheezing sound just before she found her voice again. "And here I thought you were an educated gentleman. Come to find out, you're just a . . ."

Her words were cut short as they were both thrown forward. Winslow's face smashed into the seat in front of him. He felt the bridge of his nose snap and bit down on his tongue. Vision blurred and face throbbing, he barely grabbed hold of the seat before the train car pitched leftward. He was airborne a second later as a violent jolt slammed through the car.

The fabric of the seatback tore under his grip and Winslow finally came out of his daze. Summoning his magic, he tried to prepare for the next crash. An instant later, the car behind them came barreling through the rear end of the cabin.

His body bounced off the ceiling and he was tossed out of his seat.

He hit the next set of seats at a horizontal angle. His temple knocked into the corner of an armrest with unforgiving force. Searing pain flashed through his vision and he saw dazzling sparkles just before his entire body got wedged into the foot space between two rows of seats. Grunting in pain and trying to find his focus, Winslow was almost too late in noticing the threat.

The force of impact between the two train cars made an accordion out of the iron and copper frame. He felt the pressure of the seat legs against his back and knew he was about to be crushed.

With a shout of mingled fear and anger, Winslow shoved back against it, calling on his Witch-Born Talent for more strength than he'd ever summoned before. Metal screeched against metal and the grind of derailed wheels against rocky ground throbbed through the iron floor. He concentrated on his Talent as the car began to fold around him. And somewhere else, somewhere close by, Winslow heard the distinct sound of Cosata Divenhurst-Lorlain choking on a terrified sob.

Gritting his teeth, Winslow prayed the Fates would be merciful.

***

Valeda Quinlan hurtled through the entrance of Delgora Hall, propelled forward by the hem of her borrowed skirt—which she had just managed to step on. She heard the wretched thing rip, which caused her to gasp, but she was too busy trying to catch herself to care. Her beloved but much-worn portfolio flew out of her hands just seconds before she fell headlong onto the marble floor. The impact smacked into her palms, jolted through her arms, and bruised her left knee.

By some miracle, she had managed to keep from landing on her nose, and praised the Fates that she wouldn't have to meet with House Witch Delgora with a purple and swollen face. After a dazed moment she realized that her papers had snapped free of their hemp binding and were now littered across the floor. Two Delgora servants rushed to help pick them up, more concerned with clearing the marble walkway than the order they should be in.

Valeda made a valiant effort not to curse at them because they were only trying to help, and hurried back to her feet. The unfamiliar heeled boots—also on loan—made her left ankle roll and she hissed in mingled irritation and pain. So help her, she was going to throttle Margaretta for insisting that she wear the outfit.

"Thank you," she said, flustered. She checked the far end of the grand hall before taking the piles of leaflets. To her relief, the large, plush House Seat was empty, meaning that House Witch Delgora had not been witness to Valeda's tumble.

"Are you all right, Miss?"

"Yes, thank you." Valeda paused, startled to find so few bodies occupying the room. While she was pleased that she hadn't just made a fool of herself in front of a score of well-to-do Untalented Court members, it wasn't normal to have only six people inside a great hall. Especially if two of those six were servants. She spotted three black and white chainmail tunics at the far end of the room, signifying that the men wearing them were Warders, which only heightened Valeda's curiosity.

"What is going on?" Valeda looked to the servant beside her, only to discover that he wasn't a servant.

Being the lead writer for the *Tormey Regular*, her job required her to know the faces of every dignitary in Magnellum. Her embarrassment resurfaced as she recognized the blunt-toothed smile and slick blond hair of Montgomery Taven; Ambassador of House Witch Minne Orzebet.

"Honestly? I've no idea." Montgomery nodded to the House Seat. "Vicaress Leona mentioned something about opening the gardens for tea."

"Where is House Witch Elsie Delgora?"

"I've heard rumors that she is overseeing the construction of an ark."

Valeda felt a thrill shoot up her spine. *So it's true,* she thought. *House Witch Delgora really is building a haven.* Montgomery shook his head in bafflement, clearly unaware of what sort of madness could force a Witch to such an extreme. Valeda, however, had a clue. Or, well, it was a hunch, really. But it was a hunch that she believed with every fiber of her being.

Magic, the God of Magnellum, was gone.

Valeda could sense his absence as though she were a Witch-Born herself. She just couldn't prove it. Yet.

Forcing herself to laugh, she busied her hands by making a neat stack of her papers, "I thought that was a joke."

"No, no. No joke. It's about six miles south of here." Montgomery's mouth seemed to tighten for a moment. "I've been waiting two days to speak with the Witch or the Consort, but they will not allow 'outsiders' to visit the construction site."

She mentally noted the wounded pride in his voice. "Two days?"

"But I hear the Witch and Consort are to be present for the tea gathering, so I suppose that's something."

"Yes, that's something." Valeda fought a wince because the words sounded so lame. She was distinctly outclassed by the Ambassador and she knew it. She'd interviewed such well-known men and women before, but was always reminded of her little one-bedroomed apartment when they stood so close. Men like Ambassador Taven had apartments in manors where their respected House Witches resided, as well as private homes of their own.

The Ambassador seemed to sense her discomfort because he gave her a compassionate smile and bowed his head, "How rude of me, jabbering away without proper introduction. My name is Montgomery Taven, though you probably already knew that. Friends and pretty young ladies, such as yourself, are permitted to call me Monty."

There was nothing lascivious about the introduction from the tall, dignified man beside her, and Valeda decided almost instantly that she liked him. He was older in the refined sort of way that most Witch-Born grew into, as though time itself had nothing but kindness to offer the man. His smile was gentle, crinkling his eyes into a warm, blue twinkle, and though she knew him to be ten years her senior, Valeda couldn't help but think him handsome. Immaculately dressed in shades of navy, Monty was trimmed with coppery tones. The fringe of his waistcoat was lined with the color, and she was fairly certain that the buttons on his jacket were, in fact, made of highly polished copper. The handle of his cane matched the buttons, glinting up at her in the sunlight.

Copper was apparently in fashion, or so Margaretta had informed her, and House Witch Delgora had a keen eye for such things.

"*You can't go insulting the Witch before you've even opened your mouth. You'll do enough of that when you begin to harass her with your questions.*" Margaretta had said it all so sensibly that Valeda had listened.

Thus, she'd allowed her friend to festoon her in the cream and caramel two-layered skirt. Margaretta could not afford the actual color copper, which she'd bemoaned for half a day before settling on the outfit Valeda now wore. Cream underskirt of satin, showing class and modesty, and a lacey caramel overskirt, to show color and vibrancy, added to a terrifyingly low-cut bodice of matching cream. Valeda had tuned the woman out, which she lamented because if she'd been listening she might have paid more attention to the fact that the skirts were an inch and a half too long.

By Fates, Valeda was never going to let another woman dress her again.

Realizing that Monty was waiting for her own introduction, Valeda blushed and stammered, inwardly kicking herself for getting distracted by something as inane as fashion; "Valeda Quinlan, from the *Tormey Regular*."

"The *Tormey Regular*?" Monty sounded genuinely surprised. "Is Tormey House planning some kind of alliance or union with Delgora?"

"Oh, no, no," Valeda said, feeling her face color even more. "That is, I'm not acquainted with House politics enough to say. I'm here on . . . other business."

A blond eyebrow quirked up at this and Montgomery hummed. It wasn't an altogether unpleasant "hum", but she recognized the curiosity in him and searched desperately for a distraction. In truth, her boss would be quite displeased to learn that her three-week vacation was really following the one lead to the one story he'd demanded she forget. *The one story*, she thought, *that affects every House Land in Magnellum.*

It had been eight years since the last time Magic, the man-god, had walked in plain sight of his people. Eight years since he had attended a noble Witch-Born birth and bestowed the Talent onto a new subject, and while Magic was known as a capricious sort of god, he'd never been absent from Magnellum for so long. Valeda could sense that something was amiss. There was an ominous feeling to the very air around her, a churning in her gut that couldn't let the story go. Korman Poutre, owner of the *Tormey Regular*, could threaten her with her job all he liked, but Valeda had to know the truth.

Spotting the tear in the hem of her skirt, Valeda seized the change of topic, "Oh, Margaretta is going to kill me. She spent a month's salary on this outfit."

"Ah, the vagaries of borrowed clothing," Montgomery clucked his tongue at the ripped fabric. "If it helps, I can testify to Miss Margaretta that the skirt plotted against the toe of your shoe and lost the battle."

Laughing, Valeda shook her head, "I doubt it would help."

"Ambassador Taven," a soft, feminine voice intruded on their conversation.

Valeda turned, startled to find that Vicaress Leona had managed to approach them without her noticing. Dipping into an instant curtsy, she heard Montgomery greet the Vicaress with something that sounded like affection in his voice.

Copper was not a highlight in Leona's garb, Valeda noticed that straight off. The girl was resplendent in rich greens, so deep and constant that Valeda imagined she'd sprouted from the jungles of Delgora. To Valeda's envy, Leona's hair shone healthy and bright in the sun, making perfect golden ringlets that brushed her shoulders.

No one should be allowed to be so beautiful, she thought.

"The gardens are prepared." Leona gestured toward the western side of the grand hall, a hall that, to Valeda's dismay, only served to feed her sense of inadequacy.

Great, high windows, all of them open, with massive pillars running the length of the room to the raised dais and ornate House Seat. Everything was a mesh of marble and brass fixings and Valeda thought again about her little apartment.

Outclassed, she told herself, definitely outclassed.

"If you will both follow me," Leona half turned but paused at Valeda's squeak of alarm.

"Oh, my Lady, I mean Vicaress, I am just . . ."

Monty interrupted her by taking possession of her elbow. "Miss Quinlan is my guest. An Untalented, but purely charming guest. I trust the House Witch will not mind the added company?"

"No, not at all." Leona appeared highly amused by this turn of events and gestured for them to follow.

At the suave and also amused gesture from Monty, Valeda began to do so, allowing him to escort her through Delgora Hall. Korman would wheeze with laughter at the sight of his pants-preferring, mud-diving, get-dirty-if-you-have-to, star reporter being treated like a dignitary. Valeda herself was having trouble with a fit of nervous giggles, but somehow managed to keep her reactions limited to a smile.

"You didn't have to do that," she whispered to Monty.

They passed through the garden doors and into a canopy of large, jungle leaves. Flowers bloomed everywhere, peppering the greenery with bright splashes of pink, yellow and purple. Were it not for the humidity, which made unpleasant prickles of sweat bead over her spine and pool in the hallow places of her body, it would have been the most beautiful thing she'd ever seen in person.

"Nonsense," Monty whispered back to her. "We cannot have Miss Margaretta's best skirt sacrificed for nothing. Besides, I've been here two wretched days. In my estimation, the Witch owes me for my time."

CHAPTER TWO

It was the dripping that woke him up. Warm and wet, he couldn't see what it was that kept splattering against his neck, but in the darkness of his metal cocoon Winslow could hazard a guess. He'd managed to make a pocket of space with his magic, just big enough that he hadn't been crushed to death. But as his Talent had waned, the train car had collapsed around him.

His right foot throbbed. Sharp metal tore into his skin when he tried to move it.

"Mother, Maiden and Crone!" he hissed and tried to relax.

He needed to concentrate. He needed to breathe. But the breathing part was hampered by what felt like two tons of pressure aimed directly at his chest. In the blackness of his little space, he could hear an alarming crackling sound in his shallow breaths. Leaning back against the bite of cold metal, Winslow closed his eyes and summoned his Talent again.

He could sense it at the core of his being, faint from over-use but still there. Slowly, meticulously, he took an inventory of his injuries. His magic led him, pinpointing several lacerations, a fracture in his left elbow, a large contusion on the left side of his skull where the seat had snapped free of the train and hit him. *Concussion, more than likely, but not nearly as disconcerting as the collapsed lung,* he thought. His right leg was broken in no fewer than three places, mostly near his foot, where the floor of the train car had been sandwiched against the wall of the train.

"Have mercy," he winced and wheezed at the same time.

Another droplet hit his jaw and Winslow focused. The map his magic had made of his battered body consumed his mind. He could see it, feel it, as he commanded his Talent to mend the lung. It was an agonizing moment as he bent time, speeding up the recovery process for the injury and he cried out from the pain of it. The sound of his own voice seemed very small, as though the train had swallowed him whole.

His lung patched and inflated and he took his first full breath of air since the crash.

After three deep breaths, Winslow concentrated his Talent on escaping from the train. The window would have been near his feet, or at least, that's where he estimated it would be. When he'd landed on the floor, his head had been half in the aisle and his body managed to lodge itself there. He could feel indentations in the metal floor where his elbows pushed back against the crumpling train.

He heard a small whimpering sound, muffled through the metal surrounding him. Winslow flinched, his heart twisting at the anguish he heard. It came again, originating from somewhere to his left. Craning his neck back, he squinted at the dark, calling on his magic to pull his vision into sharp focus.

A jagged tear made a vent in the iron floor, exposing shadowed ground that looked impossibly far away. The tear was a good two feet from him, but by the angle of it Winslow could calculate that their car was jammed up on top of something.

"Hello?" His voice was raspy, sounding eerie even to him.

A sniffle and a light movement came from just beyond the tear, and Winslow's stomach dropped. *The little girl and her mother,* he thought.

"Hello?" He said, more forcefully this time.

"My hand is stuck and Mother's asleep."

Winslow closed his eyes again, his chest locked in grief. *Fates have mercy,* he prayed, *may that woman just be unconscious.*

"What's your name?" He tested his moving room, hissing as his fractures came roaring to life.

"Mirabella."

"It's nice to meet you, Mirabella. My name is Winslow."

Gritting his teeth, he forced his Talent to mend his body. He had to go one injury at a time, but none of the fractures were quite as agonizing as the lung had been. His magic still needed rest, but little Mirabella needed rescuing now, too. And if he was fully honest with himself, Winslow was starting to get claustrophobic.

"Are you hurt?" Mirabella asked.

"Only a little," he bit back a curse when he realized he couldn't fix his leg until he freed it from the bent metal.

"Mother says men swear a lot when they're in pain because it makes them feel better."

He smiled briefly before pressing his palms to the seat half folded on top of him. "I don't know that it makes us feel better, but it certainly lets us focus on something else. Are you hurt, Mirabella?"

"My hand is stuck and I can't feel my fingers."

"What's it stuck in?"

"I don't know, I can't see around Mother's head."

Winslow fought back the images that brought to mind. Imagining the girl staring at her dead mother for however long he'd been unconscious, he felt terrible that he'd been so frustrated with her before. Of course, he didn't know that the mother was dead. He prayed she wasn't, but someone had lost enough blood for it to drip into his face. It seemed uncharitable to hope that fate belonged to Cosata Divenhurst-Lorlain.

"Mirabella, I'm going to move the seat that's on top of me. There's going to be a lot of noise. Try not to be frightened."

He waited for her to acknowledge him before he pushed at the seat. It was a joint effort of his natural strength and his Talent to move the thing, straining muscles and magic to an almost painful point. Iron scratched into iron, screeching in a spine-tingling pitch. Something shifted higher up in the train car, slamming into the row of seats as it came free. Winslow felt the shock of it rattle into his arms and through his shoulders but didn't let go.

Mirabella screamed in pain and Winslow stopped, panting and alarmed. "Mirabella?"

She continued to cry, great gasping wails, and Winslow panicked. He tore his foot out of the vice it was stuck in, shouting in mingled fear and pain as the metal tore deep into his leg. All the fractures in the offending appendage shifted to squeeze through the opening. He fought his way up to the tear in the floor, placed his good foot on the jagged lip and shimmied his way up to where Mirabella should have been.

He found a booted foot first: feminine, with a half an inch of pointed heel and several dainty buckles up the side. By its size, he could tell that this was the mother. Carefully, trying not to jostle the train any more than he already had, Winslow reached out and circled the woman's ankle with one hand. He concentrated on the sensation of touch and tried to ignore Mirabella's hiccupping cries.

A rapid, stuttered pulse beat into his palm and he exhaled in relief.

The mother was alive.

"Mirabella?"

"My hand . . ."

Fates alive! He wished he could see through metal. "I know you're hurt, but I need you to be brave. Can you be brave?"

"Mother says being brave means you look at the thing that scares you most and tell it to scram."

Winslow smiled and wiped blood and grease from his brow. "I like your mother. Do you think you can be brave?"

"Yes."

"Good." He paused and bent to duck his head through the hole.

Their train had leapt the tracks. In the shadow of their particular car, Winslow could see the railway tracks more than five feet away. The ferny, mountainous landscape of southern Clenci meshed with the white-washed gravel that held the train tracks. He was grateful for the sudden brush of late autumn air through the vent on two accounts. For one, it smelled a damn sight better than the wreck of the train; and for another, it meant less of a chance of a fire. At the moment, he had quite enough trouble to cope with.

"Mr. Winslow?"

"One moment, Mirabella."

He didn't want to move anything on the inside of the train again. Fates only knew what else might fall on top of them if he did. They didn't have time for him to climb on top and work his way down to them, either. Pulling his head back inside the train, Winslow glanced between the snaggle-toothed metal and feminine boot. There was no way to help Mirabella or her mother until he could see what he was dealing with.

Setting his hands against the edge of torn iron, he summoned his magic once more, growling as he ripped the train floor further. He kept tearing, folding the iron away, ignoring the sharp bite of broken metal in his palms. His own blood started a slow roll around his wrists, soaking into the sleeves of his dress shirt. The tan, linen material turned a rusty color at the cuffs and for a moment he turned his attention to that instead of the strain. Then he redoubled his efforts, widening the hole until he reached the mother's knee.

Pausing for breath, Winslow balanced on the shredded floor and considered the tangle of iron and woman before him. The best way to get the girl and her mother out of the train was just to continue ripping the hole in the floor, and then lower them down. But Mirabella's hand was stuck on something and he had to get around the mother to see properly.

With a resigned sigh, Winslow got back to work. Bracing himself on either side of the hole, he peeled back the floor, pushing warped curls of iron away until he encountered Mirabella's leg. Then he continued further, inch by painstaking inch, scooting his own body along for better balance.

He found the trapped hand first. A little arm in pansy-printed sleeves led up to the seat just beside them. A seat that had come loose and now sandwiched Mirabella's hand to the train floor. Gingerly, slowly, Winslow worked the metal away from her hand. It was more than broken, he realized with a pang of sympathy, it was crushed.

"Mr. Winslow?" Mirabella's voice was closer now, and he could hear the tremble of fear in it.

"Just call me Winslow." He freed the hand and carefully pulled it away from the seat.

"Are you a Witch-Born?"

"Would it matter if I was?" Grunting in effort, he pushed at the metal caging them in, dragging it back and away, and shoving with his shoulder when it got too high.

"I can't imagine an Untalented man staying behind to free me."

"Nonsense. There are some perfectly sensible Untalented men who would do everything they could to save you." His fingers found a shock of curly hair and he breathed in relief. With another two bends and rips he revealed her face and, panting, tried to grin at her. "Hello there, Miss Mirabella. Would you like to get out of the train now?"

She nodded at him, her green eyes blinking.

"Excellent. Scoot closer to me and I'll show you the way out."

Careful not to jostle her mother too much, Mirabella shimmied her way toward him. When she reached the lip of the hole, her eyes grew wide with surprise. He knew she was still in pain; she had to be with her hand the way it was. Still, she didn't cry out when he took her by the arm and lowered her down. Even with his body stretched as far as it would go, it was still a drop, but aside from a small *oof* on impact, Mirabella kept calm.

The mother—Fates be praised—wasn't stuck on anything. Winslow pulled her by the waist, then fought to sling her limp form over one shoulder. When he was confident she was secure, he lowered himself until he dangled from the awkwardly positioned train car.

It really is a drop, he thought, as he stared past his boots and at the ground. He tried to calculate if his magic could withstand a time-bend, and realized that if he tried that, he'd never recover from it. Grimacing, he took a deep breath and let go.

His still broken foot hit the ground first and he yelped. His body collapsed under the weight of Mirabella's mother and jolts of pain shot up and down his leg. Dizzy sparks overwhelmed his vision when his head smacked into pebbly ground. Dazed, hissing in anguish, Winslow stared up at the underbelly of the train car.

"Mother, Maiden and Crone," he muttered.

CHAPTER THREE

She's important.

Elsie tugged on her earlobe, knowing the voice hadn't been audible to anyone else, but feeling self-conscious just the same. Despite the rumors that she was going crazy, Elsie knew this voice; had known it all her life. From the moment she was born, magic had been a part of her, growing with her, sharpening as she'd learn to use the Talent inherent to her race. But until recently, it hadn't manifested itself in such a clear, undeniable way.

Her.

Looking up, Elsie watched Leona escort Ambassador Taven and a mousy-looking woman into the gardens. Since she knew Magic wasn't trying to point out Leona, Elsie focused on the other woman.

Cropped dark-brown hair with tints of red that warmed under the sun curled in disarray around the woman's head. She looked stylish without appearing to fuss over it, which meant there were more important things on her agenda. Dove-gray eyes flicked over the gardens, widening as though she were startled and impressed. There was a bird-like quality to the woman, gentle and small curves in her oval face, a slightly pointed chin, and a mouth that looked a smidgen small, but when taken with the rest of her face was proportioned just right.

As they neared the gondola where the table had been arranged, Elsie relaxed in her lattice chair and surveyed the woman openly. She was, after all, the House Witch of Delgora and did not have to apologize for taking an interest in an uninvited guest.

Whoever had dressed the poor thing should have been shot. The caramel-colored skirt didn't complement her hair and the cream lacing almost exactly matched her skin. Something red would have looked better.

"You've got that displeased look again."

Elsie smiled just as Dorian's hand squeezed her shoulder. She'd known he was coming but hadn't heard his approach. With a fluid movement he bent to kiss her cheek before settling in the chair beside her. For a moment, Elsie allowed herself to bask in the feel of her husband's presence. Reaching out, she took hold of his hand and felt the purr of his magic through his skin. He smiled back at her before turning his attention to the approaching emissary.

"Montgomery Taven." His mouth twitched down and she sensed his annoyance. "No doubt bringing more recriminations from my stepmother."

"He could be here on your father's business." Elsie squeezed his hand in what she hoped was reassurance.

"Father would have come on his own."

They quieted as Leona presented their guests, gesturing first to Montgomery, who gave them a perfect bow in greeting. His copper buttons gleamed in the sunlight and Elsie calculated that his beautiful coat was going to have him sweating before the tea was served. As nice as he looked, the thickly embroidered material wasn't practical for the Delgora tropics.

No, Elsie thought. *Poor Taven is better suited for the high woodlands of Orzebet House.* Situated on the furthest northern border of Magnellum, Orzebet lands had some of the longest winters around.

"You look splendid, Ambassador Taven," Elsie said. "Those buttons are quite clever."

"You flatter me, Lady Delgora." Montgomery's cheeks flushed, either from heat or pleasure, and he bowed again.

With deliberate movements, Elsie turned to regard the woman beside him. Up close, there was an undeniable shine to her, something unnatural that seemed to warm out through her skin. Elsie met her gaze directly and held it, seeing the anxiousness in her but nothing that could explain the strange glow.

She's Fated.

Startled, Elsie reflexively tightened her grip on Dorian's hand. She'd never known an Untalented to be Fated before. The Fates normally delved into the lives of the Witch-Born, leaving the Untalented to their own devices. Dorian squeezed her hand back, helping her to focus on propriety again.

"And who is this?" Dorian nodded to the woman in question.

"Ah, I do beg forgiveness. This is Miss Valeda Quinlan of the *Tormey Regular*. She has been a delightful distraction in the waiting hall." Montgomery emphasized the word "waiting", letting them know he was peeved about how long they'd left him.

Elsie ignored the implied accusation.

"The *Tormey Regular*?" Elsie smiled and gestured for them to be seated. "I've read several articles from that distinguished paper."

"You have, my Lady?" Valeda's eyes widened in surprise, but she managed to take her seat beside Montgomery.

"Yes, we Witch-Born do learn how to read, Miss Quinlan." Elsie continued to study the woman, who flushed a painfully bright pink under the scrutiny.

"No, of course, my Lady. I only meant that . . . well, Tormey is so far away. I wouldn't have thought a person of your distinction would have the time to bother." Valeda bit her lower lip, glanced at Montgomery, then Dorian, and finally back to Elsie.

Her mind mapped out Magnellum. *Tormey House,* she thought. Eastern Magnellum. She really didn't know much about the Tormey family. However, those lands were very popular with the Untalented and Elsie had a particular interest in its Universities.

"I take an interest in all of Magnellum, Miss Quinlan," Elsie said. "Isn't that right, Ambassador?"

"It would appear so," Taven said. He was too well-bred to squirm, but she had the distinct feeling that he wanted to. The attention of the table moved to him and Elsie spotted a bead of sweat rolling from his temple. The poor man was sweltering in that coat. If she asked him to, he would likely take the thing off, regardless of the social faux pas that would make. One did not dress down in the company of a Witch.

Elsie felt a wave of humid air pass over her and glanced at the garden. Strong purple and pink hues overwhelmed the greenery in the space, still keeping the jungle feel with the hibiscuses in constant bloom. There was only one bush that looked awkward in the bunch, set nearest to the gondola and small by comparison; a rose bush. Her mother had determined to have one many years ago, but it was Brochan Delgora-Fie, Elsie's father, who had managed to bring a potted rose into the tropics.

Leona kept the thing alive, mostly by her gentle willpower, or so Elsie thought. For years it had been a symbol of pain for Elsie; a dark reminder that the ambitions of men could end in murder. Her heart ached for her parents and she took a deep breath.

"Tell us, Ambassador, what news my stepmother sends." Dorian slouched in his chair.

"Lady Orzebet wishes to meet with you both at Winter Tournament." Taven remained poised but sweating, inclining his head just-so as he made the request.

"We were not intending on going to Winter Tournament," Dorian said, glancing at Elsie.

Elsie's mind went to the ark. Seven long years of construction and they were nearly done. There was an ominous growling in the back of her mind, a warning that they might not be done in time. That she would fail all of them, that she had somehow misinterpreted Magic's guidance, but even as she contended these thoughts, there was a greater fear. The ark was a colossal, sprawling, floatable dome of brass and iron, built to house many people and withstand any assault; and the Fates only knew why she'd had to build it. Magic only told her so much, shedding light only when it pleased him. She wasn't certain if he was just capricious or if he was hiding something from her.

Maybe she really was going crazy.

***

On a scale of one to ten, with ten being the most bizarre, Valeda decided that House Witch Delgora qualified for an eleven. She was beautiful, make no mistake, with the richest, blackest, shiniest hair Valeda had ever laid eyes on, and exotically curved features offset by lush eyelashes, perfectly arched eyebrows and a full mouth that seemed always to be half-smiling. But there was something preoccupied in the steady, umber gaze the woman sent her, something that made Valeda nervous.

Rumor had it that Elsie spent time as a Bedim Assassin prior to her ascension to House Witch. The league of assassins that plagued Magnellum for so long had suddenly disappeared from society—again, some eight years ago, around the time that Magic, the man-god, had last been seen. No one could say how or why they had gone and the noble Houses of Magnellum were just as tight-lipped about it as they were about the matter of Magic Himself.

With House Witch Delgora steadily appraising her from across the table, Valeda swallowed hard and tried to remember the last time an Untalented had been assassinated for political reasons.

By Fates! What was I thinking, travelling all this way for a story no one wants me to tell. It's ludicrous!

"We're in the middle of a project that requires special attention," Dorian said.

Consort and husband to the House Witch, Saldorian Dominic Gregorian Delgora-Feverrette was as much of a mystery to Valeda as his wife. While there was nothing peculiar about his direct gaze or his cagey smile, Lord Dorian had a manner about him that would not be crossed. His steely gray eyes remained fastened on poor Monty, who did a commendable job at dancing through the delicate politics at their table.

What Valeda knew about the people before her was a matter of public record. Saldorian Delgora-Feverrette was the son of Lord Rorant Orzebet and Lady Jessamine Feverrette, who had a scandalous affair in spite of the fact that Jessamine was married at the time. Lord Dorian's stepmother, Lady Minne Orzebet, was the leading contender against his marriage to House Witch Delgora, which made the request Monty had delivered less than friendly.

"Vicaress Leona assured me that your project was of the utmost importance," Monty said. "Otherwise you would not have left me for two full days without explanation. But nothing could be more important than representing Delgora at the Winter Tournament."

Valeda shifted in her seat and wondered where the tea was. She thought she might be more comfortable if she could bury her face in a cup and pray they forgot she was there. Beside the table was a small serving cart covered with a clean linen cloth, but there was no servant nearby to manage the tea. She could see the telltale lumps of carafe, cups and other such utensils beneath the cloth and frowned, wondering what they were waiting for.

"Thank you, Ambassador Taven, for your concern about Delgora House affairs," Lord Dorian said and leaned back in his chair. "I'm sure Winter Tournament will get along just fine without us."

Monty blustered, finally losing his composure. "But . . . will you send anyone at all?"

Elsie suddenly lifted her right hand to tug at her earlobe. Valeda blinked, startled to see that the Witch was wearing one long, sateen glove that stretched all the way to her shoulder. It was ivory, matching the breezy dress that Valeda hadn't noticed until that moment, but notable since it was the only glove the woman was wearing. Even if gloves were in fashion—which Margaretta would have made certain Valeda knew—the humidity in Delgora made the thing unnecessary.

The House Witch gently pinched her earlobe, looking distracted from the argument at the table.

"We hadn't discussed sending anyone," Lord Dorian said.

"But the Tournament is three months away!"

"Tell Lady Orzebet that we will be happy to entertain her at Delgora House during the Tournament," Elsie said.

Lord Dorian stiffened, sending his wife a sharp glance.

"We cannot guarantee when we will arrive and we certainly won't stay for long, but we will make an appearance." The House Witch stood up suddenly and Valeda gasped at the speed with which the men moved to follow her.

Realizing that she was the only one still seated, Valeda blushed and carefully got to her feet. All eyes were on her, she knew, but she was captivated by the gaze of Elsie Delgora. There was a troubled look to the woman, something that made Valeda shiver in apprehension.

"There are things I must attend to now," the Witch said, keeping her focus on Valeda as she spoke. "Tomorrow morning we will discuss what you came here for, Miss Quinlan. Until then, you will be a guest here in Delgora Manor. Leona will see that you are properly cared for."

"I do hope I have not caused you any distress," Monty started to apologize, but Elsie cut him off.

"No, indeed. I always enjoy when an Untalented presumes to school me in Magnellum politics, Ambassador Taven. It quite makes my day."

"That was not my intention, my Lady. You have my sincere . . ."

"It does not matter, Montgomery Taven." Elsie turned away from them, but her last sentence carried over the sounds of birds and gentle brushing of leaves through the garden. "The prattling of society at large will make little difference to anyone very soon."

As she walked away from the table, the Witch waved her gloved hand, sending the serving cart into sudden motion. The cloth flipped back, the tea set lifted and floated, settling on the table with exactly the right place settings. Delicate saucers, pansy-blue patterned cups, all of it arranged itself without any noise or fuss. Valeda had a creeping sensation crawl up her spine as she stared at her own cup, now filled with amber, cinnamon-scented liquid.

"My wife does not care for tea," Lord Dorian said, mostly to Valeda. "But she knows the apple spice is a favorite of the Ambassador."

Beside her, Monty squirmed and pulled a kerchief from his vest pocket. He wiped the sweat from his forehead and muttered a further apology. Valeda glanced between Monty and the Consort, sensing the unspoken challenge that drifted between them. Monty had been terribly rude, but the Witch had abused the Ambassador's time by forcing him to wait. Valeda understood the precarious alliances that held Magnellum together. Each House brought different bits of trade, different engineers and resources to the table, and each one was out to secure their own power and prestige.

With thirteen distinct House Lands fragmenting Magnellum, there were no fewer than sixty-seven embargos cutting the merchant business down. Of course, there was a thriving black market in every town, but the Warders were constantly raiding them. Valeda had done an article on the embargo of special soaps from Clenci in her homeland of Tormey. One particularly fidgety shop owner she'd interviewed had made the simplest and perfect summation of the problem: "I couldn't care less if Lady Tormey's got her britches twisted over Lady Clenci's marital decisions. Their personal opinions haven't got anything to do with trade."

"Please extend my apologies to the House Witch," Monty sighed and shook his head. "Your announcement took me by surprise and I thought . . .”

“You thought her years living as an Untalented might have blinded her to the politics in Magnellum,” Lord Dorian finished for him.

“Well, yes. She does seem out to defy everyone.” Monty stared at the place she’d left through. “There are many in the Council who would like to befriend Delgora, but she is making that very difficult.”

Valeda listened raptly. House tensions were nothing new, but Elsie Delgora was still a figure of speculation. *Years living in disguise as an Untalented,* she thought. *So not all of the stories I’d read had been exaggerated.*

“Let me make something very clear,” Lord Dorian leaned forward to adjust his teacup, pausing before he continued. “My wife may have lived humbly for many years. She may have been forced to endure more than any Witch-Born has ever conceived of in her lifetime, but she is nobler than any member of the Council because of it.”

The force of his statement caused Monty to rock back on his heels. With a nod of his head, Lord Dorian bid them good day and left.

CHAPTER FOUR

He woke with the train still hovering overhead. There was warmth and light where there shouldn't be and Winslow's groggy mind struggled to catch up. Beyond the train, just to the left, he could see starlight and the moon shining through high treetops. The train itself was a smudge of tangled iron in the shadows above him, looking like a jagged, toothy mouth gaping wide.

Shuddering, Winslow rolled to his left, flinching as pain shot through his leg.

He still needed to fix that.

He'd been about to access his magic when he spotted Mirabella. The little girl scurried out of the tree line with an armload of wood. Depositing the wood in a pile just beside a small fire, she propped her hands on her hips and harrumphed. She hadn't noticed he was awake yet, she was that intent on her job. Apparently deciding the fire wasn't right, Mirabella took a bit of wood from the pile and carefully pushed it into the fire. She bent so close to the flames that he feared she'd get singed.

"Hello, Miss Mirabella," he said, levering himself onto one elbow.

Gasping, she whirled to face him. "Mr. Winslow!"

She charged forward, throwing herself onto him and nearly sending him back down. Surprised, Winslow caught her with one arm, realizing a second later that she was hugging him. Not only hugging him, as she buried her face in his shoulder, but crying.

Awkward and uncomfortable, Winslow gave her little form a tight squeeze and tried to murmur something reassuring. "Did you build that fire all by yourself?"

She nodded against his shoulder and tightened her arms around his neck. Her voice was muffled when she spoke, "I used Mommy's matches. She'll be mad when she wakes up."

Winslow spotted the still unconscious mother near his feet. "No, no. I'm sure she'll be very proud of you. How's your hand?"

Mirabella sniffled and pulled away from him. Tilting her head to the side, she gave him a puzzled look. "It's been better since I moved you."

He blinked in surprised. Normally he had to be conscious of accessing his magic, but as Mirabella showed him her hand it was clear that she was healed. She turned it over, stretching out all of her fingers, each little bone set perfectly where it should be. Winslow focused inward, suddenly afraid that he'd spent the last of his Talent without meaning to, but he recognized the healthy purr of his rejuvenated magic and relaxed.

"You really are a Witch-Born, aren't you." Mirabella's green eyes were wide with wonder.

"I am." Winslow carefully sat up. His fractured leg throbbed to life and he grimaced. With one hand on the aching limb, he commanded his Talent to mend the wounds.

Several soft, unsettling pops resounded from his body as bones shifted, correcting themselves. He felt each one of them and did his best not to swear in front of the girl. The sudden relief from pain left him shaky, but he winked at Mirabella anyway. She gave him a wobbly smile before glancing at her mother.

"She woke up but didn't talk," Mirabella shifted on her feet nervously. "Can you help her?"

Winslow patted Mirabella's shoulder and moved to kneel beside the mother. She looked alarmingly pale and pasty, strong bones in a broad face that bordered masculine. He'd thought at first that there were too many shadows playing across her features, but realized that her lips really were tinged blue.

With a deep breath, he splayed his hands over her chest and belly and summoned his magic. Each injury glowed in his mind, showing him the ruptured spleen, the blood collecting where it shouldn't be, and Winslow got to work. Just under his left thumb, he could feel the steadying beat of the woman's heart. It stuttered at first, and then leveled out, increasing in strength as each torn bit of tissue repaired itself.

Several vertebrae had snapped along the woman's spine and he had a sudden vision of her covering Mirabella with her own body as the train careened off course. *She's the best kind of brave,* he thought, letting his magic spiral through her body. Each of her toes snapped back into place, audible enough that he heard Mirabella make a small, distressed sound.

"She will be all right, Miss Mirabella," he murmured.

Winslow immediately regretted his words. What his Talent showed him next made every part of him cringe; a fracture in the back of her skull, severe hemorrhaging throbbing pressure against the wound. As Talented as he was, even Winslow knew his limits. Fixing her was going to take an incredible amount of time and focus, and if he didn't do so now, he risked her death.

Opening his eyes, he looked at Mirabella. "You should rest now. This next bit is going to take some time."

The little girl shook her head and plopped on the ground beside her mother. Cross-legged, she pulled her mother's limp, blunt hand onto her lap and continued to watch. Winslow smirked. He should have expected that response. Then he closed his eyes and devoted his attention onto the woman's head injury. He had to go slow. No bones could just snap into place here, it could disturb the delicate brain tissue beneath.

In his mind was only the contusion, the spider cracks webbing away from the impact point—a crater that terrified him enough that he avoided it for the moment. Magic swirled through the spot, oh-so-carefully mending the cracks, taking it a centimeter at a time.

If they were very, very lucky, he'd be done by sunrise.

***

"So now we *are* going to Tournament?" Dorian tried to hide the annoyance in his voice. It had taken him the better part of an hour to track his wife down, and what he found her doing was just as baffling as her sudden announcement at tea.

In her old workshop, outside of Delgora Manor, Elsie had snuck away from all of the guards and

Warders without even leaving him a note. It was only by relying on his Talent that he'd been able to find her. He left footprints through heavy dust on the floor and tried to ignore the drape of cobwebs in the corners. She'd abandoned this shop when she'd ascended to House Witch and, to be quite honest, he'd forgotten about it himself.

One of the dress forms had been stripped of its sheet and placed prominently in the center of the room. Likewise, she'd bared one of the worktables and sat sketching plans for a new dress. The only magic present in her current task was shown in the bright candelabra light fixtures. Dorian knew the electric lights were faulty, normally flickering and dim, but Elsie made them shine.

"It would appear so," she said without looking up.

"Is this another premonition?" Dorian self-consciously glanced at her right hand.

She'd taken off the glove in order to work, revealing the gold, shimmering tattoos that curled around her skin, looping between fingers. Eight years married and the sight still jarred him. He could still hear the pitch of Magic's voice as the Dellidus creature attacked, could feel the shared agony as it began to feed on their god.

"I wouldn't call it a premonition so much as an order." Elsie frowned at the sketch. "Lavender. Lavender would be better, she's too skittish for red."

Dorian took a moment to digest her words. Leaning against the doorframe, he shoved his hands into his trouser pockets and squinted at her. "Elsie."

She stared at the sketch for another long minute before looking at him. The haunted, tormented look on her face only confirmed his suspicions. Things were getting worse. A mere month into their marriage, she'd started having nightmares. A week later, she'd taken to pacing through the Manor in the dead of night, not asleep but not totally awake, either. Dorian was aware of every shift in her, his Talent was so attuned to hers that he could feel the gnawing, ever-present fear she harbored. A fear she had no name for and precious little understanding of.

The ark project had mollified her, given her something to do, but it was almost finished. He hadn't understood what the thing was for at first, but he'd taken a tour three weeks ago and finally caught on. Inside the massive thing were rooms upon rooms, three large kitchens spread out to accommodate a lot of people. She'd made eighteen gardens inside the structure, all of them engineered to use artificial light. But perhaps most frightening of all, was that she'd made certain none of it required magic.

The pain in her eyes stabbed into him, but he stayed where he was. "He's talking to you now, isn't he?"

Her gaze fell to the tattoos and he watched her flatten her hand over the paper. "I should have known I couldn't hide it from you."

"I'm a little hurt that you wanted to."

She looked back at him and their eyes met. "I was afraid at first," Elsie smiled remorsefully as she explained. "I was afraid that I really was going crazy."

Dorian let go of the breath he'd been holding and pushed himself away from the door. He took the room in three strides and crouched down beside her. Covering the offending hand with one large palm, he endured the zaps that needled into his skin on contact. It was several moments before the unpleasant prickle subsided and they both looked at each other again.

"Elsie, I love you whether you're crazy or not." Holding her gaze, he tightened his grip on her hand and tried to give her a reassuring smile. "But we both know you're not. Something terrible is coming and you're the only person who can see it."

"I'm tired of being the only one, Dorian." With a shaky, unhappy sigh, she leaned over until her head was on his shoulder. "Just saying it out loud can't capture it all. Something is driving the Wild to breech our borders. When the Warding Pillars fail—and they will fail, Dorian—it wants nothing short of our complete annihilation."

"The ark . . ."

"The ark will preserve a few, but it will only buy them time." He felt a shiver pass through her and turned to kiss her forehead. "Something else has to be done. I just don't know what."

"It would help if the Council quit fighting. Maybe that's why we're supposed to go to Tournament."

She made a disgruntled sound. "They won't listen. They want to maintain their power and we threaten that."

"Right now, the Wild threatens that more."

"If they wouldn't listen to Fate eight years ago, they aren't going to listen to us."

Dorian grunted his agreement. "Does that mean we shouldn't try?"

Her sigh brushed across his throat and she nuzzled closer to him. Dorian pulled her out of the chair and half into his lap, balancing carefully on his haunches. She settled into him, her slender form relaxing against his and he held her tighter. He wanted to shake her, to get her to tell him everything, but he couldn't do it. If there was one thing he knew about his wife, it was that Elsie Delgora required her privacy. Even after eight years of marriage, she still had to keep secrets.

He couldn't blame her. Not after all she'd been through. But he still wished she'd let him in completely.

His attention caught on the sketch and he paused. "Those aren't your measurements."

"No," she said, sounding almost amused. "This is for Valeda Quinlan."

"You're making a dress for the Tormey reporter?"

Elsie looked at the sketch too. "She's Fated."

"But she's Untalented."

"I know," Elsie shifted back into her chair. "Which makes me doubly curious to know why she's here."

CHAPTER FIVE

After an awkward half an hour at tea with Monty, Vicaress Leona had come to collect Valeda. The economy with which the Vicaress managed to arrange the cleanup, the necessary accommodations for the Ambassador, and Valeda's own needs, left Valeda dizzy. She had never seen a woman so perfectly suited to their profession before. Leona was gracious and kind in a bubbly way that made complaining impossible. Which was why Valeda found herself chin deep in fluffy, light-weight sheets, her body held snugly in a luxurious mattress that made her wish she really was a dignitary.

When she'd tried to say that she had lodging in town, Leona had reiterated that the Witch insisted Valeda remain as a guest. Servants were parked right outside her door, giving Valeda no need to depart. She needed night garments—they were provided. She needed toothpaste—it was already stocked in the room. Messages had already been sent to Miss Margaretta Orianne explaining where Valeda would be staying, which made her nervous. She couldn't remember using Margaretta's last name at any point during tea, which begged the question of how they'd known.

From start to finish, Vicaress Leona would have had no more than one hour to discover who Valeda was and where she was staying. Delgora House lands were relatively small compared to the Houses on the Mainland of Magnellum, but there were still a significant number of people who lived here. Surely there were more than a dozen Margarettas who called Delgora home.

Troubled, Valeda turned on her side, snuggled her pillow, and tried to replay the day's events.

The touch of moonlight set the walls in a soft glow. There were shadows under the table at the far wall, outlining the painting that hung above it, but for the most part it was bright in her room. Bright enough that she could make out the twists and curves of the banyan tree in the painting, and the copper glint of basin and pitcher on the table. A matching copper bathtub was set into a niche in the western corner, its pipes ran the height of the wall and disappeared into the ceiling.

She knows, Valeda thought. *The House Witch knows why I'm here. Why else would she put me in a gilded cage and pamper me?*

Elsie Delgora's golden eyes burned through her memory and Valeda shuddered. If the cursed room wasn't guarded by servants, she'd have tried to run for it. The thought crossed her mind that she could lie, make up a false story as to why she'd travelled to Delgora, but Valeda imagined the Witch would see through something like that.

When dealing with her fellow Untalented, Valeda was known as a stubborn sort and prided herself on that. But having direct contact with a Witch-Born was something else. They were relatively similar to the Untalented by way of physical traits, needs and temper tantrums, if a tad more refined than the common man. Not that they would deliberately harm someone without due cause, just that they could.

Remembering clearly the precise manner in which the tea had set itself that afternoon, Valeda decided that the terrifying thing about the Witch-

Born was the choices they made. Or rather, the choices they could make if they wanted to. It was a matter of walking or flying for Elsie Delgora, with both being just as easy as the other. Valeda imagined that the Witch could silence her forever with a wave of that imperial, gloved hand.

The light suddenly altered in her room, from pleasant silver to a deep crimson and back again.

Blinking, Valeda sat up.

It came again—silver to red—and she got out of bed. Barefoot, she padded across the sturdy wooden floor to her open window and peeked out. Three flights up in Delgora Manor, Valeda could easily see the town proper. Sprawling in chaotic, curling lines, the town blended in with the jungle. Here and there she could see the flint of brass or copper in the moonlight, rooftops peeking out above the tree line. The marketplace was easier to spot, all of its tents and little shops closed up for the night, leaving an abandoned circle of pale cobblestone in the landscape.

The light came again, illuminating a tall structure high up on the ridgeline of mountains in the south. Valeda gripped the window frame and leaned forward, squinting to try and make out the particulars through the distance. The ruby glow dimmed and faded out, only to build up again in a slow, constant pulse.

"What in Fates is that?"

Her voice sounded small and unfamiliar in her lonely room, but she was too overcome with curiosity to feel self-conscious. She could only make out the framework of something massive, with one giant spire at the center. The spire's peak was the source of the cynosure, and she had the sense that it was turning.

A few moments later the slow blinking stopped and the ridgeline fell into shadow. She could still vaguely make out the structure, but it blurred in with the natural curve of the mountains.

The ark, Valeda thought.

Fear slid down her spine as she continued to stare. A sticky breeze rustled the skirt of her borrowed nightgown, brushing it up against her ankles. She thought she should probably move. Someone down below might spot her in the thin, barely modest material. It would be her luck that the person to spot her was some prude of a courtier, too. But she couldn't move because her mind was racing instead.

Elsie Delgora really was building an ark.

No Witch-Born had been blessed by Magic, the man-god, in eight years. If he didn't bestow the Talent on anyone else, the Witches would die off one by one until there was no one left to keep the Warding Pillars in place.

And if the Warding Pillars came down, then the Wild would come in.

Valeda turned from the window. Staggering to the bed, she sat down and tried to catch her breath. She'd broken out into a fine sweat. Nursery rhymes drifted through her memory, old warnings given about what lay beyond the Pillars, traditions rooted so deep that no one could specify where they had come from.

It has been and ever shall be
The plight of the Witches to live for thee

The Pillars stand tall
For one and for all
And the Wild has no place to flee.
Beyond the vale
Where the Wild prevails
Lies death for you and for me

Her mind conjured childhood horrors; beasts twice as tall as a man, with teeth flashing deadly sharp in a snarl, claws raking through the air with great whooshing sounds. Unnamed animosity was focused on every Untalented in Magnellum, insatiable and unstoppable, held in check only by the Warding Pillars.

Valeda closed her eyes and tried to will the images away, but it only made them clearer. Thick, long vines rampaging through towns, swiping away buildings and homes and people like so much rubbish from a table. Feline and wolf-like beasts, she could make them out now, sleekly muscular but still snarling, hunting down every breathing member of their society.

With a strangled, distressed cry, Valeda opened her eyes and stood up. She was right. She knew she was right. Wherever he had gone, Magic, the man-god, was no longer in Magnellum and all of their lives were at risk.

People had to be warned.

***

Winslow knew when the woman woke up. He'd managed to repair the head injury, but no amount of magic could predict what lasting repercussions would come of it. He'd once seen his friend Bartholomew heal a man's hip, but the deterioration of the subject's bones had kept him limping.

Head trauma like the mother's could result in a lasting problem. She could wake and not remember who she was. She could forget how to eat or walk, or have any number of problems. For most of the day Winslow had feared she'd never wake at all. So he'd kept his Talent focused on her breathing while he and Mirabella had seen to the necessities of food and better lodging. Sleeping under the wreckage was unappealing on several fronts. For one, he was constantly afraid the thing would fall. For another, there was something morbid about the thought of Cosata Divenhurst-Lorlain's body being so close.

The thought of Cosata brought more issues to mind. He couldn't figure out how Mirabella and her mother had managed to survive the wreck at all. He knew the only reason he'd made it was because of his Talent, and even then it had been a close call. Mirabella's mother might have been in terrible shape and probably would have died without his help, but compared to everyone else on that train she was lucky.

Every instinct in him had screamed that something else was going on, he just couldn't figure out what. And he wanted to find out what it was before the rescue came. He estimated that the depot in Three Points would have figured out that they were missing by now and would have started to mount a search party. That gave him a day at best, maybe more, depending on whether they risked taking a train out to find them.

The late autumn air had the bite of encroaching winter to it, so he'd known they would need some sort of cover. He'd taken the walls and roof from the train car two sections down from theirs to make a small shanty. They'd positioned it a little way from the wreck, under a cluster of trees for added cover. Mercifully, their train had been scarcely populated, so the casualties weren't quite so high. Not a lot of people wanted to catch the 4 a.m. nonstop from Drewhaven, Clenci, to Three Points, Broska. Winslow imagined that that had everything to do with the outrageous hour and nothing to do with the destination. Three Points was a hub of commerce, sitting on the borders between House lands Broska, Clenci and Tormey.

"Mirabella?" The woman's voice was raspy but clear, carrying easily through the make-shift building.

Winslow watched Mirabella dart into the structure and prayed the girl wouldn't hurl herself at her mother. Slowly, giving the two a moment for their reunion, he started for the domed shell. It wasn't perfect, but it was sturdy. If snow fell at night, they'd be covered. He'd bent the metal into long curves, allowing a hole in the center at the very top so that they could have a fire inside. Mirabella had torn up the padding from some of the seats for bedding.

"Mr. Winslow used his magic to get us out of the train," he heard Mirabella rushing through an explanation. "Then he healed you, but he said you were hurt so bad that you needed to rest. So we built this house until you woke up."

"Mr. Winslow?"

Taking his cue, he ducked into the iron dome. "Ahem," he blinked as his eyes adjusted to the light. "Winslow Agoston, Madam."

The mother was still lying down, but her eyes were open and she was holding Mirabella's hand.

"Lord Winslow Agoston, of Agoston House?" She kept her hazel gaze on him, something akin to fear passing her features.

He couldn't blame the woman. It was unlikely that she had any personal dealings with Witch-Born. "The one and same, Madam."

Mirabella settled down beside her mother. "He's not at all like a Witch-Born, mother. Not like Daddy says they should be. Mr. Winslow is very brave and very caring. He healed my hand while he was still sleeping!"

Embarrassed, Winslow rubbed the tip of his nose and cleared his throat. "We were just debating the matter of food, Madam. If you're feeling up to it, I wondered if you could keep Miss Mirabella company while I go out for a little hunt."

"How long have I slept?"

"Almost a full day, mother."

Winslow saw the distress in the mother's face as she processed this information. Because he couldn't think of a way to comfort her, he looked out through the folded doorway and took a deep breath. Ferns overran the landscape outside their make-shift lodging. If he had his bearings right, they were at least on the right side of the Dorshin mountain pass. They could follow the tracks all the way to Three Points. He could run there and back with help faster than they could walk it together, but his Talent recoiled at the idea of leaving the two of them alone.

He hadn't ventured far enough down the line to see what had caused the crash, but he had a sinking suspicion it wasn't natural. There was the occasional accident when one of the great, iron trains would jump its tracks, but this had felt different. Winslow had the unsettled sense of malice ebbing off the forests around them, the feeling of many unfriendly eyes watching him.

"I am indebted to you, sir," the mother said. "How can I ever repay you for what you've done?"

Winslow felt his cheeks burn with further embarrassment and sheepishly rubbed one shoulder. "We're not quite safe yet, Madam. We've a long walk to Three Points. It should take us a day and a half on foot."

"But why don't you just fly there and come back?" Mirabella asked.

Chuckling, Winslow looked to the girl and winked. "I'm a male Witch-Born, Mirabella. I'm afraid I can't fly."

"That doesn't seem fair." Mirabella's face scrunched up with displeasure.

"Yes, well, Magic had his reasons for favoring the females of our race." Winslow flinched involuntarily at his own words. His memory flashed to Delgora Manor at the mention of Magic, the man-god, to that moment he'd been forced to catch Bartholomew before his friend could hit the ground. There was a smear of movement in his memory, the sounds of combat drifting back to him with horrifying clarity.

"Surely you can run to Three Points faster." The mother sat up, grimacing as she did so. She touched the back of her head gingerly, blindly probing around the spot he'd healed. There was a bump there, he knew, a residual effect of the injury.

"I do not feel comfortable leaving the two of you." Winslow moved closer to the door. "It's safer for us all to travel together. But for right now, I will get us some food. I'll stay within hearing distance. Call for me if you need to."

He nodded to the mother and ducked outside, giving her no opportunity to argue. They would speak later, when Mirabella couldn't hear. There was no sense scaring the little girl, but her mother would need to know the danger they were in. She seemed a sturdy sort of woman, and by her actions on the train he knew he could count on her to keep Mirabella safe.

Three strides from the doorway, Winslow summoned his Talent and took off running. Weaving around trees and leaping small bushes, he let his magic guide him on the hunt. There were fresh rabbit tracks and he followed them, concentrating so hard on locating the animal that he almost missed the Warding Pillars. Stopping just on the verge of crossing, Winslow caught his breath in his chest.

At some point in his run he'd pushed his magic to show him the unseen, the reality just beyond what the Untalented could see. It was the place where the Warding Pillars dwelt. Only the Pillars in front of him were crumbling and deteriorated.

"Mother, Maiden and Crone!" He blinked up at them as fear chilled his body.

On the other side of the barrier, he could see a feline creature staring back at him. Large and magnificent, striped with orange and white, it prowled outside of the Pillars, pacing. Winslow could feel its great paws as they struck the ground, could sense its hateful gaze through the thin vale.

“Fates have mercy,” Winslow stared back at it, feeling suddenly small and insignificant.

Elsie Delgora was right.

CHAPTER SIX

Elsie took some small enjoyment in the curious manner that Valeda Quinlan presented to her. The girl was genuinely interested in nearly every facet of Elsie's life; from her humble upbringing to her fight against Vicaress Reonne. Valeda showed dismay at the thought of the late Vicaress's murderous appetite, and was baffled about the creature known as the Dellidus. The insatiable wild serpent known as the Dellidus was a thing of legend, a nightmare told to children at bedtime to keep them away from the Warding Pillars.

Elsie could sense the shocked disbelief coursing through the woman as they hiked through the jungle. Pausing for a moment, Elsie flicked her long braid over one shoulder and considered the steep slope in front of them. For reasons she couldn't fathom, she'd decided to take Miss Quinlan to Witch-Eater Lake by foot. Horses would have been preferable, there was no one to hide from anymore, but it seemed that old habits died hard. Even after eight years, Elsie had trouble not glancing over her shoulder. She always took note of every exit in a room the moment she entered it, sized up all threats that might be presented from the people around her, and covered her own tracks through the moist Delgora dirt.

"Is it much further?" Valeda asked. "Not that I mind walking, My Lady, just that the tropics feel heavy."

It was in that moment that Elsie noted how breathless her companion was. The red in the woman's hair shone out defiantly among the dark brown locks, and several curls looked damp in the humid air. Valeda's angular, bird-like features were flush from heat and exertion, and as curious as the girl was, she was also quite annoyed at her current situation.

That odd brilliance to her, the mark of being Fated, seemed to burn more brightly in the private setting. At first, Valeda had been reluctant and uncertain, not wanting to accompany a House Witch on a trek through the jungle, alone. There was mistrust and not a small amount of paranoia in her. Elsie didn't like that, but she didn't know how to fix it, either.

"Just a bit further, yes."

Valeda paused to catch her breath, propping both hands on her hips in a manner that exemplified her irritation. Elsie became distractedly pleased by the fit of the woman's trousers, blouse and bodice-vest. Elsie was proud of the outfit. The vest cinched tight around Valeda's torso, accenting feminine curves in a subtle sort of allure, and the colors were more appropriate for the woman's skin and hair; a deep briny green with swirls of maroon throughout.

She smiled in spite of Valeda's increasing agitation.

Elsie had whispered a truth spell into the thread, encouraging her Talent to permeate the garment. If the girl was a spy from another House, Elsie needed to know. While the spell couldn't outright tell her such a secret, it could show the nature of the woman. The internal aspects of Valeda were reflected on the outside, plain for Elsie to see. And Elsie was happy with what she saw.

Rather than twisted and wretched, as a mean-spirited person might appear, Valeda's features had not changed. If anything, Miss Quinlan looked sharper, more focused, with a nervous smile and an almost unsettling honesty.

"Are you taking me to the ark?" Valeda asked bluntly.

Elsie smiled some more, careful not to show her surprise. Regardless of her good nature, Miss Quinlan was a reporter. The last thing Elsie needed was another news report about Delgora matters. "I'm sure I don't know what you're talking about, Miss Quinlan."

"I saw it last night. From my window." Valeda's soft gray eyes narrowed at her. "On the southern ridgeline."

Elsie chuckled and turned away, resuming their hike before she answered. "First of all, Miss Quinlan, you'll notice the position of the mid-morning sun is directly to our right. You, being an educated woman, are well aware of the sun's rotation from east to west, which would make our current trajectory due north of Delgora Manor."

From the corner of her eye, she saw Valeda look to the sky and frown. "That doesn't deny what I saw last night."

"Secondly," Elsie continued without acknowledging the comment, "even if I were inclined to divulge Delgora House matters to you, Miss Quinlan, my better sense knows that your profession cannot be trusted."

"I'm a reporter, not an idiot. If you required my silence, you would have it. I'd never cross a Witch."

“A person’s sense of self-preservation can only keep them quiet for so long, Miss Quinlan. It has been my experience that the only thing you can fully rely on in this life is the greed of the people around you.” Elsie crested the hill and stopped again, waiting for Valeda to catch up.

“His Lordship . . .” Valeda panted as she reached the top of the hill, “His Lordship might take offense at that viewpoint.”

Grinning, Elsie winked at the woman. “Dorian would be an exception to that rule. But I applaud you on your growing sense of confidence around me. There are few Untalented who would risk such a comment.”

Valeda blushed and squirmed, glancing away from her. “It’s the miserable heat. It brings out the testy side of me, My Lady.”

“I thought it might.” With an easy gesture, Elsie directed Valeda’s attention to the clearing before them.

Valeda opened her mouth as though to protest, but suddenly stopped. Sharp peaks and hundreds of waterfalls stole her attention. Elsie stood back and watched, all too familiar with the deceptive beauty surrounding them. Witch-Eater Lake commanded the center of the clearing, churning its depths with many waterfalls that scattered about the cliff face. Each mountain peak was dark with greenery, looking as though in constant shadow, defiantly tall and treacherously steep. The Warding Pillars were several miles to the north, but the presence of the Wild raged through the landscape.

Elsie felt when it started to lure Valeda in. It was a distinctly welcoming feeling; a warmth that promised safety to the subconscious levels of Valeda's mind. The reporter took a step forward and Elsie grabbed her shoulder. Valeda blinked up at her, confusion clear on her face.

"This is Witch-Eater Lake, Miss Quinlan. It will happily drown you."

"It's Wild?"

Elsie nodded.

"But that's impossible." Valeda looked back at the lake and froze.

It's here.

The ominous announcement from Magic felt like a growl over her skin and Elsie was acutely aware of the tattoos on her arm. Under the long sleeves and gloves she could feel them, a constant prickle, like someone was stabbing her with a sewing needle over and over again. Magic never liked it when she visited the lake, but at least this time she'd known what to expect.

Elsie knew what she would find when she looked back at the lake, but his nearness still startled her. Standing just four steps away from them was the ghost-boy Baldemor Delgora.

He looked solid, though Elsie knew him not to be, and his movements were all jerky. She watched as he tilted his head to one side, which only amplified the sense of wretchedness about him.

"Who are you?" Valeda asked the boy.

Elsie heard the nervousness in her voice, but didn't try to support her. It had been three years since Baldemor had spoken to anybody and she wanted to see what might happen. Because Valeda was Untalented, the outcome might be different. His last reported words were by far the most alarming. Dorian said he'd paused to see the ghost, just checking on a hunch. Baldemor was normally seen playing at the shores of the lake, but this time the boy had stopped. Dorian described it as though the child had suddenly been struck by something unseen, and then he stood straight—rigidly straight—and moved to the edge of the clearing.

"It's time." Those were the last words.

But time for what? Elsie wondered, gazing at the blue-tinged apparition.

No one in Magnellum had ventured past the Warding Pillars in any of their recorded history. They left the Wild alone, unless it somehow got through the Pillars like the Dellidus had. She couldn't understand where this animosity came from.

***

Valeda had the disturbing sensation of something very cold sliding down her spine. The only sound came from the waterfalls crashing into the lake just beyond, though Valeda could swear she heard a low, deep humming from the boy in front of her. He hadn't answered her yet and the House Witch had given no explanation, so Valeda kept quiet. If she was being honest, she was terrified.

There was something malicious about the boy, something intense and powerful that clung to him.

"In truth, Miss Quinlan, I'm not sure how to introduce you," Elsie said at last. "The form before you is that of Baldemor Delgora. Baldemor, however, has been dead for centuries."

Valeda swallowed down her fear. "Centuries?"

"Until recently he talked. Sometimes he would warn people away from the Lake. But he's changed now. He's more Wild than anything else." The Witch tugged at her earlobe and frowned. "The Wild is coming, Miss Quinlan. Very soon, I'm afraid."

Turning to look at her, Valeda rallied herself for her questions. It was the best opening she would have to confront the Witch and she had to take it. She found the boy's constant stare to be more than disturbing and had to concentrate to formulate the right words. In the end, the right words failed her and she reverted to bluntness.

"Magic is gone, isn't he," she stated.

For a Witch who had gone through as much as Elsie Delgora, Valeda was surprised at the lack of theatrics. Elsie didn't try to pretend not to know, she didn't hide the flash of pain in her eyes or the haunted way she looked at her gloved arm. The glove, peculiar as it was, caught Valeda's attention again and she wondered if the woman had been disfigured in some way.

"I am not permitted to speak on such things," Elsie said.

"Why not? If he's gone, then people need to know. We're all in danger."

"The people can be a danger to themselves at times."

"Poppycock!"

Elsie sent her a chilling glare that stopped Valeda from further argument. "Attempt not to insult me, Miss Quinlan. I of all people have seen the Untalented do great and terrible things for their own prestige."

Valeda flinched, remembering the horrid tale of how Vicaress Reonne had smuggled a Dellidus into Magnellum. It wasn't just murder that the serpentine creature had delivered, it was an ongoing torture for its victim. Valeda had thought the creature a thing of myth, until Elsie had disclosed how she'd had to garrote her father in order to get the Dellidus to detach from him. Only after her father's physical body was dead, was Elsie able to destroy the creature itself. Her matter-of-fact way of describing the death of her own father had the gravity of truth behind it.

Then her mind hooked onto the one important thing Elsie wasn't saying.

"Magic really is gone."

"Oh, no. I didn't say that. Magic is here. He's just . . . preoccupied."

"Why hasn't he blessed anyone with Talent in eight years?" Valeda pressed, glancing at the still staring form of Baldemor Delgora.

"Has it been that long?"

Valeda sensed the story here, all her instincts as a reporter throwing caution and propriety aside in the pursuit of the truth. "The last time he was seen was here in Delgora, eight years ago. On the day of your ascension to House Witch. You know more than you're telling me, Elsie Delgora."

"Of course I do, I'm a House Witch. Really now, Miss Quinlan, you've got to have a better argument than that."

Valeda stammered and flushed, feeling altogether overwhelmed by her own boldness and the Witch's frustrating evasiveness. Beside her, the creepy ghost continued to glare and she wondered for a moment why Elsie had brought her here. Of all the places in Delgora, the Witch had taken her to a murderous lake where a ghost could silently hate her. The seething, angry boy didn't even blink, he stood so still.

Valeda wasn't certain what she'd meant to do, she just wanted the boy to stop looking at her, so she raised her hand. It moved so fast it blurred and an icy grip clamped tightly around her wrist. A sudden, forceful tug nearly took her into the clearing, but Elsie moved just as fast.

"*Fellata!*" the Witch commanded, and just as fast as it had grabbed her, the ghost let go. The form of Baldemor Delgora flew away from them, pushed back by whatever spell Elsie had cast. He was swallowed up by the lake a moment later, the water eerily undisturbed by his passage.

Stunned, Valeda glanced from the lake to the Witch and back again. "I..."

"I have several jobs for you, Miss Quinlan, which you will do without question." Elsie continued to stare at the lake, frowning deeply.

"I beg your pardon?"

"The first of which is to go to Master Walter at Walter's School for Unfortunates in Lorant. You have to travel through Lorant to get home to Tormey, so this should pose no problem."

"Except that I already have an employer and don't wish to work for you." Valeda wasn't certain why she was being so obstinate, but there was something infuriating in the smile on the Witch's face.

"Oh, you want to work for me, Miss Quinlan. Because I'm going to give you what you want."

Elsie finally turned from the lake. "Do these few things for me, and I will give you the location of Magic."

CHAPTER SEVEN

Winslow adjusted his hold on Mirabella's legs, amused by the way she propped her chin on his right shoulder. He'd been carrying the girl on his back for the better part of the day as a means of expediency. Fayree, Mirabella's mother, managed to keep pace with him, understanding that there were dangers present that she couldn't see. He hadn't gotten a chance to speak with her on the matter of the Pillars, but when they'd passed the front of the train it had been evident.

The crash hadn't been a matter of technical malfunction or even a sudden jumping of tracks. Their train had been yanked off the railway by a twelve-foot vine. The giant, slimy green tentacle originated in the Wild and somehow crossed the Warding Pillars long enough to attack. It was apparent that the thing hadn't been finished, either. The engine and half of the first train car had been dragged through the Pillars and into the Wild before Magic won the battle.

Grimacing, Winslow fought back the images of mangled train, dead conductors and passengers, and continued the trek toward Three Points. His mind, however, kept returning to the distressing scene. The long, glistening vine stretched across their path, severed at the Pillar point. They'd had to step over it to move forward.

The Wild is coming, he thought grimly. *It's really coming, just like Elsie predicted.* When she'd first sent him on his quest Winslow assumed she just wanted to keep him busy. In the years since Bryva's death, he'd been restless and discontented.

Even now, his heart ached at the thought of her. Bryva Gelgova, his vivacious, beautiful, perfectly Untalented lover, felt just as near to him as the day he'd met her. There were moments he swore he could hear her laugh, and dreams where he could still touch and taste her.

Perhaps it was predictable of him, but Winslow welcomed her haunting. He wanted nothing more to do with noble society, so he was more than pleased to take Elsie's assignment.

"Check the boundaries," she'd said. "All of them."

Since she paid all the expenses, Winslow hadn't balked at the enormity of the task. Honestly, he wouldn't have balked if she needed him to pay for it, either. He just wanted to move, to have something to do . . . to matter.

And now I do matter, he thought. Because a vine breaking through the Pillars to attack a train was exactly what Elsie needed to know. She needed to know that she was right, the Wild was coming, and hopefully they wouldn't be too late to act against it.

"It's too bad you can't fly, Mr. Winslow," Mirabella said. "If I were a witch, I think I'd fly everywhere."

"Oh?" Winslow said. "And where would you go, if you could fly anywhere?"

From beside him, he could see Fayree smile at her daughter, but the woman stayed quiet. She did look a trifle flush, now that he really looked at her, but he thought that had more to do with the exertion of walking than anything else. At first he'd been afraid the woman would need more rest, what with the head injury still so fresh, but then they'd come upon the front of the train and pushed ahead. By silent agreement, they tried to put as much distance between themselves and it as they possibly could.

"They say the Kelemen mountains are so tall they touch the sky," Mirabella said after a moment. "I think I would like to see them first."

Winslow smiled. "You'd best go in the summer, then. It gets terribly cold that high up."

"You've been there?" Mirabella squealed in delight, making him flinch.

He covered the pain of having his ear blasted with a peal of laughter. "My dearest friend was a Kelemen before he wed House Witch Caresse Feverrette. Perhaps you've heard of Bartholomew Feverrette-Kelemen?"

"Do you know all of the witches in Magnellum?" Mirabella wiggled on his back and Winslow had to struggle to keep his footing before they both fell over.

"I know of them," he said with amusement, "but I certainly haven't met them all. Magnellum is a very large place, Miss Mirabella."

"Father says all Witch-Born are lazy and ineffectual. That you all enjoy tea and ignore the rest of us."

"Mirabella!" Fayree scolded her daughter, unable to hide the distinct pitch of dismay in her voice.

"Well, he does."

He stopped them at the base of a hill, his mind torn between the promise of another long climb, Fayree's waning strength—he could sense that from the woman—and Mirabella's accusation. It wasn't the first time he'd heard that sentiment from an Untalented and he doubted it would be the last. The Great Houses were, in fact, too busy squabbling over power and trade to focus on the dangers becoming apparent in Magnellum. A few more "accidents" like the train wreck and the Wild might not have to bother attacking because the people would riot and their whole society would be torn apart.

"I can't say that I like your statement, Miss Mirabella," Winslow lowered the girl from his back and knelt before her. "But I won't deny it, either. There are too many Witch-Born who can't see beyond their own pocketbooks. Your father is right about some, but not all of us."

Mirabella smiled at him. "You're a good man, Mr. Winslow."

From beside them, Fayree let out a sudden and terrified scream. Startled, Winslow looked at her and then at what had caught her attention. Just to his right, the striped, feline creature prowled out of the forests. It looked defiant and imperial and huge, soft fur vibrant in the daylight. He saw it hunch, all of its muscles coiling, and knew it was about to leap.

"Mother, Maiden and Crone," he cursed, shocked.

Fayree grabbed Mirabella and yanked her back at the same moment that the great cat attacked. It let out a horrifying, primal roar and for a dumbfounded moment Winslow couldn't react. The teeth alone were shocking; sharp, pearly and big enough that one bite would go straight through his forearm. It was the claws, however, that snapped him into reality. The creature wasn't aiming for him, it was aiming for Mirabella, and that, he thought with frightened clarity, would not do.

Letting out a yell of his own, Winslow launched himself at the cat. He summoned his Talent to move his body faster, crashing into the feline before it could hit the girl. The impact jarred his body and they both, cat and man, fell to the side in a jumble of limbs.

They rolled together, away from Mirabella and her mother, wrestling awkwardly. Winslow had never fought such a thing before. He tried to think of weaknesses, growling as he felt claws rake over his back. Then its teeth clamped onto his left shoulder, powerful jaws locking closed and Winslow shouted in pain.

With a sudden jerk, the cat yanked Winslow's body leftward, tearing muscle and sinew through his shoulder. Blinding pain shot through him as the cat slammed him to the ground. He felt more claws from its back legs, digging past pants and into skin, successfully pinning him down. The creature shook its head, refusing to release its grip on his shoulder and he heard, more than felt, bones snap.

Dazed, Winslow thought he could hcar the damn thing purring. It was a deep, almost guttural sound that seemed to vibrate from the heavy, powerful beast on top of him. Any moment now it was going to yank upward and tear his arm off. And there wasn't much he could do to stop it. The feline was just as strong as he was, possibly stronger, and Winslow was already using his magic. Talent could enhance his natural abilities, making him faster, stealthier, more agile than the average man, but it had limitations.

He had only one weapon left to him. Well, two if he counted his boot knife, but he couldn't reach it at present so his options narrowed to one. Winslow summoned his Talent and bent time. The world around him slowed, taking on a sheen-like, reflective quality. Slow ripples of light ebbed outward, pushing away from him as he held the moment still.

At first, he'd been afraid that the cat wouldn't be affected by the time-bend, but the furious shaking stopped and he knew his gamble had worked. It was a strain on his magic to hold Time so slow and he had to battle past the wretched agony in his shoulder to think clearly.

Boot knife, he thought, and with a growl of effort, pulled his right leg free of the creature's back paws. He felt its claws rip open the flesh just above his knee, but was too focused on grabbing the knife to care. His hold on Time was slipping, he could feel it.

Shouting in mingled rage and pain, Winslow slammed his dagger into the back of the cat's jaw just as Time snapped away from him.

The grip on his shoulder released and the startled cat reared away from him. The move forced Winslow's dagger to drag through skin and fur until it snagged to a halt on jawbone. It was an oddly silent knifing, or it might have been that Mirabella's screaming covered the sounds of ripping flesh. Either way, the damage was done. The creature roared, this time in pain, and leapt off him.

Winslow's strength failed. The dagger pulled from his numb fingers as the cat retreated, tearing off into the forest again. Colors smeared in his vision as he watched the fleeing creature; visceral red staining majestic fur. The metal pommel of his dagger glinted in the sunlight, its blade still buried into the great cat's jaw.

Mirabella slid to her knees beside him. He saw her dirty, tear-tracked face and tried to smile for her. He didn't want her so scared, didn't want her crying, but his face was as numb as his fingers and he realized belatedly how much blood he had lost. He needed to heal himself before he lost consciousness.

Gathering his Talent, Winslow tried to prepare himself for the feat, but it was too late. His eyes closed and rather than concentrating on the injuries as he'd planned, he just passed out.

***

Valeda stood in the center of a luxurious suite on board the dirigible called the *Crescent Moon.* Plush furnishings surrounded her, all in pleasant shades of honey-gold and maroon, but none of it comforted her. In point of fact, she was afraid to move any further from the commode door lest her stomach make another revolt and she throw up on the thick carpet.

She wasn't sick, not really. She was petrified.

The appeal of the room could not mask the peculiar sway of the dirigible underfoot. It could not hide the fact that she was miles and miles away from the ground, drifting through the sky toward the

House lands of Lorant. Valeda wondered if they had already left Delgora behind, but the prospect of a vast, gaping ocean underneath them seemed somehow worse.

Rushing back into the private lavatory, Valeda flung herself over the brass and wood toilette bowl and squeezed her eyes shut. Whatever was left in her stomach was not going to stay there and she refused to ruin the suite. Elsie had paid an exorbitant amount for her to fly back to the mainland of Magnellum and it didn't seem right to repay that kindness by staining the floor.

Elsie has paid for more than just my suite on board the Crescent Moon, Valeda thought miserably. The witch had paid Margaretta for services rendered, such as they were, in delivering Valeda to Delgora House, and loaded the girl down with a ton of fashion advice. For which, Valeda had no doubt, Margaretta would be eternally grateful. In addition, House Witch Elsie Delgora delivered a note of account to Master Rally Bank, transferring a tidy sum into an expense account for Valeda's personal use.

The note was sent via telegram and post since Elsie—Lady Elsie, her mind corrected—did not fully trust the newfangled telegram machine. Valeda had chosen not to mention that the telegram had been in use for over a decade now. The Witch-Born had a history of distrust for technology. They tolerated such gadgets, but Valeda always felt an air of discomfort from them when facing machinery.

Hunched over the brass bowl, Valeda tried to distract herself with questions. As much as she was humbled by the money she'd been given, the Witch hadn't specified what "personal use" it was for. There were four envelopes in her luggage, each of them sealed and labeled, with instructions once she landed in Lorant. Elsie hadn't prohibited her from reading them early, but Valeda couldn't make it to the small writing desk without fear of being sick.

Curiosity was eating at her.

Aside from their hike through the jungle, Valeda hadn't spent much time with the House Witch. Vicaress Leona saw to all of her needs, replenished a small stockpile of luggage prior to her departure and delivered the envelopes just before Valeda boarded the *Crescent Moon*. It was either luck or political maneuvering that Ambassador Taven was on the same voyage. Dependable Monty would undoubtedly try to extract all the information he could from her. She still wasn't certain how he'd learned of her private walk with the House Witch, but she knew he was itching for information.

More than itching, she thought with a groan. Monty probably thought she owed it to him. He had, after all, helped her get to the ill-fated meeting over tea. To her knowledge, the Ambassador hadn't been given another audience with the Witch or the Consort after that. Not that she blamed Elsie or Lord Dorian for that; Monty had been abominably rude.

In that aspect, Valeda was almost relieved to be sick. Monty couldn't assume she was avoiding him if the maid spotted her like this. If she got to feeling better, she would have to come up with some other excuse. Her only orders thus far were that of discretion. It was best that no one know of her private conversation with the Witch, that she appear ignorant of anything in Delgora, including the construction of an ark.

Whatever she'd seen, or thought she'd seen, on the ridgeline in Delgora, was to remain a mystery. When she completed the tasks in the envelopes, she was promised all of the answers.

Lady Elsie would not only tell her where Magic, the man-god, was, she would show her. *Exclusive rights,* Valeda thought. But in the back of her mind, Valeda couldn't shake a feeling of apprehension. She rubbed her wrist, remembering the icy grip of the ghost-boy at Witch-Eater Lake.

"The Wild is coming, Miss Quinlan. Very soon, I'm afraid."

Elsie's words.

Suppressing a shudder, Valeda thought of the hate that had radiated from the ghost. Or, it wasn't quite a ghost. It was more of a manifestation of the Wild. Which meant that the hatred was really coming from the Wild, from whatever lay beyond the Warding Pillars. There was no doubt in her mind that their quite society would be annihilated if the Pillars fell.

"*Beyond the vale, where the Wild prevails, lies death for you and for me*," Valeda whispered the rhyme and shivered. "Fates alive. I hope you know what you're doing, Elsie Delgora."

CHAPTER EIGHT

"Why would you promise that woman something you know you can't give her?" Dorian half chased Elsie around the western perimeter of the ark, thoroughly annoyed that he'd been forced to hunt her down again.

"Who says I can't give her what she wants?" Elsie kept a brisk pace, lithely avoiding the overgrowth of jungle around them. Her black hair was pinned up in a tight bun, making the exotic, angular curves of her face more prominent. If he hadn't been suppressing the desire to strangle her, Dorian might have given her a compliment.

"The Council says you can't." He had to catch himself on a fallen bit of tree when she abruptly stopped. The moist ground slid away from his left foot and he quickly found a better standing spot.

The ark was built precariously close to the edge of the ridgeline, its entire circumference taking up a four-mile wide, three-and-a-quarter-mile long declivity in the mountain range. The egg-shaped monolith of iron and steel was far enough from any towns that it looked like a shadowed lump of hillside at a distance. Up close, however, it was big and bulky and looked quite impenetrable. *Which is the point,* he thought with a frown.

Elsie turned to an iron ladder built into the side of the wall and prepared to climb. Dorian grabbed her elbow to stop her. There would be people wherever she was heading and they needed to have this conversation in private.

"You promised, Elsie."

"No," she said. "As I recall it, you are the one who promised silence, not me. I stood there like an idiot, trying to remind myself why I didn't kill them all where they stood."

"Elsie. Think of the hysteria that would happen if word got out." Dorian moved closer to her, glancing at her gloved hand and preparing himself for the battle he'd just stepped into. "If Valeda Quinlan publishes the fact that Magic is dead, the Untalented will panic. There will be riots and mayhem and a lot of innocent lives will be lost."

"Even the Witch-Born will panic, Dorian. Talented or not, all of Magnellum's fate rests on the Warding Pillars. Panic is exactly how the people should be reacting." Elsie scowled at him but didn't move, still poised to climb the ladder. "The Wild is coming, Dorian. It's coming and there's very little we can do about it."

"The Wild has been 'coming' for eight years now, Elsie!" Exasperated, he let go of her and shoved his fingers through his hair. "By Fates! I've been listening to you for eight long years. I've watched you build this . . . this . . ." He waved at the side of the ark in frustration, "this insanity, using resources you shouldn't have. Don't try to deny it, either. Delgora was rich when you ascended to House Witch, but it wasn't this rich. You've been spending more money than we've got, insistent that the world is about to end, and for what?"

Elsie blinked up at him, her caramel-colored eyes glimmering with an emotion he couldn't recognize.

“The Warding Pillars haven’t failed, Elsie. There’s peace in Magnellum right now. You cannot overturn society on a whim.” Self-conscious at his own rant, Dorian sighed and looked away from her.

Deep jungle green cast dark shadows over the landscape, interrupted by bright pink and yellow flowers here and there. Vibrantly colored birds streaked past the horizon, calling out to each other in a beautiful and vociferous sort of way. It had taken Dorian a surprisingly small amount of time to acclimatize to the tropics. The lands of his youth were rugged and tall, dry during the summer and cold during the winter, an impressively stark contrast to the year-round humid press of Delgora.

And yet, he loved it here. He loved Delgora almost as much as he loved the infuriating woman beside him.

“My whim did not kill Magic, our god,” Elsie said after a moment. “And Magic is dead. His human form is lost to us and our time is running out. Perhaps peace has lulled you into a sense of complacency, Dorian, but I would prefer to be broke and prepared than wealthy and dead.”

He turned back to her, clenching his fists and barely holding onto his temper. “Complacency? By Fates, Elsie, I haven’t known a single day of peace since I met you. First there was the fight against Vicaress Reonne and her Dellidus creature, and then the fight against the Council . . .”

“I fought the Council so that I could marry you. Are you wishing I hadn’t?”

“That’s not what I’m saying.”

“Then what *are* you saying?”

"I'm frightened, Elsie!" His voice raised more than he'd intended and he could hear a scuffle from high up on the wall. He ignored it. "You don't tell me anything. You keep repeating that the Wild is coming, you keep burning political bridges with other Houses. You send Winslow off to Fates knows where and spend nearly every waking moment confined to this damned ark. Now pardon me if I want some explanations."

For a long moment neither of them moved. Dorian felt a trifle foolish at the things he'd confessed, but he could at least admit to himself that they were necessary. Marriage required a brutal honesty, the ability to see not only your spouse, but yourself as well. By his estimation, he'd been more than fair, more than patient, waiting for the moment when she would finally open up to him and share the burden. He hadn't wanted to push her, but Fates help him, he couldn't take it anymore.

Slowly, quietly, Elsie turned to face him. She nodded slightly, as though deciding something for herself, and then started to remove her glove.

"What are you doing?" he asked, focusing on the glittering tattoos.

"I'm giving you an explanation." Elsie stripped the glove off completely and met his eyes.

She held up the tattooed hand, fingers splayed, and waited. Dorian hesitated for a heartbeat, then reached out to weave his hand through hers. The tattoos zapped him, they always did, but the jolts subsided after a moment.

"*Opawa Ayaatee,*" Elsie murmured the spell and the world around them shifted.

It was a common incantation, the vision spell that allowed all Witch-Born to see the unseen, to inspect the Warding Pillars around their domain. Dorian was a little confused by it, but then Elsie started a memory spell and he understood. Whatever she was going to show him, it existed in that realm and not the present.

Everything shifted again, their reality being overtaken by whatever memory Elsie had called forward. Rather than the ridgeline and the ark, Dorian found himself in Delgora Square, the wide circle of the marketplace bustling with activity. Merchants shouted to be heard above the crowd, venders waved their various wares at potential buyers, children zipped through the street, laughing. It looked quite normal. Dorian could even smell freshly baked bread coming from a nearby building.

And then someone screamed. It was the sort of scream that held terror and pain, as a large mass of gray fur barreled into a merchant. There was no time for a stunned silence as the creature bit into the ill-fated man. More screams rang out, several more wolf-like creatures started to emerge from the jungle, and then chaos erupted. People scattered, trying to flee, but the wolves kept coming.

A loud crack sounded just beside him as the closest building splintered, falling in on itself. Vines burst through shutters, curling around homes and yanking them from their foundations. The sight jarred him and Dorian blinked, still holding tight to Elsie's hand. In his mind he could hear her voice from eight years ago, demanding that her ark be made of steel and iron. She'd insisted that no wood be on the outside because it wouldn't hold up.

He looked to her, but she wasn't watching him. Elsie stared off to the left, to where the Manor was crushed beneath the weight of hundreds of vines. The impact rumbled through the ground, vibrating through his boots, and the deafening report of the defeated structure covered the screams of people scrambling to get away.

"Is this your premonition?" He whispered the question, fear fluttering in his gut.

"One of them."

"Fates have mercy." Dorian flinched, spotting a young man as he was tackled by one of the creatures. Blood stained the wolf's gray fur, its massive paws were slick and dark with it. Dorian watched, horrified, suddenly understanding Elsie's obsession with the ark, her sleepless nights and her irregular behavior. He'd known there were creatures beyond the Pillars, he'd just never seen one before.

The wolf let out a triumphant howl that seemed to crawl over Dorian's skin. Its counterparts echoed the call, drowning out the sounds of still crumbling buildings. There were no more screams.

Elsie's voice reached him, quiet and grim as she released the memory and returned them to their own place and time. "I think Fate is fresh out of mercy, Dorian."

***

Winslow woke up sometime in the night with a pleasant sort of numbness radiating from his shoulder. They hadn't moved him far from the scene of the attack and he knew he should be worried about that. The great cat hadn't been very wounded, just startled enough to run away. There was a good chance it would come back, but he had an odd sort of detachment about it. He wanted to be worried, yet he couldn't find the willpower to work up such an emotion.

He felt bubbly, as though he were floating on a soft surface, and curiously amused. *This is very wrong*, he thought, *because there's little humor about being on the brink of death.*

Winslow fought for coherency. He needed to wake up. He needed to heal himself again. The fact that this was the second time in a week where he'd been seriously injured was irritating. He'd gone through Winter Tournaments, sparring against other Witch-Born, and never had this much trouble. *And that,* he thought with a frown, *was decidedly more dangerous than riding a train or hiking the mountains.*

Closing his eyes, he tried to summon his Talent. To his surprise, his magic didn't respond. It was still there, at his core, he could sense it. But there was a lazy sensation coming from it. *My magic,* he thought with amazement, *is sleeping.*

He opened his eyes again and peered at the wounded shoulder. They had stripped him to the waist in order to tend the wound, but he was strangely comfortable. He should have been cold, he knew. If he had a fever, he would have noticed by now. But he was neither warm, nor cold, just comfortable.

If that wasn't strange enough, Winslow was baffled further by the dressing on his shoulder. No bandages, not even a makeshift one from clothing, just a strange, gooey green glob on the injury. Whatever it was, it covered all of the torn flesh and he had the sense it had been lathered inside the wound as well.

Something was different. Winslow frowned up at the leafy canopy and tried to discern what was bothering him. Well, what was bothering him beyond the wounded shoulder and threat of attack. The great cat was still nearby. Winslow could sense his presence, just beyond the Warding Pillars.

Which was, now that he thought about it, an oddity. He hadn't been able to sense the creature before, so why was he able to now?

No amount of urging or summoning could get his magic to wake, which heightened his anxiety considerably. If the great cat returned, Winslow would be unable to protect Mirabella and her mother.

Turning his head, Winslow sought out the girl and spotted her by the campfire. She was poking the embers with a stick, her chin propped in one hand. Winslow squinted at the glistening goo on his shoulder and wondered if he had the strength to sit up. It didn't feel like his shoulder or arm even existed. He could see them there, right where they should be, but when he prodded the appendage, he couldn't feel it.

Confused, Winslow searched the campsite for Fayree. He knew she was there, could sense her, but couldn't see her anywhere. Frowning, Winslow realized that the same sense he had for the great cat beyond the Pillars was what alerted him to Fayree's presence. He tried to concentrate, to define what was letting him know these things. It wasn't his

Talent, he double-checked, but still only caught the sense of slumber from his magic.

He sighed and then stopped.

He could *smell* them.

Inhaling again just to test the theory, Winslow not only smelled the cats, he could taste them in the air.

"Mother, Maiden and Crone," he breathed.

Fayree was a great cat.

But that was impossible. He'd healed the woman. She had the same bone structure as any Untalented. True, he'd been a little disoriented at the time, what with having just survived a train wreck, but he was certain he would have noticed any discrepancies.

"Mr. Winslow?" Mirabella perked up at the sound of his voice. "Mr. Winslow, you're awake! Are you hungry?"

He shook his head. He probably was hungry; he was just too focused on being confused. "Where is your mother?"

"Here, Lord Agoston," Fayree called from the tree line.

Winslow had to crane his neck to see her approach. She was exactly as he remembered her, female parts all where they should be, but now that he watched he could see a litheness to her movements. As blocky and hard as her features were, Fayree was graceful. She had a shorter frame, built a bit stockier than the average female, but the difference wasn't so substantial as to be noticed at first glance. Her dark hair was down, curly locks flipping wildly around her shoulders, which only seemed to accent a sense of strangeness about her.

For a second he thought he might be going crazy, but the look in her eyes told him otherwise.

She was different and they both knew it.

"I cannot summon my magic," he said. It seemed important that she know he was vulnerable, but he couldn't fathom why. If she wanted him dead, she could have killed him in his sleep, or just left him to bleed to death after the attack.

"I thought that might happen." Fayree stepped beside Mirabella. "The methods of the Tre`ow are unknown to your kind. I fear I may have traumatized your Talent."

"Madam," Winslow couldn't stop a wry laugh, "you are dangerously close to traumatizing me as a whole."

Fayree smiled and crouched beside him. Leaning over, she began to check on his wound, keeping herself busy as she stumbled through an explanation. "There is a wild plant called the verue. It has several medicinal properties when used correctly. Specifically, it slows bleeding and promotes the healthy mending of tissue in the body. But it is a difficult plant to find. Very wild."

"Where did you get it?" Winslow glanced at the gooey substance coating his shoulder. "Did you . . . did you cross the Pillars?"

"No. I can never cross the Barrier again. Outside of Magnellum I am considered a traitor to my own kind and the Wild would kill me." Fayree nodded to his shoulder in approval and settled back on her haunches. "But the space between the Pillars, where the Remora stones grow, there are sometimes such plants. You are lucky I was able to locate one."

Winslow regarded her carefully. He knew of the space between the Pillars. The Warders, the sect of society meant to keep both Witch-Born and Untalented in order, hunted the spaces for their Remora stones. A stone could render a Witch-Born talentless, thus putting the nobles of society on equal standing with the Untalented. But they were rare and hard to find. It was dangerous to enter the space. The Wild was active there, capable of attacking if you entered it, which meant that Fayree had taken a rather large risk in order to produce the healing plant.

The methods of the Tre`ow, she'd said. Her people. None of the history lessons he'd been taught as a boy had ever mentioned such a race. In fact, history seemed to take for granted that the Warding Pillars had always been there. The hatred harbored by the Wild was never explained, just accepted as unalterable truth.

Staring at this woman, who was so obviously not Untalented or Witch-Born, Winslow felt a little like an uneducated oaf.

He looked to Mirabella, who fidgeted beside her mother and appeared to be doing her best to behave. He sensed none of the cat in her, but there was something else. *Something different*, he thought restlessly. Seeming to read his mind, Fayree spoke again.

"My daughter is an anomaly. She is not full Tre`ow and she is not full Untalented. Time alone will show us what she is, Lord Agoston."

"And when will I have command of my Talent again?"

"I do not know," Fayree stood, smiling at Mirabella as only a mother could. Then she refocused on him. "When I used the verue on you, your Talent rejected the Wild in it. There was a battle between your magic and the wildness of the plant. I cannot tell which of them has won."

"You have a little Wild in you." Mirabella bounced twice, beaming as though this were a good thing. "Just like me!"

Unsettled, Winslow couldn't return the smile.

CHAPTER NINE

Valeda surveyed Walter's School for Unfortunates from across the street. It was, by all appearances, a mansion that had been converted to hold the school. The four-story building commanded its half of the street, unapologetically austere behind the wrought-iron gates surrounding it.

At first glance it wouldn't be a place that you would expect to see children, especially happy children, and yet they were there. Just to the right of the building, in a wide patch of grass, several children of varying ages rioted about the place. Their bubbling laughter could be heard above the clap of horses and carriages, and Valeda couldn't suppress her smile.

The sight and sound tugged at her heart and for the first time in several weeks, Valeda felt her unease lessen. Inasmuch as she didn't like Lady Delgora's cryptic movements, Valeda had a sense that she was on the right side of things. Whatever was happening behind the closed doors of noble society, House Witch Delgora was obviously fighting for the Untalented. And since Valeda herself was Untalented, it seemed a good idea to support the Witch rather than expose her.

That was why she hadn't shared anything with Monty. The Ambassador managed to wedge her out of her stateroom on board the *Crescent Moon* just once, exclaiming how unhealthy it was for her to remain cooped up for so long. She still wasn't certain how she'd managed not to be sick in front of him. Whatever he'd seen on her face seemed to convince him that she wasn't faking, but Monty would not be deterred from his answers.

At least it had been a pleasant sort of interrogation. He needled and pried, but covered it all with laughter and compliments. In retrospect, Valeda thought his company had been welcome in spite of her illness. For the hour he'd spent at tea with her, Monty managed to keep her distracted from the fact that they were flying.

Still, she'd kept her responses vague, especially when he asked about her private walk with Lady Elsie. House Witch Minne Orzebet didn't need to be kept abreast of movements in Delgora, and Valeda was well aware of the fact that Montgomery Taven would relay everything to his own Lady. That was, after all, his job.

Glancing both ways, Valeda made certain the road was clear before crossing. She blessed the Fates that she was back in her trousers and suit-jacket, nimbly avoiding horse droppings and muddy puddles in the cobblestone. While she saw the necessities of wearing a skirt on occasion, Valeda much preferred trousers. It wasn't considered stylish, but she wasn't a fashion mogul.

No, she thought, as she reached the front gate of the school, *she was a fencer and a reporter, capable of handling herself if need be*.

A plump old man sporting a chest-long white beard waddled out of the gatehouse on the other side. Valeda was caught off guard by the lush beard. It was braided, of all things, and the pointy triangle the braid produced should have looked absurd, but somehow, on this man at least, it complimented his features. His matching white hair made a pleasant sort of wave at his shoulders, accenting the deep tan peeking out from the beard, and his round, sturdy frame lent him an intimidating presence.

"Hello, I'm Miss Quinlan. I've an appointment with Master Walter this afternoon."

The big, white-haired man had an icy-blue glare that seemed to bore right into her. She made certain not to qualify herself as a reporter since she was still, technically, on leave and far out of Tormey Lands. While it wasn't uncommon for a newspaper to send reporters under cover to other House lands, it was generally frowned upon by the Witches. It appeared the Witches did not appreciate having the troubles of their homelands under the scrutiny of their peers.

"Miss Quinlan?" The big man's menacing demeanor melted into a big smile. "Ah, the newspaper woman. Lady Feverrette said to expect you. Come on in."

He unlatched the gate and held it open for her as she passed through.

"Lady Feverrette?" Valeda eyed the front porch of the manor house with a frown. She was getting quite tired of feeling outclassed.

The sooner she got her answers, the sooner she could get back to her quaint little apartment and her regular life. She had four distinct tasks to carry out for House Witch Delgora, the first of which this strange meeting with Master Bernum Walter. Valeda had no idea what she was supposed to say or do in this meeting, just that she had to be there.

"Yes, Lady Feverrette is our patron," the man said, his bearded smile somehow widening.

"Lovely woman. She deals with all the financial particulars of running the school. Master Walter says she's a verifiable mathematical genius."

Confused, Valeda glanced up at him. "Perhaps I'll have the pleasure of meeting her in the course of the meeting."

For all intents and purposes, Valeda had assumed Lady Elsie was the school's patron. That seemed to make sense anyway. Why else would she have been sent there?

"Oh, no. You'll not be seeing Lady Feverrette here. She prefers to stay in town, closer to Fortress Lorant." He locked the gates behind her and turned toward the Manor. "But look at me, forgetting my manners. I'm Jakob, the gatekeeper. Let me show you in."

Smiling her appreciation, Valeda followed him down the cobblestone path. He didn't talk beyond that, just took to humming an unfamiliar tune as he waddled forward. It was slow-going. Jakob had a severe limp on his right, which only enhanced the dramatic waddle.

In an attempt to appear like she hadn't noticed the awkward gait of the man beside her, Valeda focused on the children again. They were closer now and some of them had stopped to watch her approach. The four smaller ones took a particular interest in her, hurrying up to the path before she could reach the porch. They were all very well-groomed, if a little disheveled by their play, and wore matching uniforms of green and white. Lady Elsie would have been pleased by the neat little button-down shirts and tailored pants.

"Mr. Jakob, who is this?" asked a dark-haired boy of about six, who kept pace with them. He kept strictly to the grass, as if the cobblestone path were an unbreakable barrier.

"Well now, Chuckabee, it's not nice to talk about someone when they're right there. Why don't you ask her yourself?"

"Madam Hilden says we're not supposed to talk to strangers," Chuckabee said, earning a few encouragements from his friends.

Jakob paused and blinked down at the boy. Then he laughed, which sounded quite a bit like a hoot and was loud enough that Valeda jumped. The children, apparently used to the big man's laughter, joined him in a chorus of giggles.

"You've got that right, Chuckabee," Jakob said after a moment. "This is Miss Quinlan. She has some business with Master Walter."

At the mention of Master Walter, the children gave a hushed and reverent coo. Thoroughly amused by the display, Valeda kept quiet as she was led up the stone steps and onto the mansion's porch. Jakob, just as entertained by the children around them, sent her a friendly wink that immediately settled her nerves. Perhaps she didn't know what she was doing here, but the so-called "unfortunates" were charming. There was a warmth here, an open welcome that she hadn't noticed on first approach.

"Children!" a female voice called from the other side of the yard.

All four of the boys jerked upright, their eyes going wide with alarm. With barely a goodbye sent her way, they tore off in the direction of the call, their little green and white uniforms disappearing around the corner of the building. Jakob chuckled from beside her, which was loud in its own right, and then gave her another broad smile.

"Chuckabee was a right hellion when he first got here. Madam Hilden has done quite a job on him. Tucks right down when he's told to now." Jakob turned toward the massive door and gestured her forward. "Afraid I can't leave the gatehouse unattended for long, Miss. The housekeeper can show you the way."

Thanking him, Valeda stepped through the door and entered the single most contradictory house she had ever seen. The front vestibule was larger than she expected, nearly the size of a full room, with two elegantly padded benches flush against the east and west walls. Underfoot, her flat-soled boots reflected off the highly polished wooden floor and directly in front stood a glass wall that was entirely impractical for a school of children. Etched in golden patterns along the glass were mountain scenes, creating an oddly disorienting symmetry between the picture and the hallway beyond.

Glass double doors stood open in the center of the strange wall, but the mountain patterns continued throughout, making a giant mural that probably made more sense with the doors closed. Valeda blinked twice and then moved into the hallway, turning so that she could see the other side of the mural. It was possibly the oddest thing she had ever seen in her twenty-six years and she wanted to remember it.

"Ahem."

Startled by the voice, Valeda spun around to face a razor-thin man with a head of thinning blond hair. His long face was wrinkled up into a welcoming smile, his tall, suited frame stood out against the pale walls and Valeda flushed. There was a door to his right, which she hoped he'd just come through. The idea that he might have been standing there the whole time she'd been puzzling over the mural made her self-conscious.

"I'm sorry to startle you," he said. "I heard the door open."

"Oh, I just . . . well . . ." Flustered, Valeda gestured to the mural. "I was a bit ..."

"It is extraordinary, isn't it?"

"Quite, yes."

"There are several rumors about where it came from. All of them boil down to the idea that the former owner of this manor house wasn't altogether sane."

Valeda smiled. "Well, as beautiful as it is . . . it does seem a bit impractical."

"Indeed," he agreed and reached out one hand. "I'm Bernum Walter. I imagine you would be Miss Quinlan?"

His grip was gentle as they shook hands, soft and scholarly.

"I am," Valeda spared the mural one last glance before focusing her attention on the man.

"I'm so pleased to meet you." Walter stepped back and invited her into his office.

By all appearances, Walter was a practical sort of man. In spite of the luxury of the manor, his office was simple. Only one window, she noted, with a clear view to the gatehouse. His desk was positioned in such a way that he undoubtedly had seen her approach up the path. The desk itself wasn't impressive, but the scattered paperwork covering it proved that Master Walter was a very busy man. She could see educational plans, calendar schedules, food orders and basic-necessity inventories.

Given that all of these were in plain view, Valeda didn't feel that she was prying into anything that might upset the man, who ushered her toward a set of chairs beside the small fireplace. In fact, if he noticed her curiosity, he certainly didn't acknowledge it.

Settling into what Valeda equated to a spare kitchen chair, she relaxed as Master Walter sat in the chair opposite. For once, she didn't feel outclassed.

"Now then, Miss Quinlan, I was quite pleased when Lady Feverrette contacted me about your visit. She said that you would be more than helpful with the articles we wanted to place."

"Articles?" Valeda faltered. "Master Walter, I must be frank, I have no idea why I'm here. I was told I had a meeting with you today, but I was given no details what it was about."

Master Walters looked shocked for a moment, and then he puffed a rueful laugh. "Oh, dear. I thought you were better informed than that."

"I'm afraid not." She had to fight the annoyance out of her voice. A part of her understood that Lady Elsie couldn't trust her, especially given that she was a reporter, but a little more information would have been better.

"Well then. It's really very simple. The school needs teachers. Particularly in Engineering and Mathematics." Master Walters slouched in his chair, his lanky frame somehow shrinking with the movement. "Mrs. Hilden is a wonder, she truly is, but the school has room for many, many more children. We've already petitioned several of the orphanages across Magnellum to send us their overflow and we're expecting two dozen more by the end of the month."

"So . . . you want to place ads in a newspaper advertising job opportunities?" Valeda spoke slowly, her mind trying to discern what was going on. This couldn't possibly be as simple as writing an advertisement, could it?

"Not just a newspaper, Miss Quinlan. The *Tormey Regular*. Tormey is renowned for its engineering program."

"But . . . surely you can do that on your own. Putting out an article is really quite simple."

"Alas, I have no money. The banking of the school is done by Lady Feverrette, and she assured me that you would have resources to make this happen." Walter lifted a finger and stood up, moving to his desk in two strides. "I have a list of what we're looking for. There are specific requirements that the candidates must meet."

Resources, she thought. Holding her shoulder bag in her lap, Valeda had to suppress the urge to roll her eyes. House Witch Delgora's trust fund really did have a purpose, though the sum that had been transferred into Valeda's name was far more than what would be necessary to run an advertisement in the *Regular*. The other tasks she was meant to perform were low budget as well, unless the Lady meant for Valeda to travel in high style. Her travel to Lorant was a moot point since getting back to Tormey from Delgora required that she cross through Lorant lands.

She was always given an assignment in Lorant during the Winter Tournament and her newspaper normally paid for that, so the requirement that she meet with House Witch Feverrette wasn't a problem, either. *Fifth day of the first week of Winter Tournament, at Feverrette House lodgings in Lorant, at precisely three in the afternoon*, her mind recited. Documents would be sent to her prior to that date to carry to the meeting.

The meetings were the only tasks she'd been given that worried her. This meeting and the meeting with House Witch Feverrette were the only two, but neither of them had specified what they were for. Though Master Walter, who was circling and underlining the salient points in what he needed in teachers, wasn't near as intimidating as her imagination had made him out to be. She was certain Lady Feverrette would be more frightening.

Her third task was the one that would be difficult. She was to seek out the whereabouts of Lord Winslow Agoston and report his location to Lady Elsie immediately. Valeda was baffled about this matter because it was well-known that Lord Winslow Agoston and Lord Dorian Feverrette-Delgora were close friends. It seemed to her that two such friends should always know where the other was. *Or at least have a clue*, she thought.

"Here we are." Master Walter returned to the chairs and handed over a sheaf of paper. "I understand that advertisements cost per letter, so I'll leave it to your discretion on how it's done. It's imperative, however, that the Engineering teacher has a specialty in water pumps."

That statement drew her attention. "Water pumps?"

"Indeed."

He didn't elaborate further. In fact, something flashed in his eyes that told her not to question further. As she rose to leave, thanking him for his time and promising to see to the advertisement as soon as she got home, her mind flashed to Delgora Manor. To the night she'd stared out the window at the ridgeline in the south, watching the light rotate and overtake the darkness, she remembered.

The ark, she thought. *By Fates, this was how the Lady was gathering the people she needed to build the thing.*

CHAPTER TEN

Elsie growled in frustration and tried the summoning spell again. Salt and fire whirled around her, hiding from view the trappings of her bedroom. Though she couldn't see him, she knew that Dorian had entered at some point and was standing just beyond the whirlwind. Still, she had to try one more time.

"I, Elsie Varene Delgora, House Witch, call forth Magic to my side."

In answer, the swirl of flame and salt stopped, poised midair, and waited. Elsie could see Dorian now, a silhouette through the fog of orange-speckled salt. It was comforting to know he was there, and at the same time, she cringed. He knew what she was doing, or trying to do, and her failure would only cause him pain.

"Find for me Lord Winslow Agoston."

Her command sent the salt back to spinning, whipping through the air with the force of fire behind it. She concentrated, barely able to see an image forming in the chaotic swirl before her. But the image was a blur and the most she could make out was a vast forest of coniferous trees. There was no strain on her magic, though she knew there should be. Her union with Dorian stretched her Talent beyond the normal capacity of any Witch-Born. This was the main reason the Council had attempted to block their marriage. There was a different sort of power growing between Dorian and herself, something that frightened the noble Witches.

And yet, as powerful as she and Dorian could be together, Elsie could not clear the vision. She couldn't find Winslow, and no matter how long she stood there, the picture before her wouldn't change.

Flinching, she released the spell.

It's very likely, she thought, as the flames returned to their candle wicks, *that Winslow is dead.* The blurred trees, the blobs of what she assumed were boulders, were probably his final resting place. And Fates forgive her, it was her fault.

"Still nothing?" Dorian asked. The grimness in his voice cut into her heart.

"Nothing. Just those cursed trees." Because she couldn't bear to look at him, Elsie turned away.

With one sweeping motion, she commanded the candles and salt back to their respective places. The candles swished through the air, stacking themselves neatly into a chest on her vanity table. The salt gathered and deposited into a small sack just beside the candle box, and then there was silence..

Dorian was debating what to say, she knew. The poor man was stuck between defending her actions and the prospect of a dead friend. *Dead*, she thought with a great deal of self-condemnation, *because of a silly order I made*.

In her defense, Winslow had been miserably restless.

"Perhaps Miss Quinlan will uncover something," Dorian said quietly. "By all accounts, she is a determined reporter. She won't rest until she has answers."

"As demonstrated by her appearance here at Delgora Court," Elsie murmured.

Another long silence cloaked the room. Elsie remained at the center of their room, staring at the cream and blue quilt stretched across the bed. Leona had commissioned it from a notable quilt-maker in Three Points, Broska. It had probably cost a year's stipend, which made Elsie vaguely uncomfortable. She was used to being the giver, not the receiver.

In fact, Elsie felt far more comfortable in her little old shop down in the township than she did in the Manor. Everything was on display in the Manor. She felt vulnerable, open, and not at all like a House Witch. Though, to be fair, Elsie wasn't certain how a House Witch was supposed to feel. Eight years in the position and there was still an awkwardness about her.

Dorian moved to stand behind her, pulling her into a firm, reassuring embrace. "This is not your fault," he said.

She felt the rumble of his voice and closed her eyes. "It certainly feels like it."

"Winslow needed something to do, even I know that. If he'd stayed here, he would have continued to mope."

"I'd rather he be moping and alive than missing and possibly dead."

His grip tightened on her at the statement. He didn't move, didn't try to contradict her, just held her. *That*, she thought, *is the remarkable thing about my husband*. Dorian had such control, such quiet command of himself that he could speak to her even in silence. He agreed with her, at least in the desire to see Winslow safe, but could offer no words of encouragement. What he could offer was strength, security and compassion.

Fates bless the man for his patience. True, he'd shouted at her earlier, finally demanding the truth of what they were fighting, but Elsie had expected that fight years ago. He had quite a lot of fortitude in waiting so long.

Seeming to sense her distress, Dorian ran his hand over her arm, barely hissing as the tattoos zapped him. Elsie knew the pinpricks of gold peppering her arm were defending themselves, she could even understand that Magic didn't like to be touched, but she needed to feel Dorian's hand in hers. There were moments it felt like the entire arm didn't belong to her anymore, and she needed the normalcy of this small act.

Sighing, she determined to enjoy the quiet moment and turned to face Dorian. He smiled down at her, though he looked more tired than anything else. Reaching up, she brushed his jaw with her knuckles and smiled back. It was unfair that she couldn't push the worry away from her mind. Dorian deserved a peaceful, warm life. He deserved better than the insanity she had put him through over the years.

"I can sense the regret in you," he said. "Quit it. I chose the woman I love over being pampered at court. Deal with it."

Elsie breathed a faint laugh. Sometimes she forgot that their Talents could communicate. He knew her on a deep, quiet level that spoke beyond the physical realm.

Giving her a real smile, Dorian kissed her. She leaned into him, forgetting about Magic and the ark and Winslow.

CHAPTER ELEVEN

Winslow wasn't certain what bothered him more: the fact that he still couldn't heal himself, or the damned walking stick he was forced to use. By mutual agreement, they had decided it was time to move again, injury or no injury, and he clumsily negotiated the tracks with the thing. He'd never endured a wound for this long and he suddenly had a healthy respect for the Untalented.

Pain spiked through his leg and shoulder at every step, and he imagined his body was justifiably angry with him for the movement. Not even the verue plant concoction slathered over his shoulder was much help.

"Tell me about the Tre`ow," he grumbled, grunting as the toe of his boot snagged on a bit of rock. He over-corrected, jarring his body and intensifying the pain. "Mother, Maiden and Crone!"

"Do you need to rest, Lord Agoston?" Fayree asked.

"No. If I rest I might not get up again." Winslow continued forward and slanted a glare at her. "Distract me. Tell me who the hell you really are."

Fayree glanced down at where Mirabella kept pace beside her. The little girl's green eyes were wide with wonder. He got the distinct feeling that this was a story she hadn't been told before. That seemed a bit curious, but Mirabella was still very young. It was possible that Fayree was trying to shield her daughter from the revelation. Still, he couldn't feel any remorse for asking. Even at their slow pace they would reach Three Points by midday the next day, unless a rescue train came for them.

He wondered what was taking the personnel at Three Points so damned long to get out there.

"I'm not sure how to explain this to you," Fayree said after a long moment. "Your own history books cannot recall a time without the Pillars. You have no concept of the culture you come from, and even if you did, you wouldn't recognize it. Magnellum has grown into a culture of its own, with customs and traditions far removed from its origins."

Winslow kept hobbling forward, frowning as he digested her statement. "You mean to tell me that Magnellum was once a part of the Wild?"

"Yes," she said. "A very important part."

"Is the land sacred or something?" Winslow could picture some kind of religious motivations spurring the Wild to attack them. *It would explain why the Wild continued to assault the Pillars*, he thought. But it also meant there would be no end to that assault.

"No," Fayree said. "But there is something sacred to us here."

"Well, what is it?" he asked. "Whatever it is, I'm sure we can return it. Anything for peace . . ."

"Magic," she said grimly and he faltered. "Magic itself is what we hold sacred."

"But . . ."

"And time."

"Time?"

"Outside the Pillars, time has stopped."

Winslow paused to lean on his stick some more. His shoulder flared with dizzying pain and he had to take several breaths to steady himself.

"That's impossible," he said. "You can't stop time. Life would cease to exist."

"Nothing grows," Fayree said quietly. "We live and breathe and consume, but nothing new grows. There are no new births. Our children do not age. If time has not stopped for us, then it is moving at such a slow pace that we may never see our old age."

Winslow felt a shiver crawl over his neck. Somehow, this seemed far worse than religious motivations. *But how?* he wondered. *How could they have lost time outside the Pillars and what good did it do them to attack Magnellum?*

"How is that possible?" he asked.

"It happened the day Magic was taken from the Host tree," she said. "We were a great people once, the Tre`ow. Skilled farmers and tradesmen, much like Magnellum is today, but with a far simpler political system. We all used the Talent you Witch-Born possess, just in smaller portions. And we all paid homage to the Host tree . . . the place where Magic dwelt."

He didn't like where this story was going. Magic, according to Fayree, originally belonged in the Wild and the Wild wanted Magic back. There wasn't a Witch in Magnellum who would willingly give up their Talcnt, and even if there were, he doubted that would appease the Wild. Besides, Magic Himself had been stolen from them, too. They literally had nothing to give the Wild.

"A woman named Median devised a way to extract Magic from the tree," Fayree said. "The intention—or so she said—was to give us a chance to speak to Magic. To give Magic a voice. She took a young man named Brasen and tattooed him with wards in the finest gold."

Winslow could remember those wards. He'd seen Magic up close the day the Dellidus attacked. Even in the horror of the moment, the man-god had been beautiful, shimmering golden light as power was drained from him.

"When Brasen touched the Host tree, Magic poured into its new corporeal form. We were all of us amazed," she continued, as they resumed hiking. "We'd lived for centuries with Magic, but never had the opportunity to speak with it. In the months that followed, we all took our turn with Magic, learning how best to harness our Talent. But the longer Magic stayed in Brasen, the darker the Host tree became.

"Our Talent started to change. Instead of being able to work our craftsmanship, we began to . . . shift. At first we couldn't predict it. One moment we would be ourselves and the next . . ."

"An animal," Winslow said, realization hitting him. Fayree really was a great cat.

She nodded at him and smiled sadly.

"I've never seen you as an animal," Mirabella said suddenly.

Fayree brushed curly hair away from her daughter's face. "I've had a lot of practice learning how to control it."

Mirabella seemed to accept this answer and continued walking. He watched her for a moment, thinking of Fayree's description of the timeless world outside the Pillars. He wouldn't want to raise a child that couldn't grow. That would be heartbreaking to the extreme.

"Mirabella . . ." he started to say but Fayree must have anticipated his question.

"My daughter was born in Magnellum. She isn't like the rest of us."

"Ah," Winslow said. "So . . . what has time got to do with this?"

Fayree sighed and shook her head. "We demanded that Median put Magic back."

"And . . . she refused?"

"No, she tried." Fayree frowned, her whole face pinching in concern. "But when Brasen touched the Host tree again, something else happened. Some say Median was standing too close. Others say she misplaced a ward on Brasen. The theories vary, but whatever it was that went wrong, it cursed Median. And through her, we are cursed."

"I don't understand. What kind of curse?"

"Median is stuck. She is constantly pushed through Past, Present and Future. You know her as Fate."

Winslow stopped walking again, this time out of shock.

"Mother, Maiden and Crone," he said reflexively.

"Her body shifts because it cannot stop. She is constantly in flux, you see?" Fayree said.

"Let me get this straight," Winslow said. "Fate, the Deity that all of Magnellum worships, is really a cursed Tre`ow named Median who may or may not have intentionally stolen Magic from a tree in the Wild?"

"The Host tree is not merely a tree, sir. Please do not take it lightly," Fayree said stiffly. "For thousands of years it protected us and brought us prosperity. Without Magic it has continued to decay, slowly dying right in front of us. And believe me when I tell you that any Tre`ow would gladly give their life to heal it."

"Is that why you're here? To find Magic?"

Her expression suddenly closed. "No, Lord Agoston. I already told you. I am a fugitive from my own people."

A hollow hooting belched into the air and Winslow glanced down the tracks. Another train was coming.

Though it had taken them a disgracefully long time to send it, the depot in Three Points had finally come to see about their missing passenger train. Winslow could feel the rumble of it through the tracks and hobbled for the side, quickly ushering Mirabella and Fayree out of the way. The hurried movement jostled his injuries, but he was too pleased at the prospect of rescue to grumble about it.

He didn't know what he was going to say about his sudden lack of magic and he really didn't care. The other Tre`ow was still tracking them and he wanted Mirabella safely away. He looked from the girl to her mother and then at the approaching train. Fayree had taken a big risk by saving his life and exposing herself. Damned if he knew all the consequences to it, but he could smell the fear in her.

"Your secret is safe, but if you have any hope of survival you will go to Lady Elsie Delgora." He had to raise his voice against the roar of the locomotive. "At the very least, she can buy you a little more time."

CHAPTER TWELVE

Cringing, Winslow hobbled down the short steps and onto the platform. For various safety reasons, not the least of which was a concern to keep Fayree's secret, he'd been forced to scrape off the verue goo. He'd done this in the privacy of his cabin, insisting that the Untalented physicians were unnecessary in spite of the gaping wound. He'd expected the pain to double without the numbing agents of the plant, but Winslow had grossly underestimated the damage to his shoulder.

Now that he could feel it, the entire arm was only barely attached. His bones shifted every time he moved; like they were floating in a viscid sea of torn muscle and cartilage. Giddiness made the world swirl in his vision as his feet settled onto the wooden deck and for a horrified second he thought he might faint.

"Winslow!" a familiar voice shouted above the throng of people.

Winslow hadn't really noticed the crowd at first, he'd been too damned focused on not vomiting all over himself. The unpleasant prickle of fever made his skin damp and his vision fuzzy, and he suddenly wished they hadn't been rescued. The verue plant was far better than dealing with the unnatural tide of heat, the nausea threatening him, or the confusion of bodies just below the platform.

"Winslow!" The voice came again and he tried to concentrate.

He was holding up the line of people behind him who wanted to disembark the train, but if he wasn't careful he thought he really would pass out.

So he used the unidentified caller as an excuse and scanned the crowd. His vision blurred at the edges, smearing people together and making them indistinguishable from storefronts and streets and grungy market tents. Blinking hard, he finally located the voice in his memory.

An instant later, Bartholomew Feverrette-Kelemen broke free of the crowd. He was intercepted by a Warder, who was obviously trying to quell the fascination of the crowd. It had been twenty years since the last train accident, making this an unprecedented debacle. There were a scant few, however, whose anxious faces gave away the hope of finding a loved one among the survivors. Winslow wondered which one was Fayree's husband.

"Sir." Bart's voice cut through the clamor with cold authority. "I am Lord Feverrette, Consort of House Witch Caresse Feverrette, and you *will* stand aside."

The Warder looked conflicted for a moment, but conceded. Tugging once on his suit jacket, Bartholomew strode forward, clearly angry but too gracious to complain. Winslow found himself smiling, though he knew it must look weak to his friend. Bart reached his side, took in his battered state, and then grabbed his elbow.

"Fates alive, Winifred, if you tell me you've strained yourself out of Talent, I will kill you where you stand."

The reprimand was quite serious but for the use of Winslow's teasing name. He couldn't remember exactly when he'd earned the title "Winifred"—sometime during his University years—but he was fairly certain Dorian was the instigator. The rest of their little group had taken to the nickname shortly after.

"Oh, you know me, Barty," Winslow mumbled as Bart began to lead him out of the way.

"Curse you, Winslow Agoston. When I heard about the accident, my heart nearly failed." Bart took a slow pace away from the train, toward the private stairs that would take him into the depot. "You could try to have more consideration for my nerves, you arrogant, thoughtless man."

Winslow was too ill to argue. In fact, given the last few days, he was honestly pleased to hear his friend's voice again, irate as it might be. He found weird comfort in Bartholomew's tirade. Winslow didn't catch it all, just the familiar rumble of his friend's voice as they proceeded into the station's formal offices designated for nobility.

The building around him was a dizzy swirl of wood and brass fixtures, but he caught the privacy of the room they stopped in. Bart helped him settle into an overstuffed sofa that seemed utterly out of place. They were in an office, not a lounge. The fraying, brown catastrophe that he sunk into belonged someplace else. The overwhelming scent of stale smoke wafted from the thing, and he had to take a moment to fight his nausea down.

Winslow decided instantly that the sofa needed to be burned and put out of its misery.

"Now then," Bart said, returning from closing the door and reaching for Winslow's shoulder, "let me have a look."

He knew his friend meant to heal him, and for some reason he became alarmed. He jerked to the right, and his shoulder snapped to life with sudden, acute pain. He lost control and wretched all over the couch. Bart swore, which was funny because he never swore, but Winslow was too busy being sick to laugh.

"Fates alive, Winslow! Just let me fix it!"

But all Winslow could think of was Mirabella, proud as a shiny whistle, declaring that he had a little Wild in him. He wouldn't risk hurting Bartholomew, not even if it meant the end of his misery.

"D-don't," he wheezed.

"What?" Bart hesitated. "Why ever not?"

"Just . . . don't."

"To hell with you, Winslow Fagen Agoston. I'm not watching you bleed to death. Now quit whining and let me help . . ."

"Crone's teeth, Bart! Leave me be!"

Obviously shocked by the outburst, Bart stepped back. *There was cursing*, Winslow thought wryly, *and then there was 'cursing'*. "Fates preserve us", "Fates alive", even the unsavory "Mother, Maiden and Crone" could almost be construed as a prayer or a plea. But "Crone's teeth" was something you only heard muttered in a black alley somewhere with murder in the air. Given what he knew now about the Fate's origins, Winslow couldn't work up the superstition to apologize, either.

Someone knocked on the door but Bart didn't move, he just kept staring at Winslow.

"You really have lost your magic, haven't you?" Bart said quietly. "I thought maybe you'd just been resting it after helping the other survivors, but . . ."

The knock came again.

Winslow met his friend's light blue eyes and held them. He trusted Bartholomew with all his might, but he couldn't part with Fayree's secret. *Not here*, he thought. If someone else heard him, he'd have more to worry about than his silent Talent. He could be branded a heretic for revealing Fate as no more than a cursed Wild woman. Now that he thought of it, Winslow had no idea how to tell his friends—especially Elsie—what he had learned. They would have to know, and soon, if anything was going to be done about it.

But Fates help him, he wasn't certain they would believe him.

Just before the door opened, Winslow nodded to his friend. He consoled himself with the fact that it was only partially a lie. At present, he really was Talentless. He wasn't certain how he was going to explain to Bart why he didn't want to be healed, but he hoped he would think of something soon. Bartholomew's expression turned pained and he closed his eyes, ignoring the fact that their privacy had been intruded.

"My Lord Feverrette," a professional needle of a man said from the doorway, "are we to assume that the gentleman is indeed Lord Winslow Agoston?"

"He is," Bart said quietly, opening his eyes.

"Excellent. We have arranged lodging at the Pinnacle and Pyre." The man glanced at the soiled sofa, but his face never faltered from its polite, careful expression. "We will, of course, want to hear His Lordship's version of events so that we can discover what happened."

"I'm certain that can wait for a day," Bart said.

"Yes, of course."

"Wait." Winslow fought another bout of nausea before he could finish his sentence. "Mirabella and Fayree . . ."

"Mrs. Cornelius was met by her husband. They are filling out some forms for us and are free to go."

"Give them my room number at the Pyre," Winslow said. "I . . . wish to see them again. Before they go."

The man looked puzzled at this but nodded acceptance. A moment later the door was closed, presumably so that Bart could heal him in privacy. It was sometimes funny, the things society took for granted.

"They're going to notice if you won't let me heal you," Bart seemed to read his mind.

"I know."

"You're not the first Witch-Born to strain himself out of Talent," Bart continued. "From all appearances, you did it to save those two females. That's as noble a reason as any to lose your magic."

"Barty," Winslow struggled to his feet. He swayed until Bart steadied him with a hand on his good elbow. "Stop trying to cheer me up."

"I'm not trying to cheer you up, I'm trying to make you see reason." Winslow heard annoyance in Bart's voice now. "Just let me heal you."

"Bartholomew," Winslow grabbed his friend's shoulder, shook off another wave of dizziness, and met his eyes again. "Swear to me that you won't try. No matter what happens, don't do it."

"What the hell, Winslow? This is insane. What do you mean 'try'? You know perfectly well that I can do this." Bart stopped suddenly, a new flicker of understanding in his eyes. "By Fates! What has happened to you?"

"I can't explain right now, Bart. I just . . ." Glancing at the door, he lowered his voice. "It could be dangerous for you."

Bartholomew's mouth tightened into a grim line. "Fine," he said. "But when I'm castigated from one end of Magnellum to the other for not doing my compassionate duty, I want you to remember this moment."

***

"We've been dragging the water up here in buckets," Forvant grumbled and pointed at the southern slope beside the ark. "It's a pain, but at least the greenhouses inside are healthy. There'll be herbs and food, just like you wanted. All they'll have to do when the ark is sealed is maintain it."

"Master Walter is interviewing an engineer for the water pumps tomorrow," Elsie said with a frown. "Hopefully we can solve the issue of water soon."

"Another engineer?" Forvant grunted, his weathered face contorting into a scowl. One bushy, white eyebrow shot upward in question. "How many more you plan on bringing in?"

Any other day, with any other person, Elsie might have ignored the question. But today was her anniversary and she had pleasanter plans occupying her mind, which put her in a far better mood than normal. And this was Forvant, one of her last surviving friends and confidants. The man had known her as a child, helped her fight for Delgora when she came of age, and she could not disregard him as she would any other servant.

"The water pumps are the final issue with the structure. Everything else works," she said, turning away from the ark.

Where was Dorian?

"The more people you bring in, the more rumors are going to spread about this thing."

"The rumors don't concern me, Forvant. This ark needs to be functional, and quickly."

The sun was nearing the horizon; dusky purples and vivid pinks sprawled across the sky. Shadows stretched and beckoned, inviting her into the obscurity of night. Standing in riding pants, blouse and vest, Elsie suddenly missed the comfort of her assassin's garb. She hadn't worn it in years. Not since the night of Bryva's death, actually.

Her heart pinched at the thought of her dead sister. The years had not managed to dull the loss for her. Most days she was so preoccupied with what she had to do that it was barely noticeable. But then there were moments, like this one, when Bryva haunted her as clearly as Magic did.

Elsie wondered if it was like that for Winslow. The poor man had been in love with Bryva before the assassination. True, it had been a brief love affair, but there was an intensity between them that couldn't be denied. It was, if Elsie wasn't mistaken, the source of Winslow's discontent, and the reason she had sent him on his mission.

"Elsie."

Something in Forvant's voice made her turn to him. His expression seemed conflicted, though she couldn't determine what it was about. He'd never hidden his opinions from her in the past, why should he start now?

"Elsie, I know you've worked with rumors before. But these ones are dangerous. You're not just trying to confuse one woman like you did with Lady Reonne for the House Seat. Now you're upsetting a lot of nobility."

"If you're expecting a Bedim Assassin to come and kill me . . ." She stopped when he shook his head.

"No, I know most of them were killed." Forvant's long mouth twisted in displeasure. "Look. You're scaring important, powerful people. That Ambassador Taven . . ."

"Monty?"

"Yes, him," Forvant said with another grunt. "I took the liberty of going through his things. He had a whole dossier hidden in his luggage."

"What?"

"It was all about you, Elsie. You and that arm of yours. He knows it's special."

That was to be expected. It wasn't like she could hide the whole appendage. Someone was bound to comment on the gloves she wore. What worried her wasn't so much that Taven had been studying her intently enough to create a dossier, but rather, to whom he was going to deliver that dossier. Lady Orzebet harbored nothing but ill will against her and Dorian.

Her Talent suddenly coiled in anguish.

Looking up sharply, Elsie searched the ark for Dorian again. She knew this pain. It wasn't coming from her, but from her husband. It wasn't physical, but deep and powerful.

"What's wrong?" Forvant asked.

"Where has Lord Delgora gone?"

"Eh? He said he was headed to the town proper, to the telegram . . ."

Elsie summoned her Talent before he'd finished speaking and whispered the command for transportation. To any normal House Witch, this was a dangerous and difficult spell, but to Elsie it had become as natural as breathing.

"*Yetakupo,*" she commanded, and in an instant the world was gone. For a fraction of a second there was nothing, just the elemental sense of self wrapped up in her Talent, and then she was standing in the center of Delgora market. Several people gasped at her sudden appearance, distancing themselves from her immediately. The churn of people made it hard, but Elsie managed to find him.

Dorian stood outside a small, squat building. The sign above it read "Bosman's Telegram." Elsie hurried to his side, sensing his distress even more acutely now that she could see him.

"Dorian?"

He looked at her bleakly, his face an ashen gray that alarmed her further.

"Winslow has lost his Talent," he said. His words were so quiet that she almost missed them.

Stunned, Elsie gripped his forearm. "No!"

"Bartholomew caught up with him in Three Points," Dorian continued, misery painting his words. “There was some sort of accident and Winslow is injured. Bart fears he won’t survive.”

“But why doesn’t he heal him?”

“Winslow doesn’t wish it.” Dorian turned to her and gripped her shoulders, suddenly clear and awake. “He’s asking for me. Elsie, I have to go.”

“Yes, of course.” The words were out of her mouth before she could register them.

Yes, of course he had to go.

But this was their anniversary. But she needed him nearby, for support and counsel. She warred with herself, gazing into his steely gray eyes, already missing him before he’d even parted. She thought for a moment that she could go with him, but knew that she couldn’t. A House Witch could only leave their lands twice a year, at the height of Winter and Summer. For reasons no one had cared to explain to her, these were the two points when her magic was at its best. The Warding Pillars were stronger, the people safer.

They were still six weeks away from Winter Tournament. If Dorian travelled by boat, he’d reach Lorant in three. If he travelled by dirigible, he’d get there in one. It was expensive, but considering the wounded man waiting for him, well worth the money. Truth be told, Elsie wasn’t concerned about costs. There was far more cash at her disposal than Dorian knew about, money that had been taken from the league of assassins known as the Bedim. She kept it hidden because she knew Dorian wouldn’t like it. He’d spent half his life hunting the assassins down, he certainly wouldn’t want to be funded by them.

Blood money.

Yes, she knew that. Every cent earned by the Bedim came at the cost of someone's life. She had, after all, been a Bedim before Dorian had entered her life. There were moments she thought he struggled with the knowledge that she'd been an assassin, but he seemed to justify her actions as necessary. After all, if she hadn't been a Bedim, she would have died before she could claim the Delgora House Seat.

"I think the *Crescent Moon* is due back early in the morning," Elsie said quietly. "We will get you on it."

Something flickered in his eyes. He reached out to cup her face, gingerly rubbing his thumb across her cheek. "I will bring him back here if I can."

"There isn't much time. You need to go pack."

His hand slipped behind her neck and he drew her closer. Elsie leaned into his solid warmth and closed her eyes. It did not escape her that she was about to be alone for the first time in eight years. His kiss drowned the thought from her mind. She didn't care that they were standing in the middle of the marketplace, didn't care that there were giggles and gossip around them, she only cared about the promise his mouth was making.

I will be back, it said.

As he pulled back and turned to escort her to the manor, Elsie felt a block of icy fear settle in her stomach.

Yes, but will you be back in time?

She wasn't certain if the voice came from herself or from Magic.

CHAPTER THIRTEEN

Valeda walked down Grandeur Street, a thin layer of snow muffling her footsteps. The pale dawn was brightened by a fresh blanket of snow; the first fall of the seasons, if she wasn't mistaken. It was cold enough that she'd donned a scarf and mittens to accompany her navy-blue suit jacket, but it wasn't bitter.

She could almost hear the bellowing laughter of her father and three older brothers echoing through the empty street. They played hard and often in the winter, trouncing through the frothy white stuff while the neighbors looked on in horror. To them, snow was a prison guard, keeping them safe inside their homes with blazing hearths and hot drinks. But to Jeremiah Quinlan and his family, winter was the apex of freedom.

Stopping in front of the elegant double doors of the Pinnacle and Pyre, Valeda pushed her fond memories aside. Her father was a newspaper man. Before earning himself a cozy editor's position at the *Daily Prime*—her own paper's direct opposition—he had been a reporter like her. In fact, everything she knew about the business came from him. She could hear his voice even now, coaching her to remove her own bias, to make herself like a sheet of blank paper, unprejudiced against whatever story she was about to find.

But there was a problem this time.

This time, the story she was meant to get dealt with the very man Lady Delgora had sent her to find. It was too bizarre to be coincidence. Lord Agoston hadn't been seen in months. His erratic behavior had estranged him from his own family and pushed him from the public eye. How he had ended up in Three Points, Broska, hundreds of miles away from Agoston House lands, left quite a bit up to speculation. The cursed man wasn't doing anything to stem that speculation, either.

She glared at the shiny brass doors and tried to fathom a man who allowed the rumor mill to slander him. Most of the Witch-Born would relate some sort of public statement, if only to calm the nerves of the Untalented. But from Lord Agoston there was nothing, not even when the gossip suggested that Winslow himself had caused the train accident.

Taking a deep breath, Valeda pushed open the doors and stepped into the warmth of the Pinnacle and Pyre front lounge. Everything was cream and brown inside, promoting a sense of cleanliness, warmth and class that might have intimidated her before. Now, however, she was too focused on her goal to care if her jacket wasn't flush with fashion.

Lifting her chin, she made her way to the polished front counter. No one greeted her in the lounge, which was expected this early in the morning, but the silence still unsettled her. Perhaps it was unseemly for a girl to call upon a wounded man like this, but she needed to bring something back to her boss, Korman, or she'd be out of a job. The other two survivors of the train accident disappeared hours after their arrival in Three Points, making Lord Winslow Agoston her only chance at keeping gainful employment.

Ringing the little bell on the counter, she prepared herself for a fight. An immaculate man walked stiffly out of the back offices. The curls of his dark hair looked somehow stern, waving to the left in a precisely curved arc. He had a flat face, as though perpetually pressed against a bit of glass, with a long, pointed nose and flaring nostrils. Valeda smiled as winsomely as she could when his black eyes settled on her.

"I am here to meet with Lord Agoston," she said, trying to adopt a casual manner.

"His Lordship has given strict instructions that he is not to be disturbed."

Valeda had anticipated this. More than one of her colleagues had moped about having been turned away from the place. They, however, did not have a patron.

"His Lordship will accept me, sir. House Witch Lady Elsie Delgora put me on this errand. Please express this to him."

The man eyed her narrowly, but set off for the back rooms. Presumably, he was going to relay her message to the Lord in question, so she waited.

Sunrise glowed fiery orange through the windows, setting the lounge into vivid shades of gold and honey. The ivory floor rug tinged an opaque pink in the reflecting light, and the deep cherry wood on the furnishings warmed until they looked black. *Simple, classy and clean*, she thought. *It was no wonder why every nobleman and ambassador lodged here.*

"His Lordship is prepared to see you now, Miss."

As the man turned away from the room, she gave him a pleasant smile and followed him into the comfortable hallways that made up the Pinnacle and

Pyre. He stopped in front of door number twelve, knocked twice, and stepped back. A muffled voice called for her to enter. Valeda nodded to the manager, seized the brass handle, and admitted herself into the room.

Winslow was on his balcony, reclining in an armchair that had obviously been moved for his comfort. All of his windows were open to the dawn, revealing a large room of the same cream and brown tones, an unmade bed, and a side table crowded with an alarming array of bloodied bandages. Her eyes fixed on the bandages for a moment as she closed the door behind her. She'd only ever seen that much blood at Winter Tournament, when she'd interviewed Lord Bravyn Ibolya about his controversial decision to raise the price of healing.

She only had a moment of confusion.

Winslow Agoston was wounded, and by the looks of it, quite badly. *Not only is he wounded*, she thought as she walked carefully through the room, *he's unable to heal himself like a normal male Witch-Born. In the effort for survival, he has likely strained himself out of Talent.*

Fates be praised, she thought. *Korman's going to get a brilliant story.*

"For someone on the business of a House Witch, you certainly dawdle a lot."

Affronted, Valeda marched onto the balcony, half aware that it was snowing again and half surprised at the appearance of the young lord. She used the word "young" in a loose sense. Winslow Agoston had to be five years older than her own twenty-six, but he was certainly younger than

Montgomery Taven. He was so sickly pale that he matched the snowflakes gathering on his blonde head. Even the dark circles that outlined his hazel-green eyes seemed subdued under the stress. He wasn't gaunt, not yet anyway, but the angular bones in his face promised that such a destitute state was forthcoming.

"For a Witch-Born, Lord Agoston, you certainly look close to death," Valeda blurted before she could check herself.

Agoston smirked at her, his wide mouth curving in a devilish manner that belied any illness. "Death has been hanging about me for days, Miss. As I am still breathing, you can see that it hasn't won yet."

"Well, it's certainly doing its best to try. Why in Fates haven't you let someone heal you?"

"I fail to see how that question has any pertinence to your business here this morning." He closed his eyes and for a moment Valeda was struck by how fragile he looked. Not just sick, but frightened, as though all of Magnellum were crushing down on him. "Since you failed to leave a name with the manager, you have me at a disadvantage."

"Valeda Quinlan. Of the *Tormey Regular*."

His eyes snapped open. The withering glare he gave her was neither sick, nor fragile, and she realized at once her mistake. She took an involuntary step back, though he hadn't moved from his position.

"You are either incredibly clever, or dangerously stupid." His voice and demeanor were just as cold as the flecks of snow peppering her face.

"We could try something more flattering than that," a cultured voice said from the doorway. "You are a gentleman, after all."

Trying not to show her surprise, Valeda turned to the balcony doorway. A freckled man with curly, orange-blonde hair leaned casually on the doorframe, his highly tailored clothing giving him away at once.

"My Lord Bartholomew Kelemen-Feverrette," she said, dipping into a quick curtsy.

"Well, at least you remembered to curtsy to him," Lord Agoston said with a scoff.

"He was not busy insulting me," she retorted.

"Yes, and you weren't plotting how to charm an interview out of him, either."

She flushed and glanced at the balcony railing. He had her there. "I won't deny hoping you would relate your adventure to me, Lord Agoston, but I really am here by the direction of the House Witch."

"Which House Witch?" Lord Feverrette asked.

"Elsie," Lord Agoston struggled to sit up. He grunted and hissed his way to a standing position, looking somehow paler as he straightened.

He was a good head taller than she was. She noticed this as he swayed, half turning toward his room. Lord Feverrette pushed himself away from the door. Winslow's first step was unsteady, and the second step sent him reeling. He toppled backward, directly into her, and Valeda's yelp of alarm was cut short as they both toppled to the ground.

The wooden porch rattled under the impact of their combined weight. Her left hip struck first, pain bursting into her awareness a split second before Lord Agoston's body smacked into her again. Something hard—likely his head—crushed her nose in a single, sickening snap.

After several moments of confused struggle, trying to determine whose limb belonged to whom, ignoring the pain throbbing out of the center of her face, with Lord Feverrette grunting in effort somewhere above her, Valeda finally sat still. Lord Agoston's head was in her lap, heavy and limp. By instinct, her left hand pressed against the oozing wound in his shoulder. Lord Feverrette crouched beside them, his concern evident as he stared at his friend.

"What are you waiting for?" she asked, unable to stop holding the man in her lap. "Heal him."

"He made me swear not to."

"He's bleeding to death!"

Lord Feverrette's face twisted into a conflicted scowl.

Had she been in a right state of mind, Valeda might have been able to see the oddity of the moment. While she'd done all manner of reports for the *Tormey Regular*, she had never once held a dying man in her lap. Help was literally an inch away, and yet, Bartholomew Feverrette still did not move.

"He's your friend!" she tried again.

"I know who he is!" Feverrette snapped. "But he made me swear . . ."

"To hell with your oath, sir!"

The look Feverrette gave her was hard and angry, but he suddenly grabbed hold of Lord Agoston. She'd seen healing done before, so the concentration on Feverrette's face wasn't a surprise. The sudden slam of pain, however, stole her breath. It was a deep pain, coursing from Agoston and into her own body, sinking into her bones. A sliver of coherency helped her realize that this had nothing to do with his shoulder. This was something else.

The ache intensified. She felt suddenly hot all over, as though she might combust if it continued. She didn't know when she'd closed her eyes, but she forced herself to open them again.

A purple mist clouded them, sparkling in the morning sun. She saw four bodies where she knew there should only be two. Bartholomew crouched over Winslow, his face contorted in surprise and determination. The other two forms were more like shadows, no facial features and yet, she could recognize them. She knew instantly that she was looking at their Talents, though the rational side of her said it was impossible.

Witch-Born magic wasn't really seen, just the affects when the user accessed it.

The alarming thing, beyond the burning pain, was that these Talents looked like they were fighting. Valeda watched them churning about in the mist until her vision dimmed.

***

Frowning, Winslow sat up. Melted snow soaked through his dressing robe and trousers, freezing his left hip in an uncomfortable manner.

That discomfort, however, paled to the sudden realization that he was healed. He rotated his shoulder, stripped the robe away from it, and searched for the wound.

A crescent shaped scar ran from his collarbone to his shoulder, jagged and puckered a deep pink. Running his fingers over the soft skin, Winslow fought between joy and horror. The jumble of bodies on his balcony was an inch deep in snow, testifying that they had been there for quite some time. Bart and the Quinlan woman were both passed out, tangled together on top of his own body.

He knew, without looking, that they were alive and not dead. He could hear their heartbeats, steady with slumber; could see their soft puffs of breath through the frigid air.

Winslow called on his Talent.

Deep in the recesses of his core, his magic still slept. But there was a sense that it had been used recently. He could feel the residual effects of it in his body, the healthy strain of muscle and quiet clarity of mind. But he could also feel the Wild in him. It was a constant purr in his blood stream, just out of his reach and yet, tauntingly close.

Shifting carefully, Winslow gathered the woman first. The snow stood out in her reddish-brown hair, looking somehow soft when it connected to her. Everywhere else it was cold and sharp, but when it came in contact with Valeda Quinlan, snow itself relented. Winslow had noticed, and appreciated, the intelligent beauty who had come to interrogate him in spite of the pain he'd been in. As he lifted her, small weight pliant in his arms, he got an even closer view. A perfectly oval face framed by dark curls, dark eyelashes, short but prominent against the fair skin. Her mouth was a thin, pink line, the same shade as his freshly discovered scar, and he was tempted beyond all reason to kiss it.

He frowned, shoving that impulse firmly away. Carrying her into the room, he laid her on the bed and went to retrieve Bart. His friend was not as easily lifted. Grunting and struggling, Winslow managed to drape Bartholomew's arm over his shoulder and drag his limp form into the warmth of the room. He took one step toward the bed and stopped.

Bart would not thank him if he woke up in bed with a woman who was not his wife. Innocent though it may be, Bartholomew Kelemen-Feverrette took great pains to ensure his honor could never be called into question. Redirecting his feet, Winslow lugged Bart to the settee on the other side of the room. It was a ridiculously flowery contraption, obviously meant to appease the gentler sex by way of aesthetics, and located in the coffee nook. He tried to lower his friend gently, but Bart outweighed him by at least ten pounds and was taller by several inches. His friend slipped from his grasp and collapsed into the settee, every bit as unconscious as when Winslow had picked him up. Winslow suspected Bart would now have a bruise on the left side of his head.

Wincing apologetically, Winslow arranged Bart into a more comfortable position and straightened. He stepped back and surveyed his work, looking from Valeda to Bart and back again. Satisfied, he harrumphed and turned to the bathing nook. It didn't look like either of his guests were likely to wake soon and he'd been too injured to attempt a bath when he'd arrived. Honestly, he didn't care if Miss Quinlan woke while he was bathing.

It would serve her right for her impertinent behavior, he thought.

He still wasn't certain why she was unconscious. By all appearances, she was Untalented. He assumed that he'd knocked her senseless when he fell over. *It seems the most plausible reason*, he thought, as he turned the brass knobs and started the bath. Pipes rumbled against the wall just before steaming water burst from the faucet, pouring into the copper tub.

Taking his time, Winslow shut the balcony doors, closed the drapes, double-checked on his two slumbering guests, and returned to the tub. It was halfway full by the time he stripped off the dressing robe. Deciding it was best to maintain some form of modesty, he turned his back on the room before slipping out of his trousers and stepping into the bath. He groaned as his body submerged into the warmth and he closed his eyes.

"Mother, Maiden and Crone," he muttered.

Inch by beautiful inch his muscles relaxed. Winslow scrubbed travel, illness and dried blood off his body, reveling in the feeling of being clean again. He knew he was being silly. He'd never paid this much attention to a bath before, but suddenly every little pleasure in life was monumentally important.

His stomach growled, startling him with its loud protest.

Reluctantly, Winslow unstopped the tub and got out. Snagging his dressing robe again, he checked on Valeda and Bart, but neither had moved. He only got the robe halfway on before the scent of stale sweat and blood assaulted him. Offended, he dropped the garment and searched the room for an alternative.

His eyes found Bart's travelling trunk at the base of the bed. Given that the dressing robe had been leant to him, Winslow doubted Bart would be upset if he borrowed something else. Still naked and dripping, he moved to open the trunk, not caring about the small puddles he left in his wake. It wasn't until he had selected a pair of pants and a shirt from the trunk that Winslow recognized the oddity of the moment.

He was nude and he wasn't alone.

Even though his company was sleeping, polite society dictated that he at least keep a modesty wall between himself and the woman. Bart's presence didn't matter over-much. The university showers had little privacy, after all. But poor Valeda Quinlan would be scandalized to know he'd wandered about in such a state.

Quickly donning the pants and shirt, Winslow shut the trunk and sat on it. His stomach growled again but he didn't move. There was something altogether wrong with his thinking process. Winslow was known as a flirt and a bit of a cad, or he had been up until eight years ago, but he was also a man of honor. The idea of flaunting his naked self across a room was shocking, appalling, but a disjointed part of his psyche kept asking why.

Why? he thought again.

Because it was wrong.

But why was it wrong?

He hadn't been born with clothes on. Why was the wearing of clothes such an integral part of society? Aside from the sumptuary laws that showed the station of the person wearing the garments, Winslow was bereft of an answer. There was warmth, of course. Though, for the first time since he could remember, Winslow didn't mind the cold. *It feels natural*, he thought. *Like it ought to be.*

His stomach growled a third time and Winslow stood up. He moved to the bell-pull and tugged, still puzzling over his own train of thought. There was something very wrong here and he knew it. He waited for a knock on his door so that he could order something to eat.

Meat and potatoes, he promised his stomach. *Lots of potatoes. And fruit. Any kind of fruit.*

Just before the knock came, Winslow realized what was bothering him. His line of questioning had touched on the most basic law of society—that of wearing clothes. It was, by his estimation, one of the fundamental elements that separated man from beast. It was unquestioned. One simply did not go about Magnellum without clothes on, but in his mind, Winslow fought to hold on to this simple concept.

He opened the door slowly as the knock came again. For a long moment, he just stared at the servant who stood there.

"You rang, sir?"

Winslow blinked, remembering where he was, and relayed his order. The servant bowed and ran off, glancing once over his shoulder as he went. Winslow closed the door again.

"Fates alive," he whispered. "I'm losing my sense of humanity."

CHAPTER FOURTEEN

Valeda woke to the sound of a man's voice. Disoriented, she didn't move for a long moment and tried to determine where she was. She was safe, she knew that much, though she didn't know why she knew it. Soft pillows and warm blankets held her snug and secure, but she had no recollection of going to bed. In fact, the last thing she remembered was Lord Agoston falling on top of her.

"Oh, good. You're awake."

Blinking, she found him standing by the door, wearing pants that were too long and a shirt that was half unbuttoned. She was at once struck by a healthy sense of virility flowing from him. Valeda wasn't certain if she was relieved or horrified at the fact that he'd been healed. It was one thing to call on an injured man in order to get his testimony, it was quite another to be alone in his bedroom when he looked so . . . 'Good' was the first word that came to mind, but she shoved it away. 'Hungry' was the second thought, but that was even less appropriate and she scowled.

"On my honor, Miss, I apologize sincerely for the harm that came to you," Lord Agoston said quickly. "Naturally, I didn't wish to leave you on the porch."

They both looked at the balcony door as he added, "Gathering snow."

The awkwardness of their current situation hit her full force and she sat upright. The sudden movement, however, sent a needle of pain piercing through her temples. With a soft groan, she closed her eyes and held her forehead, counting her heartbeat in time with the throb in her head. She heard Agoston move and felt the bed sink at her left.

"I'm afraid I can only offer you a towel for the headache," he said sympathetically. "But the good news is your nose stopped bleeding."

Valeda opened her eyes again, startled to find him sitting so close. She stared at him for a moment, taking in the warm hazel-green of his eyes, the lean structure of his face and the wicked curve of his mouth. Virility or confidence, she wasn't certain what it was that made him so appealing, but she nearly leaned forward to kiss him.

Shocked at her own brashness, Valeda forced herself to look away from him. Something deep inside her rebelled at this, urged her to turn back, but she kept herself strictly in place.

He'd been leaning forward too, she realized.

What was she thinking? The man had been near to death an hour ago, and she was still in his room, on his bed, and alone. *Or not quite alone*, she realized, spotting Lord Feverrette in the far corner. The other gentleman was either sleeping or unconscious, his long body half hanging off the settee.

"You . . . you really have lost your Talent, then?" she asked, needing something professional to say to take the intimacy out of the moment.

Winslow smiled wryly. "Who is asking? The *Tormey Regular* or the agent of Elsie Delgora?"

"Both, I imagine." She stiffened and frowned at the coverlet. "Whichever answer you want public, tell that to the reporter. Whichever you want Lady Delgora to know, tell that to the agent."

"Very well," he said, standing up. "Miss Quinlan of the *Tormey Regular*, I have strained myself out of Talent. To my knowledge, I am the first Witch-Born to do so in thirty years." He began to pace through the room, stopping by the settee, then doubling back to her, all the while answering the stock questions any trained reporter would ask before Valeda could ask them. "It happened sometime during the train accident as I tried not to become a human griddle cake. No, I don't think it could have been helped. No, I have no idea how the train jumped the tracks. Yes, it was a very grueling experience to be suddenly Untalented and unable to heal myself. No, I don't think I shall ever get used to the lack of magic. Yes, I would do it again if it meant keeping Mrs. Cornelius and her daughter alive."

He stopped by the balcony doors and lifted his eyebrows at her.

"Almost convincing, Lord Agoston, but you have one glaring hole."

He looked taken aback, "Oh?"

"If you lost your Talent in the middle of the train accident, how did you heal Mrs. Cornelius?" Valeda smiled at his flustered expression. "Little Miss Mirabella Cornelius made certain that everyone knew of your heroic efforts toward her mother. Which means you had your Talent when you left the train but lost it somewhere else. Something else happened on the road to Three Points, Lord Agoston. Something that took your magic and nearly your own life. What exactly happened out there, my Lord?"

If he thought he could distract her with a half-truth, then he'd seriously underestimated her professionalism. Valeda had been doing this sort of investigating since she'd been able to put two words together in a sentence. Witch-Born or not, Winslow Agoston would give her the interview she needed. She'd keep her job, report to Lady Delgora, and find Magic, the man-god, before Winter Tournament was done.

"Well, answer the lady, Winifred," Lord Feverrette said from the corner. "We're all in suspense."

"Bart." Agoston's voice was full of relief as he moved to see to his friend. "How do you feel? Are you all right?"

"I'm whole and hale, Winslow. You needn't fuss."

"But your magic is still intact?"

Valeda perked up at this. Lord Agoston feared transferring his ailment? That was interesting.

"Of course it is." Feverrette glanced at her. "I'm rather astounded that you would think otherwise."

"But there was the . . ." Agoston looked at her too. "The struggle."

Valeda squirmed under their scrutiny. Deciding it was best that she get out of Lord Agoston's bed, she moved to stand up. The pleasant mahogany floor seemed to tilt under her, and her head still throbbed but she stayed upright.

"Indeed." Feverrette stood as well. "At first I was confused by the fight. It seemed quite rude of you to take me on in an elemental battle like that.

But then I remembered that our magic doesn't work that way without a conduit."

Both men continued to stare at her. Valeda felt as though she'd missed something vastly important. Her mind was trying hard to process all of the information. The noble Witch-Born tended to guard the secrets of their magic, so she wasn't certain what Lord Feverrette meant. Common sense, however, told her that every Witch-Born's magic was constricted by the flesh around it. Nobles fought each other hand to hand; they didn't pit their magic against one another. It wasn't done because it couldn't be done.

"What exactly is your relationship with House Witch Delgora?" Lord Feverrette asked her bluntly.

***

"The exact terms of my arrangement with House Witch Delgora are private. Suffice to say, she sent me on an errand to locate Lord Winslow Agoston." Valeda managed to sound prim, her stature suddenly rod-straight, and her chin lifted at an obstinate angle.

Winslow glanced at Bart, who looked mildly amused at the Untalented woman before them. To Winslow, Valeda Quinlan seemed frightened. Oddly enough, the emotion had a scent to it. *Salty*, he thought, *like he'd been submerged in the ocean.*

As a tense silence permeated the room, Winslow tried to guess at what was scaring the skittish girl. He imagined there was a natural fear in being with a Witch-Born. Being Untalented, it was against the norm for her to be in such an intimate setting with two nobles. Not to mention the gender issues apparent—it was highly improper for an unmarried woman to be in the company of a bachelor. And there was, of course, the fact that she'd been trampled by his own sick form and rendered unconscious.

No, he thought. *She has every right to be upset. And she's handling the situation with a commendable amount of decorum.*

"After having located Lord Agoston, what was your task?" Bart asked.

The girl flushed and looked away. "Only to report to the Lady as to his whereabouts. It was my hope to garner a favor off the gentleman."

This caught Winslow's attention. "A favor?"

"I am a newspaper woman, Lord Agoston. To be frank, my recent travels to Delgora have placed me in a precarious situation with my employer." Valeda looked up again and met his gaze.

She had the most peculiar shade of light-gray eyes. *Like a cloud heavy with rain*, he thought.

"The interview," Winslow assumed.

"Indeed."

"I see," Bart said with a hum.

A knock at the door startled them all. Winslow blinked, acutely aware of the food just outside the room. He moved to the door briskly, explaining as he went: "I'm damned starving. That'll be my order."

He saw Valeda reposition herself to the coffee nook, out of sight of the curious servant. Bartholomew came to help move the trolley of food in, tipping the servant before shutting them all into privacy again. Winslow's stomach growled again as he uncovered the plates. Heavy peppers, garlic, buttered potatoes and beautifully seared meat hit his senses full force and his mouth watered. Without a thought to his guests, Winslow filled a plate and took a silver fork from the trolley.

He sat on the foot of the bed and began to eat. He might have moaned a little as the first forkful of potatoes melted in his mouth, but he wasn't paying attention. For a long minute, nothing existed but the peppery grain of red meat, the warm comfort of buttery garlic, and the strange purr of Wild in his bloodstream.

"Your father isn't a Warder, is he?" Bartholomew asked.

Though the question was directed at Valeda, Winslow was startled at the sudden conversation. He looked at both of them, who were watching him with cautious stares. Winslow gestured to the trolley with his fork: "Have some. I ordered plenty."

"No," Valeda responded to Bart. "He's an editor."

"I see," Bart said with another frown. "Were either of your grandfathers Warders?"

"No." This time Valeda frowned. "Why do you ask?"

"Well," Bart took a deep breath, a sign that he was about to lecture, and Winslow contented himself with his food. "Warders are tasked with the protection of Magnellum. They have authority equal to and sometimes over the Witch-Born."

"I know who the Warders are, Lord Feverrette."

"Yes, but did you know that most, if not all, of the Warders harbor some magic?" Bart picked up an apple from the trolley. "Not as much as a Witch-Born, mind you, but enough that they can recognize the Talent in other people."

Valeda frowned a little more, her mouth puckering into a little bow as she watched Bart shine the apple on his lapel. Winslow continued to eat, waiting for his friend to come to the point. He assumed that Bart had a reason for interrogating the girl, anyway. For his part, he couldn't remember anything beyond his ill-fated attempt at walking prior to passing out.

"I had heard rumors," Valeda said cautiously, "but nothing substantial."

"Indeed, and it should probably stay that way," Bartholomew said. "The Warders guard their secrets very well. But the reason I ask is because you, Miss Quinlan, are Talented."

Winslow forced himself to swallow a large hunk of potato before he spoke. "You're joking."

"No, I'm not." Bart glanced away from Valeda with a smug smile. "Whilst you were busy passing out, Miss Quinlan and I were forced into an elemental battle with your inner self. As I said before, this sort of thing can only be accomplished with a conduit. More often than not, a House Witch serves as such, but I've only ever heard of it being done a handful of times in the last millennia."

"Fates alive, Barty! You sound like a history professor when you talk like that." Winslow set his plate aside and stood up.

"Yes, well, the University of Lorant has made several offers to me," Bart smiled again, "but I simply can't be parted from my wife for the entirety of the school year."

"You're wrong," Valeda said quietly. "I'm the only daughter of Jeremiah and Marissa Quinlan. I have three brothers and a moderately successful career. The only thing I am talented at is writing."

There was steel in the woman's voice. She continued to stare at them from her corner, but she no longer seemed frightened. In fact, Winslow thought she looked very angry.

"I'm not disputing your parentage," Bart said gently. "But something happened this morning that you can't deny."

"Lord Agoston fell on me, that's what happened."

"And what did you see just prior to passing out yourself?"

"I saw . . ." Valeda paused and scowled. Her eyes slid to the left and she looked as though she were remembering something. Her frown deepened and she looked back up. "I saw Lord Agoston's body crashing into me. Nothing more."

Winslow rocked back on his heels and whistled lowly. "That's either first-class denial or the worst lie I've ever heard."

Valeda flushed a deep crimson, squared her shoulders and stalked toward the door. "My business here is done. I will inform Lady Delgora where she can find you. I wash my hands of this incident."

"What's so bad about being Talented?" Winslow asked at the same moment that Bart intercepted her at the door.

"I did not mean to upset you, Miss Quinlan." Bart held his hand out to her. "Do accept my apologies."

Valeda stared at his hand for a moment and Winslow almost called out a warning to her. Bartholomew really was too clever for his own good. His long, slender hand looked bronze in the dim lighting of the room, but Winslow saw it for the trap that it was. The moment her skin touched his, she would feel the power in him, and she would be forced to see the power in herself.

Reaching out, Valeda grasped Bartholomew's hand in a firm grip.

***

She'd never felt anything like it in her life. Inhaling sharply, Valeda reeled at the sudden tingle that passed through her arm. It was like she'd smacked a hard surface and a hand-numbing blast of force pulsed through her. Her fingers felt as though many pins and needles prodded her just under the skin. The sensation continued up to her shoulder before disappearing.

Jerking her hand back, Valeda fell against the door.

"Forgive me," Lord Feverrette stepped back. "It was the only way I could think of to show you the truth."

"That has never happened before, I'm quite certain of it." Valeda found the strength in her voice curious. Her entire world felt rattled and off-kilter, and she sounded more like she was getting ready to order tea than break down and cry.

"Yes, well, I think that has more to do with Winslow than he cares to admit," Lord Feverrette said.

"Oh, yes. Blame it on me. Glorious!" Lord Agoston said.

Valeda looked to Winslow, who hadn't moved from his position beside the bed. She had an overwhelming desire to run over and embrace him, and nearly took a step forward, but stopped. *This is insane!* she thought. She didn't know this man and yet, something deep in her core recognized him. Perhaps it was her newfound magic, or the strange circumstance they found themselves in, but she knew better than to act on it.

"I imagine we've come to the point where I must explain myself," Agoston said wryly.

"Is it possible that I have somehow stolen your Talent?" Valeda asked.

"No. I can still feel my Talent. I just can't access it."

He was telling the truth, but she couldn't define how she knew that. She could somehow sense his magic, and felt its deep slumber. But she could also sense something else in him, something feral and dangerous.

"Miss Quinlan," Lord Agoston said, holding her gaze, "nothing that I am about to say can leave this room. We will come up with a story for your paper, if that is what you truly want, but it won't be the one you are about to hear."

"I can't lie, Lord Agoston. My reputation could be ruined."

"It's not a lie if he gives you his formal testimony," Lord Feverrette interjected. "There are always formal versus informal interviews, Miss Quinlan. Lord Agoston is simply offering you a chance to hear them both."

"And you're expected to keep one of them private," Agoston said. "Just like you keep your arrangements with Elsie Delgora private."

Frowning, Valeda crossed her arms. She didn't like the arrangement, but she had to know what was going on. She suddenly missed doing trade reports and interviewing the Untalented in her hometown. Everyone had secrets, to be sure, but none of them came with the underlying threat that emanated from these two men. Still, she found herself nodding her acceptance.

There wasn't really a choice in the matter. Valeda needed to know how she had somehow become Talented. It was no small amount of magic, either. She could feel it just under her breastbone, an ever-present, ever-moving companion. In her mind. she could almost visualize it: a golden cord, coiled and ready to be stretched and used. She couldn't determine its length, but it wasn't little, and she had the strange sense that it was introducing itself.

"Very well then," Winslow said, gesturing to the chairs in the coffee nook, "it's best if you both sat down for this."

CHAPTER FIFTEEN

Dorian hadn't been apart from Elsie in eight years. The lack of her voice, the yawning distance between them, and the empty half of his bed in the morning pounded her absence into his awareness. He felt a growing sense of anxiety the longer he stayed away and yet, he could not go home. Not before he'd seen Winslow. Fear for his friend mixed with fear for his wife put him even more on edge. He wondered if this was how Elsie felt all the time, knowing what was coming and helpless to stop it. Her nightmares had become less frequent as the ark got closer to completion, which he might have seen as a good thing if she hadn't shared that vision with him. Dorian couldn't shake the feeling that those canine creatures from her dreams were more than extensions of the Wild. They felt angry and intelligent to him.

All of his instincts were on high alert. It had been eight years since he'd been hunted by the Bedim assassins and, yet, he felt that same itch between his shoulder blades; the sensation of being carefully watched.

Frowning, Dorian glanced surreptitiously down the street. It was full night in Three Points and damned cold. His joints ached with the frigid air, despite three layers of coat, vest, and shirt. Dorian muttered his displeasure and wished fervently for the Delgora Tropics.

Wrought-iron streetlamps made pockets of light down the curving sidewalk, illuminating chill fog and the occasional passerby. People were hurrying home, closing little shops that lined the main thoroughfare of town. Dorian could see the welcome sign of the Pinnacle and Pyre just across the street and paused to let several carriages go by.

His last telegram from Bartholomew said that Winslow was still bereft of Talent but was no longer crouching on death's doorstep. While he was grateful that his friend would survive, Dorian had no idea how to address a man who had lost his magic. Witch-Born magic wasn't just a series of spells to be cast; it wasn't found in chemicals or nature or any other sort of substance. The Talent was a part of each individual—a quiet, constant companion dwelling at the core of every Witch-Born. Dorian couldn't fathom the idea of suddenly being without it.

By Fates! What am I supposed to say?

He couldn't just charge in there and berate the man for his actions. According to the papers, Winslow had acted heroically, rescuing the lives of some woman and her daughter. Still, all Witch-Born were trained to know their own limitations. Winslow had to have known he was crossing the threshold. He had to have sensed it. So why in Fates had he done it?

Scowling, Dorian stepped into the road and started to cross, determined to find out. As he reached the other side, a gunshot cracked through the street. Instinct grabbed him and he ducked, but he knew it was too late. He hadn't been expecting an attack, hadn't been prepared. Something slammed into the back of his left shoulder and he staggered forward. He felt jacket, shirt and flesh tear under the assault as several jagged items embedded themselves into his skin and muscle.

Shouting, he spun but the ground was icy and he lost all footing. He hit the ground hard, barely managing to keep from face-planting in the cobblestone. An instant later, a carriage screeched to a halt beside him. Two men barreled out of it, intent on his person.

"My Lord!" one of them said and for a breathless moment Dorian thought they meant to help.

Then a sack looped over his head and he was blinded. Recognition came fast and Dorian swung his fist. He tried to summon his Talent, tried to heal his shoulder and prepare for the fight, but his magic couldn't respond. As his fist met with open air, throwing his body to the right, Dorian understood: he'd been shot with Remora stones.

Strong arms took him, wrestling him up and into the carriage. Dorian fought all the way, shoving elbows and knees anywhere he thought his attackers might be. He struck the side of the carriage with an elbow and felt his arm suddenly go numb.

"Dorian!" He heard Bartholomew's voice come from somewhere high.

Pain exploded through his skull as something hard hit him in the side of the head.

***

Bartholomew flung the window wide and leapt out, causing several of the dining room patrons to gasp in alarm. Winslow himself might have been startled if he hadn't seen what had caused his friend to make such a dramatic exit. As it was, Winslow couldn't tear his gaze from the sight of Dorian's limp body being shoved into the awaiting carriage.

"Fates have mercy," he breathed, watching as Bart landed roughly on top of the carriage.

"What is it?" Valeda asked.

"Someone is attempting to abduct Lord Delgora." Winslow got to his feet and leaned out the window.

"What?" She sounded more than a little startled.

"Not to worry," Winslow said, inwardly trying to calculate if he could make the three-story jump safely. He'd never tried something so brash without his Talent and he highly doubted his legs could survive the feat. "Lord Feverrette will handle …"

Three shots rang out in succession, stopping him mid-sentence. Bart dodged the first two, but the sudden noise spooked the horses and the carriage jolted forward, throwing him off balance. The third shot struck Bartholomew in the thigh and Winslow hopped onto the windowsill.

"Lord Agoston!" Valeda cried just before he leapt.

It was a terrifyingly long drop and he thought he'd resigned himself to a fracture or two, but then *it* came alive. Like flint igniting flame, his Talent burst awake, wrapping itself around that Wildness inside him, fusing the two powers together in a disorienting and overwhelming way. Every sense he had flared to life. He saw the porous grooves of frosty cobblestone rapidly approaching him, felt the sting of frigid air rushing past his body as he descended. He smelled the acrid gun smoke on the air and could taste Bartholomew's blood in the wind.

Winslow landed with unnatural grace—feline grace—and charged forward. Bart fell backward as the carriage continued to flee, but he managed to grab hold of the edge before toppling to the ground. He hung there, flopping awkwardly against the back of the carriage as it bounced down the street. Winslow ran faster, praying Bart would keep hold long enough.

Someone shot at him but Winslow ignored it. He got close enough to the carriage that he could see the panicked expression of one of the inhabitants through the back window. A second later, the man's face was replaced by the muzzle of a pistol and Winslow jumped, shoving forward with a Talent-propelled push that sent him straight up and onto the carriage roof.

Landing lightly, he managed to balance on the jostling roof and reached instinctively for Bartholomew. Bart sent him a surprised look, but collected his wits enough to climb back up and onto the roof. Grinning, Winslow winked at his friend and turned toward the front of the carriage. The driver took a sharp turn to the left and they both had to hold on with all their might to avoid being thrown off.

"I've been shot with a Remora stone!" Bart shouted above the clop of hooves and ballyhoo of speeding carriage.

Still clinging to the roof, Winslow glanced at him. His friend's expression was a mix of rage, pain and resignation. They both knew that Bart could be of no use here. Until the stone was removed, Bartholomew would be unable to access his magic and therefore be unable to fight. Winslow nodded once in acknowledgment of the problem.

"Try not to break your neck when you get off!" Winslow shouted.

A sword pierced through the wood directly between them and Winslow cursed. Bart rolled to the right just as a muffled gunshot reported from inside the cab. The bullet missed Winslow's arm by an inch and he was forced to roll away as well.

Darkness swallowed them as the carriage careened through a tunnel. Winslow held his breath, praying the occupants inside didn't try anything more while he was blinded by shadow. He could hear them arguing, muffled at first, but when he focused his Talent he could distinguish the argument.

"The assignment was for him to be taken alive!"

"I ain't dying here for no Witch-Born! Leave him!"

Lamplight came again as they emerged from the tunnel. Winslow spotted that Bartholomew was missing, then turned back to the driver. The man snapped the reigns, driving them off the street. The wheels hit the curb and Winslow found himself airborne, scrambling for a desperate hold on the lip of the carriage. Then he crashed into the roof again, his mouth smashing into the unforgiving surface with bruising force. For a dazed second he tasted his own blood, and then he spotted the driver leaping from his seat. Two other bodies flew out of the passenger compartment, each hitting the ground in a jumble of limbs and movement.

Winslow looked back to the front of the carriage, to the speeding horses and curving street ahead. Scooting as fast as he dared, he flung himself toward the driver's seat and discarded reigns. Half in the seat and half on the roof, he grabbed the leather straps and yanked back. But his nearness only managed to spook the creatures more. Winslow smelled their fear, knew instinctively that he was the cause, and recognized that he had to think of something else.

Spotting the steering pin that connected the horses to the carriage, Winslow forced himself to move again. He let go of the reigns, fell to his knees on the footpad of the driver's seat, and leaned over. It was an unfair distance between footboard and steering pin. He had to stretch and lean, but finally managed to grasp the pin. Shouting, he yanked it up, freeing the carriage from the horses.

The horses tore off. The front of the carriage dipped down, metal and wood scraping across the ground before the triangular tip of the steering mechanism hooked into a groove and the entire carriage pitched forward. Ducking, Winslow tried to cover his head as the whole thing tilted, rolled and crashed to a halt.

***

Valeda ran as fast as her pointy-toed boots would let her. She could sense the spark of her newly gained Talent yearning to be utilized, but truly had no idea how to access it. Unlike her impetuous companions, she'd been forced to use the stairs to get to the street level rather than leap the *three stories* down. She'd been more than a little surprised that Winslow—Lord Agoston, she firmly corrected herself—was not wounded by the feat.

Left with no other options, Valeda had decided to chase the ill-fated carriage in its misadventure through Three Points.

Panting, feet aching in the silly boots, Valeda stopped half inside a long tunnel. Her chest was painfully tight and her heart thudded so loud in her ears that she didn't hear his approach.

"Think of your Talent as a friend, Miss Quinlan," Lord Feverrette said, with a pained grunt. "A relationship. Let it go. Stop holding it back."

Valeda yelped in surprise and squinted into the shadows. A moment later, she found Lord Feverrette limping toward her. He'd tied a strip of his torn shirt around his thigh and his fine blue dinner jacket was limp and ragged, hanging from his torso in defeat. A deep, jagged scratch flayed open his left cheek and as he came into the light, she swore she could see the paleness of bone through blood and tissue. Her yelp turned into a gasp and she hurried to his side.

"My Lord Feverrette, you're hurt!"

He waved her off. "It'll keep. We should get to Winslow."

"But . . . why don't you just . . ."

"Heal myself?" Feverrette's mouth twisted into a scowl. "Because they used a damn Remora stone as a bullet and it's currently so deep in my leg that it's inspecting my femur. Now," he paused to take a deep breath, "let your Talent go. You'll be more useful if you let it help."

Frowning, Valeda looked away from him. It sounded sensible enough but at the same time, she hadn't been aware that she was suppressing it. There was that image of a golden cord again, coiled at her center, waiting to be stretched, but she didn't know how to reach it. For a moment she imagined that she could touch it, and to her surprise it reacted. The little hairs on her arms stood suddenly stiff as an unnatural warmth tingled over her skin, blocking out the winter's chill. She did it again, imagining herself stroking the golden coil, and all at once her heart stopped pounding, resuming a natural pace, and her lungs quit aching, and even her toes ceased their throbbing.

"There you go," Feverrette said. "Now come along. I think I heard them crash not far from here."

He began limping forward and for a moment she hesitated. Then she remembered Winslow and the carriage and decided she could ask them later about the nuances of magic. She hurried to catch up and then matched his pace through the tunnel. They emerged on the other side to see the wreck. The road made a curve, but it was obvious by the tracks that the carriage had not followed. It had proceeded through a grassy bit of park, managed to avoid several trees, and finally crashed several yards back on the road again.

A growing crowd was converging on the wreckage, but Valeda managed to spot Winslow as he climbed into the splintered and ruined carriage. She quickened her pace and wove through the gathering of people. There were several exclamations from the unwitting audience, most of them having to do with the sight of Lord Agoston.

"—thought he'd lost his Talent."

"That ain't Agoston, that's the other fellow—"

"Saw him go under the carriage! A regular man would be dead!"

She almost paused at the last comment, her stomach knotted with the images that brought to mind, but Valeda focused instead on reaching him. She didn't know exactly why, but her Talent needed to get to him, to make sure he was solid and real and whole. Pushing her way to the front of the crowd, Valeda was forced to step onto a slat of broken carriage, where she paused.

Winslow had managed to drag Lord Delgora out of the wreckage. He stood atop the rubble with his unconscious friend hanging off one shoulder, his clothes just as ragged as Bartholomew's, and bleeding substantially from the mouth. He looked formidable and heroic, and what was more, he had stopped to stare directly at her. Moonlight flinted off the green in his eyes. His mouth twitched into that wicked smile of his and Valeda realized all of a sudden that she'd been holding her breath.

Breathing again, she hiked her skirts and climbed the rubble to get to him. She still didn't know why she had to reach him. Getting to his side at last, her ankle rolled on a loose bit of the carriage frame and she nearly fell. Winslow, however, caught hold of her elbow and drew her closer to his side.

"Careful now, Vee. I'm holding Dorian just fine right now, but I've no idea if I can carry you both down." He half whispered the words, but she heard him clearly. Heard him and felt the purr of his magic because her own Talent seemed suddenly euphoric.

"Mother, Maiden and Crone, Winifred!" Lord Feverrette shouted up at them. "Quit making a spectacle of yourself. Poor Dorian needs our attention."

CHAPTER SIXTEEN

He'd had nightmares before. Prior to marrying Elsie, Dorian had spent much of his life being hunted by assassins, so he was quite used to the weltering churn of worry in his gut. However, his nightmares were normally restricted to the general fear for his own life or the lives of his closest family. The current nightmare—the one he was fairly certain was still a dream and not a reality—was a haunting of Elsie's vision.

There were jumbled voices around him. Voices that didn't belong to the sights of wolf-like creatures and bloody assault in the vision, and that was how he knew he was still dreaming. Frustratingly enough, Dorian couldn't summon himself awake.

Someone was prodding at the wounds in his shoulder, digging the Remora stones out of him. That alone should have roused him, but try as he might he could not open his eyes. He wondered if this was how it was for Elsie. There had been many times he'd caught her pacing and tried to talk to her, only to be given that glassy, blank stare of half-sleep.

Trying to ignore the chaos of the nightmare, he thought of Elsie. He felt stronger by thinking of her, so he focused. The attacks presented in the vision had failed to show where Elsie would be during all of this.

Do you really want to know?

The voice startled him. It was familiar and foreign at the same time, not a part of the regular vision. *Magic*, he realized. The same voice that taunted Elsie, the voice that had been missing from Magnellum for eight years.

Dorian wanted to say yes, but didn't know how. Dreams were not like reality. He had very little control here. But it didn't seem to matter. Magic understood him.

The haunting stopped. The scene changed, pulling him to the base of the ark. It was closed; he noticed that straight off. Great vines pounded at the curved iron structure, trying to break through. There were large dents in the ark but Dorian didn't see any tears. Not yet, anyway. He knew, however, that it would only be a matter of time before the Wild got through it.

His heart sank at the sight.

What was the point of all their years of building, of preparing, if they were destined to fail?

There is more at play than you see, Dorian Delgora-Feverrette.

His focus switched to Elsie. In the vision, she wore her assassins garb again. The last time he'd seen her in the black, loosely fitted pants, she'd been killing the man who murdered her sister. He remembered that more clearly than he liked; the way she'd slammed the assassin into a building so hard the foundations shook. In the vision, she was sitting, looking dazed rather than fierce.

Dorian watched as she reached for the base of the ark with her tattooed arm.

"How many more?" Winslow's voice snapped the dream away.

"One," Bartholomew said with a grunt.

Pain pierced through his shoulder and Dorian woke up.

"Oh dear," Miss Quinlan said. She was sitting just in front of him, holding a little jar that contained four small green stones in it. He was slightly disconcerted at her presence, but too focused on the sharp pain to mention anything. "He's awake."

Movement beside him and suddenly Winslow crouched into view. "Fates be praised." Winslow gave him a cocky grin. "He really is."

"He should stop tensing his shoulder," Bart said from behind him. "It'll hurt more when I pull this last bit out."

"*He* would love to but is in a cursed lot of pain," Dorian half-growled at them. Still, he made a conscious effort to relax. He felt the metal tool Bart had shoved into the wound. It slid damnably slow on its way out of him, but he could feel Bartholomew's steady hand because it didn't shake and disturb more of the wound than it had to. The final bit of Remora stone popped out of his shoulder and all at once Dorian felt his Talent burst to life. Without having to command it, his magic began mending the holes in his body.

Sitting up carefully, Dorian glanced between Winslow, Bart and Valeda, trying to think of something appropriate to say.

"Who have you gone and pissed off now?" Winslow asked.

"Winifred!" Bartholomew threw a bloodied towel at Winslow. "There is a lady present!"

All eyes turned to Valeda, who looked a good deal healthier than she did when she'd visited Delgora. That wasn't to say that she'd been sick in Delgora, but there was something extra in her glittering gray eyes. Her cheeks tinged a rosy pink at the sudden attention but she managed not to squirm. Dorian wondered how long she had been in Winslow's company and why his friends had suddenly opted to trust her in such an intimate setting.

For that matter, he wondered why the hell his wife trusted her. He couldn't see anything that would mark the woman as Fated.

"This *lady* has been helping you pluck stones out of Dorian's shoulder. She has blood on her boots and grease in her hair from carrying the poor bastard in here." Winslow pushed to his feet again. "If she can withstand all of that, I imagine she has the constitution for a bit of foul language."

"That's hardly the point." Bart moved to a side bar set into the west wall and proceeded to collect crystal glasses for use.

Still a little rattled, Dorian chose to wait and watch.

It appeared that they were in the front vestibule of a rather luxurious room. Brightly lit by candelabra, brass fixtures and a blazing fireplace, the place spoke of wealth and comfort. The velvet upholstery of the settee underneath him was printed in flowery patterns that reminded him of Delgora House in Lorant. Valeda sat in a matching armchair, quietly sealing the stones inside a glass jar and setting it aside. Winslow, curiously enough, moved to lean against the arm of her chair, scandalously close and deliberately protective. Dorian watched as his friend crossed his arms in a belligerent display of possession.

A moment later Bartholomew shoved a glass of brandy into Dorian's hands, meeting his eyes long enough to let Dorian know that he was also aware of Winslow's strange behavior. There was something familiar about the sight of Winslow and Valeda together, but Dorian was hard-pressed to define it.

"The real point," Winslow said as Bart handed him a drink, "is that someone just tried to abduct Dorian. And I would dearly like to know why."

"You never were very well liked, Dorian," Bart said, settling in the settee beside him. "But I never imagined someone would try this."

"The people who don't like me try to have me killed, not taken," Dorian said.

Winslow snorted a laugh.

"The real question," Valeda said with a pensive frown, "is where they got their Remora stones. If we can find that out, we might be able to discover who did this."

Faltering, Dorian looked at her again. Leave it to the reporter to connect the dots so succinctly. "The Warders guard the stones."

"Well, yes, but are they the only ones who can get them?"

"Technically no, but it is illegal for anyone except the Warders to possess them," Bartholomew said.

"And it's damned dangerous to try and get one on your own," Winslow said.

Valeda frowned some more and stared at her own feet. Dorian looked up at Winslow, who took a sip of his brandy and frowned as well. The room fell silent, each lost in their own musings, and

Dorian tried to will the memory of the nightmare away. He needed to concentrate.

"What if someone stole the stones from the Warders?" Valeda asked. "Would they ever report such a thing?"

"Fates, no," Bart said. "A report like that would set the Witches into a panic."

"So the only people who would actually know would be the Warders themselves," Valeda said quietly. "How many Warders do you know?"

Dorian felt the attention of the room settle on him. "Just one," he answered and drank his brandy in one burning swallow. His voice was hoarse when he finished. "But he'll be enough."

***

Winslow crouched on the rooftop of the Pinnacle and Pyre, far too restless to sleep. Dorian's near abduction had been traumatic enough that he'd managed to avoid Bartholomew's questions, but he knew he'd have to answer in the morning. Bart was too quick by half and always had been, so there was no way his friend had missed the fact that his Talent was suddenly alive and well. *Albeit slightly altered*, he thought.

He could feel it pulsing through him, this new Wildness. Combined with his magic, Winslow felt new and sharp, like a blade come right out of the forge. The cold did not bother him because something deep within kept him warm. And yet, when he stood next to a fire he was comfortable. From his perch he could see the whole of Three Points, clear in spite of the late hour, and tried to remember if his Talent had been capable of so much before.

No, he decided. His Talent had been able to enhance his natural abilities, but not to this extent.

"What have I become?" he whispered.

He thought of the great cat. How many of them were there? Based on Fayree's story, he imagined quite a few, but a deep part of him hoped he was wrong. The odds were already against them and he wanted to believe the people of Magnellum had a chance of survival. But he could sense the Pillars were failing. Magic was unraveling, and he knew why. Magic had placed those Pillars. Without Magic bodily present, they couldn't sustain themselves, not even with the help of their assigned Witches.

It was too cold for snow. His breath puffed out before him, catching the distant streetlight with the icy shimmer of crystal. He had confided in Valeda and Bartholomew about the verue plant and the existence of the Tre`ow. They'd been surprisingly accepting of his story, even with the moderately heretical points. He imagined his talk of the predator cat bought him some leeway. People were always reporting such sightings on the other side of the Pillars. This was just the first attack inside Magnellum borders.

He had left out the peculiar reactions his body was undergoing. He'd left out the heightened senses, his ability to hear and smell things that thc average man could not. He supposed he could tell Bart that his Talent had just come back, but he didn't like the idea of lying.

He wondered suddenly what Bryva would think of him now.

Conjuring an image of her in his mind, Winslow smiled to himself. It was his favorite memory of her, sitting beside him, curled up against him as she used to. His arm was around her, making a light stroke up and down her spine, and he could almost feel the solid weight of her. Bryva Gelgova had never been a small woman. She was tall and toned, all of her body fit from years of wielding a sword.

Would she have rejected him for his sudden Wildness?

Below him, a balcony door opened and his image was shattered. Winslow opened his eyes, resenting the sudden call back to reality. Valeda Quinlan stepped onto her balcony, wrapped in layers of dressing robe and blanket. Winslow felt his Talent perk at the sight of her and frowned.

What in Fates was going on here? His magic had never dictated attraction before and yet he could feel himself being drawn to her. *Lured like bait*, he thought with a scowl. Could it be possible that Miss Quinlan was doing it on purpose? She seemed too genuine for such a thing but he had to test the theory.

Rising, Winslow stepped to the edge of the rooftop and let himself drop down to her balcony. She gasped when he landed, dove-gray eyes widening in surprise. Her hands pinched the blanket closer to her body, but he could see the way her pulse quickened; it fluttered, light and quick, just under her jaw.

"Win—Lord Agoston," she gasped, bowing in a curtsy.

"You had it right the first time. My name is Winslow."

"Propriety . . ."

"I'm standing on your balcony in the middle of the night. Unless I miss my guess, you're in your night shift under that blanket. Propriety is already to hell and gone, Vee."

She frowned. "Why do you keep calling me that?"

"Vee?"

She nodded. She looked uncomfortable and Winslow decided that she could not be the source of his sudden attraction. A woman trying to win a man would display more sultry seduction and less quirky anxiety. *One mystery solved*, he thought and leaned against the railing.

Her mouth pursed into a deeper frown and she met his eyes. Winslow struggled against the sudden desire to touch her and tore his gaze away from her mouth. It took him a moment to find his place in the conversation again.

"It's easy to remember," he said at last.

"And 'Valeda' is difficult?"

"Not terribly, no. Vee is just shorter."

"So you're lazy and forgetful?" Her lips twitched into a faint smile.

Dazzled, Winslow smiled back. "I did manage to misplace my own magic for a time. Name me another Witch-Born who has managed that."

"Oh no," Valeda moved to the railing and looked down at the street. "You just want to be labeled as lazy and undependable. I know your kind."

"You do?" He turned to watch her, only half aware of their conversation anymore. He was torn between the increasing need to move closer to her and the sight of her slender neck as she tilted her head at the view. She was small and she reminded him of a bird; all elegant angles and light bones.

"You're really a good man at heart, but you're frightened of something. You imagine that by appearing aloof, even careless, you'll save yourself from the hurt of loss," Valeda said.

It was a highly inappropriate thing for her to say, but as he'd already informed her that propriety was to hell and gone, it seemed hypocritical to point that out. He was standing on her balcony, after all. He was the trespasser, and if he didn't like what she had to say, then he was supposed to leave. Winslow almost corrected her. He could have told her that he was already suffering from the hurt of loss, but he didn't. Bryva was his haunting, his memory, and he'd be damned if he'd share her with anyone else.

Instead, Winslow slid closer to Valeda. Her warmth seeped into him as their arms brushed and he felt her stiffen in surprise. He waited for her to look up at him. *Fragile*, he thought, as he ran a knuckle from her cheek to her jaw, listening to the startled intake of her breath. *Birdlike and fragile*. She didn't move. The paleness of her eyes seemed to swallow what little light there was, and for a breathless moment Winslow felt like he was drowning. He caught himself before he kissed her, his mouth so close to hers that he tasted minty toothpaste on her breath.

"Are you offering me something to lose, Miss Quinlan?" he asked, his lips just grazing hers.

He felt a shiver pass through her that had nothing at all to do with the cold. His Talent screamed for him to close the gap, and for a heartbeat Winslow hesitated. Then he let it take him, let his mouth seal on hers, and their magic sparked together. She made a gentle noise, almost like a cry, but moved closer to him rather than away, and he pulled her further until he could feel every curve of her against him. She tasted of mint and silk and something else. It was hard to think around the sensations pulling him into her, but Winslow finally managed to recognize it.

Gripping her shoulders, he stepped away from her and tried to catch his breath.

Wild, he thought with shock, *she tastes like the Wild. Just like me.*

"I—I'm sorry," she stammered.

He squeezed her shoulders in answer, unable to find his voice yet. She didn't wince, though he knew he had a bruising grip on her, and that just seemed to confirm the situation for him. Her sudden Talent really had come from him, or at least been spawned by him, and she was harboring this same bit of Wild as well.

Fates alive! Is it contagious?

"Winslow?" Valeda continued to stare at him, her face betraying her fear.

"It's all right," he said, finally collecting his wits. "It's unexpected, but it will be all right."

Her brow furrowed.

“Go to bed, Miss Quinlan.” Winslow released her and took another step away. “And, Fates help me, don’t come out again.”

She nodded once, still obviously confused, but fled back into her room. He heard the latch on the doors click into place and released the breath he’d been holding. For a long moment he stood there, staring at her closed doors, battling with the churn of his Talent. This strange attraction, the forceful pull of her, it was almost more powerful than he could handle. If it hadn’t been for the familiar sense of Wildness, he doubted he could have ended things.

Finally turning away, he flinched and thought of Bryva.

CHAPTER SEVENTEEN

Pistols had never been Elsie's weapon of choice. In fact, most Bedim avoided the flint-lock mechanized contraptions due to their bulk and noise. She'd always kept one around, mostly for intimidation purposes, but could only remember using one once in her life. They were, in her opinion, an Untalented weapon. Which was probably why she had bulk-ordered several hundred of them. While the ark was meant to keep danger on the outside and away from the people, Elsie couldn't risk leaving them unarmed.

"What do you think?" Forvant asked her quietly.

Looking up from the sample crate, Elsie had to squint against the burn of midday sun. The harbor town known as Little Delgora bustled around them, a constant movement of ships and waves and people. Beyond the merchant ship, the sea was so deep a blue that Elsie swore it was almost black. *Black and ominous*, she decided. She had travelled over it often enough that she'd taken for granted the Wildness of the ocean. In the end, even the depths would rise up against them.

The engineers she'd hired for the ark were mostly certain it would float. They'd thought she was crazy, of course, when she'd hired them to find a way to do it, but she'd paid them well enough that they'd done it anyway.

"My Lady?" Forvant asked again.

Shaking her head, Elsie brought her attention back to the weapons. "They appear sound," she said. Just to her left she saw the merchant,

Hammond Feebly, relax at her pronouncement. "Inspect each crate, Forvant, and have them moved to the manor."

"Yes, my Lady." Forvant gave a sharp whistle and moved off with a handful of servants.

"Mr. Feebly," Elsie said, turning to the merchant.

Hammond Feebly was a round gentleman, shaped like a bell, and movement was difficult for him. He wobbled when he walked and kept a sturdy cane at his side. Elsie herself was a tall woman, but Feebly managed to dwarf her in height and girth. His wealth was just as immense as his person and his garments reflected this. Elsie doubted the buff-colored suit he wore had been used more than once.

"My Lady," Feebly panted, dabbing sweat from his forehead with an ivory handkerchief, "I trust all is well?"

"It would seem so." She gestured to a covered bench settled awkwardly on the pier.

Anticipating Feebly's inability to move, Elsie had asked that the bench be placed there for easier access. It looked slightly ridiculous, what with sailors and merchants milling around it, but she was in a hurry and didn't want to spend an hour relocating for the negotiations. They both sat, Feebly's weight causing the bench to creak in protest.

Elsie started the conversation immediately. "As we had already agreed upon a price, I was more than a little startled by your message."

"Ah, yes." Hammond flashed a brilliant smile that made the chub of his cheeks bubble up around his eyes. "I received a late addition . . . three passengers claiming personal business with you. They could pay only half the price up front, but as they mentioned you by name, I was willing to take them on."

Elsie blinked at him. "Passengers?"

Her mind scrambled through her network of connections. All of the children from the school were already on their way, on board her customary ship, the *Brietta*. Master Walter and everyone on the staff at Walter's School for Unfortunates were also coming. She had no contacts meant to be coming here, not yet anyway. Everything was set for the beginning of Winter Tournament. While the bulk of society was centered on Lorant, her people would be en route to Delgora before the opening ceremonies began. Elsie herself would be in Lorant for that, to deliver one last warning to the populace that the Wards would fail. But she wasn't scheduled to meet with Dorian for another week, and the ceremony itself wasn't for another fortnight.

Who's ahead of schedule? she wondered.

"They mentioned you wouldn't be expecting them," Feebly said and nodded toward the ship just as three people were disembarking.

There was a man, woman and female child, presumably a family, and Elsie was quite certain that she'd never met them before. The man was a Warder, though he seemed to be trying to hide that fact. He wasn't in uniform, but his sword was distinctive; the glint of green Remora stone set into the pommel gave him away. The woman kept a hooded cloak on and was obviously trying to hide, but Elsie couldn't sense any malice from her. In fact, the woman exuded anxiety from her tight, tensed shoulders to the way she clutched the cloak closed. The little girl, on the other hand, was open and hard to miss. As the three neared them, Elsie focused more on the child. There weren't any striking features. She looked mostly normal: curly brown hair, green eyes, her little hands clutching a doll.

But there was something not quite right about her. She didn't glow like Valeda Quinlan had. It was the opposite, in fact. The little girl seemed rimmed with light, as though the light did not actually touch her, but more surrounded her.

"Mr. Winslow said you were pretty," the girl said with a beaming smile.

"Thank you," Elsie said with a smile. "What is your name, little girl?"

"Mirabella Cornelius." Her cheeks dimpled when she smiled and Elsie was utterly charmed. "Do we get to see your ark today? Mr. Winslow said we could."

"Mirabella!" The father moved to his daughter's side, half shielding her from Elsie. "Your pardons, My Lady. Mirabella is quite fanciful at times."

The girl's face scrunched up in annoyance, but she didn't contradict her father.

"It's all right, Mr. Cornelius," Elsie said, suddenly realizing who they were.

He bowed to her, displaying a small balding patch at the back of his head. "Adamin Cornelius, My Lady."

Elsie glanced at the still hooded mother and then focused on Mirabella again. "You must be the little girl Lord Agoston looked after following the train crash."

Mirabella nodded, smiling.

"Well then," Elsie said, turning to Mr. Feebly, "I shall pay for the second half of their bill. Make the arrangements with Forvant before you go."

Standing, Elsie gestured toward the harbor town. "We should walk for a bit, Miss Mirabella. The carriage ride to Delgora Proper is quite lengthy."

"Can we fly there?" Mirabella asked, her green eyes rounded with hope.

Further amused, Elsie began to lead them all away from the bench. "I'm afraid I have never actually attempted to fly, Miss Mirabella. I can summon a transportation spell, of course, but as a matter of prudence I would prefer not to."

"Why?"

"Well, it's the Warding Pillars, you see. A portion of my Talent is always in use, holding them up and maintaining them to keep the people safe. Even while I'm sleeping, this magic is working. I must always make sure that there is enough Talent in me to do this, you understand." Elsie wondered at her own sanity for sharing such a secret with the child, but decided there was no harm in it. "Someone might need me to do something . . . fix a roof or aid an ailing horse . . . whatever the issue, and I would not wish to deny them my help simply because I was impatient to ride home."

Mirabella nodded slowly, as though this made sense to her. "Are we going to your manor, then?"

"Indeed. You will be my guest there. Is that all right with you?"

Elsie had no idea how to manage a child, but her current tactic seemed to be working. Mirabella nodded again, her brown curls bouncing with the movement.

"I've never seen a manor house before. Mother says they're quite nasty, too many rooms with no use, but father says they can be beautiful sometimes."

The mother made a small, distressed sound. Elsie looked at her, somewhat annoyed by the hood, but chose to ignore it for now. Whatever reasons the woman had to stay hidden, Elsie would discover later, after she'd ascertained why Winslow had sent them. She was tempted to think it an act of compassion—he had just given his Talent for them after all—but she could feel the tattoos under her glove go cold. Icy cold, as though they'd been dipped in snow, and she had the unsettled feeling it was a direct reaction to the girl's nearness.

"Well then, not every room is always in use, but every room does have a function, Miss Mirabella. Still, I hope you like it at least. Delgora Manor has many windows, to let the beauty of the island speak to us."

They turned onto the main street of Little Delgora, walking leisurely toward the stables. People split off and away, giving room for Elsie and her companions to walk. There were several whispered glances, quiet rumblings, and Elsie had a sudden longing for Dorian. He would normally say something to distract her from the crowds or find some way to make her laugh at her own discomfort.

"But the island is Wild. Don't you hate the Wild?"

Glancing sharply at the girl, Elsie said, "No. I do not hate the Wild. But it does frighten me."

"I didn't think Witches got scared."

Smiling ruefully, Elsie shook her head. "Oh, we get very scared. I know the Wild means to harm my people, and that scares me very much."

Mirabella's face scrunched up again, as though she were conflicted by this news. They walked along in silence for a time, the salty breeze and general commotion of the town engulfing them. Elsie watched the girl for a moment and her heart ached for Winslow. Proud, arrogant Winslow who was somewhere in Three Points grappling with a Talentless existence. She hoped Dorian could convince the man to come to the ark.

***

Tourney Street in Lorant was crowded for such an early hour. Dorian stepped out of the carriage and frowned out at the wide, circular center of town. Arenas were being erected, large planks of wood fencing off spaces for knights to fight. In the off-season, the people of Lorant used the tournament grounds as a marketplace and the earth beneath was therefore a grassless patch of hardened mud and dirt. During the tournament, depending on the weather, that mud would loosen, become slick and miserable, and every maid in the near vicinity would lament the tracks it left behind.

It's a wonder, Dorian thought, as he watched men struggling to make another fence, *that the rest of the populace did not share in the lament.* Winter was a harsh time, a make or break time, where the destitute starved all the more and forgotten souls froze in alleyways. Once, not so long ago, Dorian had been one of those wretched forgotten, shivering against a lonely wall in a dark street.

It came to him then, the memory of bone-aching cold and empty hunger. The scent of death was distinctly different from the mere unclean, and it could be smelled even in frigid weather. At nineteen years old, Dorian had never truly faced a dead body, at least not a day-old dead body, and the shock of it had been seared into his memory. It had been somewhere in Feverrette lands, he knew. Two years after discovering he'd been targeted for death, knowing the Bedim Assassins hunting him would not care about killing his family just to get at him, Dorian had exiled himself from his home. But he'd gone back often, in secret, just to see for himself that his family still lived.

Somehow, he'd thought that the Untalented were better cared for in Feverrette lands, that there were no starving people so close to the manor he'd called home. But he had been wrong.

For a long time Dorian had tried to justify the suffering. He knew his mother to be a good woman, gentle and kind, and perhaps the need was too great for even a House Witch to fix. But then, Dorian had no recollection of his mother being concerned about the problem, either. She had officials for that sort of thing.

His stomach knotted and he closed his eyes, suddenly far removed from Tourney Street. He did not smell the crisp air or the horses five steps away. No. He smelled the decay of that dead man he had found, saw the tight way rigor mortis had frozen the man, curled against himself in a desperate attempt to stay warm.

No. As good as his mother was, as good as many of the Witches were, the wretched of their society were a clear sign that something had to change.

"Dorian, are you all right?" Bartholomew exited the carriage as well and moved to stand beside him.

"I'm perfectly all right." Dorian shook off the thoughts and flashed his friend an encouraging smile. Or at least he hoped it was encouraging. When Bartholomew didn't smile back, he knew it had failed and he dropped the smile. "I'm as all right as a man who has been shot in the back and nearly abducted can be."

Turning together, they both faced the two-story office building of the Warders of Lorant. It looked like every other building lining the circumference of Tourney Street, with its pointed rooftop covered in snow and its tall, skinny frame. All of the windows were open, but morning frost painted chilly patterns across them, hiding everything save the glow of lights inside. There was one difference in the building that distinguished it from its neighbors—a sword mounted on the front door. It was a decorative thing, far larger than the rapiers polite society utilized, and it was the only object on the building not covered in frost or snow.

Dorian stared at it for a moment as he and Bartholomew climbed the steps to the wooden porch. The point of the sword was directed downward, putting the hilt and pommel at eye level. He felt his Talent withdraw just at the sight of the large green Remora stone set into the pommel. Though he knew it to be a trick of the light, the stone seemed to be perpetually glowing, and Dorian had to suppress a shudder. Swirling patterns ran the length of its forty-inch blade, colored that same Remora stone green. He'd seen swords like it ever since his father had been appointed head of the Warders, but it still jarred him to look at it.

They'd traced Lord Rorant Orzebet to Lorant. *Well*, Dorian thought with a frown, *we practically chased him here*. Rorant had been in Three Points but departed just hours before they'd gone to the Warders Office there, heading for Lorant to prepare security for Winter Tournament. After much deliberation. they had come to the unified decision that Winslow would discreetly escort Miss Quinlan home so that she could attend matters there, while Bartholomew and Dorian tracked down Rorant in search of answers to the botched abduction.

"Do you think he'll know anything?" Bart asked.

Dorian gave him a sideways look. "Do you really think it's a coincidence that he happened to be in Three Points at the same moment someone attempted to abduct me?"

"He could have been there to investigate the train accident," Bart said. Shrugging, he reached out and pulled on the bell cord. "It's just possible that he could be as surprised as we were."

"Possible," Dorian conceded. "But I doubt it. My father is almost always five steps ahead of everyone else."

The door swung open and a sour-faced girl glared at them. Sharp brown eyes glanced them over once and she glared harder. "Witch-Born."

"Good gracious," Bartholomew breathed the words, clearly surprised.

It was painfully evident that his friend had never visited a Warders office before. Dorian spoke before Bart could remind the woman of their rank in society, which he no doubt would have done. Bartholomew wasn't vain, but he had clear societal boundaries.

"Lord Delgora and Lord Feverrette to see Lord Orzebet, if you please."

It felt funny calling Bart "Lord Feverrette." Growing up, he'd been Lord Bartholomew Kelemen, or just Bart, but now he was married. Dorian still didn't know how he felt about one of his closest friends marrying his sister, but in the grand scheme of things he imagined the alternative was worse. Caresse could have married Ibolya Clenci, and then Dorian would have had to murder the wretch, which would have spiraled into a House War.

"Lord Orzebet is not taking visitors today," the girl replied.

She was far older on second glance than he'd first thought. Under the ivory head cap, her hair was dark, with streaks of gray at the temples. She had a long, bony face, a nose so large and flaring that it would have been better suited for a man, and her mouth twisted with such contempt that Dorian was flustered for a moment.

"This is Saldorian, Lord Orzebet's son. I imagine he will make the time to see us," Bart said.

"You keep imaginin'. See if it comes true, eh?"

Bartholomew stepped back at the waspish remark, looking stung. For a baffled moment they exchanged glances. No one spoke to the nobility that way. Suddenly concerned for his father's welfare, Dorian nodded silently at Bart, who nodded back at him in agreement. They turned back to the woman and surged forward in unison. She gasped and tried to slam the door closed, but Bart blocked it with his shoulder.

Grabbing the woman by the elbow, Dorian pushed his way into the front vestibule, dragging her with him. He stopped short as three pistols were leveled at him. Bart paused beside him, just as startled at the display as he was.

"What in Fates . . ." Bart started to say, but trailed off as one of the weapons shifted to aim at him.

They were all three Warders, Dorian knew by the white chain mail tunics, and he recognized the eldest man. "Victor. How pleasant."

"Go home, Dorian. Your father has no time for you today." Victor's dark, rough-hewn features were passive, but there was a flash of fear in his hazel eyes.

Glancing at the other two men, Dorian frowned. His father always had time for him. Something was dreadfully wrong and he had the sinking suspicion that if he pushed the matter, these men really would fight. For whatever reason, he and Bartholomew had to leave.

"Did he say when he might have a moment for me?" Dorian asked.

"Lord Orzebet will be leaving tonight on the train to Fairbridge Tormey. Regrettably, he had not thought to see you here, my Lord." Victor's weapon never wavered. "Better luck next time."

The edge in Victor's voice amplified the need for them to go. Dorian released the hissing doorwoman, tugged once on his jacket, and turned to Bart. "Right," he said. "Next time."

Bart met his gaze with a baffled look but managed to compose himself. They retreated out the door only to have it slam behind them. Gritting his teeth, Dorian stormed down the porch steps and headed off for Delgora Winter House. Bart kept pace beside him but seemed to understand that they could not discuss the matter in public. Something was going on, something that had Rorant Orzebet frightened of being watched. Dorian had never known his father to be frightened of anything.

The Wild was coming. Elsie was barely holding on to her sanity. The ark was in a constant state of being almost done. Winslow had some malady from the train accident that couldn't be explained and their entire society was built by a cursed woman and stolen magic. Scowling, Dorian wondered what the hell else could go wrong.

CHAPTER EIGHTEEN

Being followed left her with a very strange sensation right between the shoulder blades. Valeda wasn't certain if this unsettled feeling had more to do with the man following her or with her newly hatched Talent; and she didn't care to speculate. Lord Agoston had not shown any inclination to repeat the actions taken on her balcony in Three Points, and for the most part, she was grateful. Apart from formalities arranging travel back home and the assurance that he would be nearby, Valeda hadn't seen Winslow since boarding the train home.

She knew he was there somehow, and not merely on account of feeling constantly watched. Her Talent told her of his nearness in a quiet, instinctual way.

Trudging up the cobblestone steps to her apartment building, Valeda felt the sludge of half-melted snow seep into her boots. Silently cursing Graham Fey, the building's keeper, for not shoveling the path, she fumbled with her key and unlocked the front gate. Gusts of sleet buffered against her shivering form, whipping her hood away from her head. She pushed the front door open and hurried inside, thoroughly chilled.

Mr. Fey had not bothered with lighting the front vestibule fireplace. Staring at the cold cast-iron hearth in disdain, Valeda thought again about writing to the superintendent. But it would be pointless. Mr. Marsh Attlewood was not particularly concerned about the comfort of his residents. The place was clean and quiet, and she doubted he would spare the expense to have the building stocked with coal and lumber.

Still clutching her keys in icy fingers, Valeda moved into the tight hallway just beyond. Stomping the snow from her feet, she veered for the stairwell and began her climb.

"That you, Miss Quinlan?" Fey's nasally voice called from the first door.

She paused, peering over the railing and at the office. It was situated just past the front vestibule, the only door that never seemed to be closed, and from the parallel staircase she could see inside. Fey was leaning back in his chair, squinting up at her. Although he was only five years her elder, Fey was already balding. The feathery brown wisps of his hair made a valiant attempt to hide the growing spot at the back of his head. He had a paunchy face, the evidence of an easy life with little care, and she knew him to be a relative to Mr. Attlewood.

"Yes?" she asked, suppressing a groan.

He made daily attempts at trying to charm her and she had truly hoped to escape unscathed this time.

"Oh, good!" Fey smiled, displaying an awkward number of teeth. He stood, reaching for something out of her line of sight. "You had a delivery today."

A moment later, he was striding through the door, carrying a large envelope. Valeda's stomach knotted. Recognizing the envelope as one Lady Elsie would use, she tried to hide the anxiety from her face as he reached her.

"The messenger was adamant that it had to be hand-delivered to you," Fey said with another broad smile. He winked at her. "Have I got competition for your attention now?"

Quelling her growing annoyance, Valeda reached for the envelope. "Don't be silly, Mr. Fey. It's likely just business."

"Good then." He handed the package over and leaned against the banister. "You know, I've got a nice fire going in the office. You could come in, enjoy the light, and I could fix . . ."

"Thank you kindly, Mr. Fey, but I must pack tonight." She tried for an apologetic smile. "I leave for Winter Tournament tomorrow."

His smile wavered, but he gave her another insolent wink. "Perhaps when you get back, then."

Not for all the House Seats in Magnellum, she thought, already turning away. "You flatter me, Mr. Fey. Do be well."

"I try," he called after her.

With her back safely to him, Valeda allowed herself to frown in distaste. He was such an impudent toad. She wondered if there was a spell she could cast to send his attentions in another direction. As she climbed the stairs to the second floor, she frowned some more. Maybe she could cast the same spell on herself. That would solve the problem of Winslow Agoston.

He's probably shocked and disgusted by your actions on the balcony. Why in Fates did you kiss him?

Reaching her apartment door, she fumbled with the keys again, this time fighting off a supremely embarrassed flush. It took every ounce of her willpower not to linger on the memory. Pushing the door open, she entered the little apartment and flipped the heavy switch for the lights. Only one of the four ceiling lamps hummed to life, dimly illuminating her beloved home, and it took several seconds before she realized what was before her.

Her apartment had been completely tossed, ransacked with uncaring violence. It looked like someone had picked it up and shaken it about, rolled it over and on top of itself several times. Stuffing littered the floor from her pansy-printed sofa, which lay gutted on its back, great slashes rent through the fabric. Her father's oak desk—given to her when she'd first been hired at the *Regular*—had all three of its drawers removed and their contents spilled onto the floor. Paper and ink scattered across the apartment, and Valeda stood frozen in the doorway.

Fingers tightening on the envelope in her hands, she rushed for the back bedroom. Here, the light turned on brightly, giving her an instant to view the continued carnage before it snapped out again. She turned back to the switch just as a shadowed figure detached from the wall beside her. Her scream was smothered in a tight grip, an unnaturally quick movement spinning her around until she was full length against the wall.

"Vee. Be quiet."

Too startled to recognize the voice or the familiar nickname, Valeda bit down hard on his palm, tasting sweat and flesh. He yelped in surprise, but instead of jerking back as she'd hoped, he pressed more firmly against her. Pinned to the wall by the solid length of him, Valeda's eyes adjusted to the shadowed room and she finally recognized who it was.

Winslow. *Lord Agoston*, her mind corrected. He met her gaze with a grim look.

Her heart actually fluttered, her relief in seeing him was so great. When he released her mouth, Winslow regarded his bloodied palm with rueful amusement. She felt the thrum of his magic as he healed the wound; felt her own Talent purr in her bloodstream. His attention lowered to where the envelope had crinkled between the press of their bodies, and he breathed in relief. She felt his breath stir the hair beside her face and she fought back a sundry of unnecessary questions.

Why did you stay away? Where have you been?

She knew perfectly well why he had stayed away. Her skin tingled at the memory of his wicked mouth, and to her mortification she looked at it. Full and firm, the pale pink of his lips twitched into a small frown, and rather than look away as she knew she ought to, Valeda continued to stare, transfixed by the memory. Her Talent seemed to coil in her chest, urging her forward.

"Valeda."

He spoke her name so softly it was a breath, his hands clasping her shoulders now as he put some distance between them. She felt a tremble pass through him and she finally looked up to his eyes again. Fear flashed in his hazel-green gaze—fear and pain.

Confused, Valeda waited, suddenly remembering her ruined apartment and the door she'd left half ajar. Gazing past him at her shredded bed, indignation ignited and she stiffened. He seemed to sense the change in her because he shook his head once, seized her by the hand and began to lead her to the window. Unlatching the foggy, snow-laden window with one hand, he pushed the glass pane open. Sleet lashed into the room, frigid wind assaulting her senses as he stepped onto the narrow ledge.

Suddenly understanding what he was about, Valeda gasped and tugged on his hand. In response, Winslow pressed a finger to her lips, urging her to stay quiet. Then he smiled, winked and ducked until he was crouched inside the window frame. She watched him for a stunned moment, her lips tingling from that brief touch, and tried to wrap her mind around what was happening.

Fear settled in her chest. He had to believe they were still in danger to insist on the silence.

Winslow surveyed the street below, then craned his neck to peer up at the roof. He looked ridiculous. His stylishly tailored trousers were the stuff for gentlemen and should not be worn for climbing in and out of windows. At least his boots seemed practical, and the long coat was thick. *Thicker than my own threadbare jacket*, she thought.

His grip on her hand changed and he pulled her intimately close. She felt his warm breath at her ear before he whispered very softly, "Trust me."

She nodded once and he lifted her. She wrapped her arms around his shoulders as he pushed them both out the window. Valeda swallowed a scream and buried her face in the crook of his neck. Wind tore at her jacket, icy flecks of rain pelted her head, and the stomach-dropping sensation of their descent forced a muffled whimper out of her. Then everything stopped.

There was no impact, as though they had landed and no jolt signifying that they had been caught by something; everything just stopped. Confused, Valeda lifted her face.

Winslow's features were set in firm concentration and he was looking down at the ground in preparation. Valeda realized a moment later that they were still moving, albeit slowly, and that the world around them had taken on a strange sheen. Snowflakes stood transposed in the air, undisturbed until they had both passed through them. Even the wind ceased its chilly barrage.

"You're bending time," she whispered.

Winslow didn't answer her. When their feet lightly touched ground, he released Time and the storm resumed, buffering against her with sudden fury. She had to shield her eyes and she cringed under the icy assault, still a little shocked at his casual use of magic. Valeda had seen Witch-Born perform such feats before, but she'd certainly never been this close. It left an altogether unpleasant knot of fear in her gut.

Reaching out, Winslow took her hand and began to lead them down the street.

***

I should have trained her like Dorian had asked me to, Winslow thought. Then she could have been more help on the trek from her apartment, instead of just scurrying along beside him. They didn't meet with any trouble, but Winslow hadn't been able to concentrate on whether or not they had been followed, either. As he led her past the front lobby of his chosen hotel, Winslow glanced at the greasy man lounging behind the front counter.

Horace had his back to them, as usual, and the snarled patch of his dark hair was slicked over the left side. A "Do Not Disturb" sign hung off the lip of the counter, with a hand-written addition just to its right: "Unless for payment."

Dutifully ignoring the night manager, Winslow pulled Valeda through the back hallway and down the near crumbling corridor that held his room. Three of the electrical lights were out and one made a constant flicker, but the darkness obscured the paint-chipped walls, and hid the passage of many rodents near the edges of the floor.

Winslow was surprised when Valeda didn't utter some sort of protest as he admitted them into his room. He had certainly grumbled about the small, creaky bed and lack of appropriate facilities. Down at the other end of the hall was a large, moldy bathing area meant to be shared by everyone on this floor. The one time he'd tried to use it, he'd been mortified by the mostly brown water that trickled out of the copper pipes. Even more startling was a slick, filmy substance ringing the tub. Winslow had forgone the necessary, opting for the more archaic basin and towel technique for washing.

Closing the door behind them, Winslow hurried to the window at the east wall. He peered down both sides of the street and finally relaxed. If they had been followed, there was no sign of their pursuers.

"Is this where you've been staying?" Valeda asked.

She shouldn't have been able to see in the dark. He hadn't turned on the lights out of paranoia, wanting to check the street before alerting anyone to their presence, and his Talent-enhanced eyesight was good enough to negotiate the gloom. Valeda surveyed the room quietly, frowning at the shabby bed and splintered nightstand. She could see, and clearly. His Talent murmured to him, urging him closer to her, and he wondered if she realized she was using magic.

Winslow forced himself to stay where he was. Leaning against the window frame, he crossed his arms over his chest and watched her. The past weeks had been a torture for him. Haunting her footsteps every day, he stayed true to his word and kept her safe, but he remained hidden in an attempt to understand their sudden attraction. It wasn't normal and he knew it.

Regardless, he didn't want to be attracted to her. He wanted to keep Bryva's memory untainted. With Valeda nearby, Winslow couldn't summon Bryva's image to mind, couldn't catch the sound of her laugh or remember the lemony scent of her.

"I was not here for pleasure," Winslow said, addressing Valeda's unspoken question. "I needed a room close enough to your apartment that I could hear you if you needed me. If there were a nicer hotel within range, trust me, I would have used it."

Valeda blushed and looked away. She seemed hurt by the cold tone of his voice and he cursed himself as a cruel bastard. But he couldn't afford to be apologetic. She was an unwelcome complication in his life, an intolerable temptation, and if he wasn't careful, he might succumb to her.

"I'm sorry it couldn't have been pleasanter for you," she said after a moment.

Whether she'd meant it as a double meaning or not, Winslow's immediate thought was of her mouth. He looked at the thin, straight line of her lips and felt his magic tug him forward. Before he knew what he was doing, Winslow found himself a step away from her. She didn't withdraw, but he thought she might have if she'd known the images teasing at his mind. *'Pleasant'*, he thought, *isn't the word for her. 'Alluring'—that's closer.*

"What news from Lady Delgora?" He summoned his voice at last and nodded down to the envelope in her hands.

Valeda looked down and started to open the envelope. Inside were two greenish tickets. Winslow almost groaned. He really didn't want to get on another train. His mind still got caught on the memory of the accident from time to time. Mostly at night, when everything was dark and there was no distinguishing between his bed and the iron cocoon he'd been trapped in. But he knew a train ticket when he saw one.

"There's no note," Valeda said.

"I imagine Lady Delgora knows we are intelligent enough to get the message," Winslow said, returning to the window.

"But how did she know you were with me?"

Winslow moved to check the window again. It was fully dark outside but the glow of lamplight reflected off the snowy streets. The storm had abated some. *It will still be a miserable walk to the train station*, he thought. Glancing at Valeda's ragged coat, he sighed.

"The Lady is very clever," he said, as he began unbuttoning his jacket. "Though I'm certain Dorian informed her of our whereabouts."

"Oh." Valeda peered into the envelope again. "Does she always do things this way?"

"That depends on the level of danger she's in. You'll notice that someone managed to track you down. They know you're involved with Delgora and desperately want information."

Her frown deepened and she gave the tickets an accusatory glare. "My apartment was searched for this?"

Shrugging his jacket off, he crossed back to her. "Obviously, they weren't aware of how innocuous the contents were. They would have been disappointed if they'd actually managed to get it."

"What are they hoping to find?"

Winslow smiled and wrapped the jacket around her shoulders. "And I thought you were the reporter here, Vee. A better question to ask is who 'they' are."

She stiffened under his hands but he continued to fuss with the jacket. He pulled the collar up, feeling the heat of her skin near her collarbone. The jacket was too big for her. It swallowed her whole, its hem brushing the dirty floor and the shoulders bunching up near her ears. She looked small and shaken, as though his very nearness might undo her.

"The only person who might link me to Lady Delgora is Montgomery Taven," she said.

"Ambassador Taven?" Winslow frowned at the news. "Lady Orzebet's pet?"

"He was at Delgora court when I arrived. To be truthful, he is the one who brought me to Lady Delgora's attention."

Pivoting on his heel, Winslow moved to collect his travel bag from behind the dresser. There was nothing valuable in it, just a spare set of clothes, but his instincts warned him that they wouldn't be back here. Elsie had to know the danger she was in. Minne Orzebet truly hated the fact that Elsie and Dorian had wed.

No, he thought, *it's more than that.*

Lady Orzebet hated Dorian. He was a living, breathing reminder that her husband had loved Lady Jessamine Feverrette. Never mind that Rorant hadn't been married at the time, Minne would never forgive that infraction. Winslow had witnessed the way Dorian was treated in the Orzebet home. As a young man, he'd even helped Dorian fight off his half-brothers when things got particularly nasty.

The fact that Dorian was now a Consort, when her own son had never managed to marry, must be driving Minne insane.

Winslow thought of the abduction attempt and fear knotted in his chest. Minne Orzebet was just crazy enough, just angry enough, to be lethal. Curling his fingers into the rough fabric of his travel bag, he looked back to Valeda.

"What time does the train leave?"

CHAPTER NINETEEN

Dorian waited in his father's private sleeping box on the train with a growing sense of apprehension and annoyance. He hadn't needed to sneak into a meeting with his father in eight years and he truly disliked having to do so now. But the way Victor had held the gun on him, the fear he'd seen in the old Warder's face, alerted him to the need for discretion.

Something had Lord Rorant Orzebet frightened enough to allow a weapon to be pointed at Dorian's head, and that concerned him considerably. Dorian could easily have avoided the bullet, but it was generally counted as bad form to level a weapon at someone.

What bothered Dorian the most were the Remora fragments that had been shot at him. The whole abduction sequence kept replaying in his mind, nagging at him that he'd forgotten something important.

Miss Quinlan was right. The Warders of Magnellum were the sole legal owners of Remora stones, which meant that either there was a leak inside the office, or the Warders themselves had tried to abduct him.

Frowning, Dorian leaned into the corner of the train car and stared at the door. He wished his father would hurry up with dinner. The longer this took, the further away from Lorant he'd be when he'd have to jump off. He'd considered riding through to the next station and then taking a new train back, but there was a gnawing sense of unease in his gut about leaving Bartholomew alone.

No, he thought. He wasn't really concerned about Bart's safety. Bart was among the more likeable men in Magnellum. *No one would want to hurt him, not even if it meant getting to me.*

What he wanted was a few extra days preparing the manor house before Elsie's arrival. Dorian was a target, but Elsie was the prize. And he'd be damned if she was hurt by anything he might have prevented.

The door slid open and Rorant stepped inside. Upon spotting Dorian lounging in the corner, his father stopped and blinked, then quickly slid the door shut. The privacy shutter was already closed on the door and the outside window, but Rorant checked them both anyway.

"If I'd known you were waiting I would have skipped the second marzipan," Rorant said and settled into the seat across from him.

"It's less suspicious that you didn't."

"True," Rorant said. After a moment of unbuttoning jacket, cuffs, and vest, he began stripping off his boots. "To what do I owe the pleasure of this clandestine meeting?"

Dorian throttled down his annoyance. The sharp glint in his father's blue-grey eyes told him more than he wanted to know. Rorant was probing him, testing to see how much Dorian had managed to piece together. In that moment, Dorian knew what had bothered him about the abduction: the voices. Combined with the Remora stones, Dorian had little doubt who had ordered the attack on him.

Still, Dorian couldn't figure out why Rorant had gone to so much trouble.

"Either you're getting clumsy in your old age, Father, or you've been trying to catch my attention."

Rorant's wide mouth twitched at the corners. "Have I?"

"Give it up, Father. I know it was you. Victor has that distinctive half-drowned cat voice and you wouldn't allow Remora stones to be stolen from the office. Now what is this all about?"

"Ironically, this is about a pair of Remora stones that have been stolen from me personally." Rorant pushed his boots under the seat and stripped off his outer coat. "But your confidence in me is quite heartening."

Dorian leaned forward. "But you *were* the one who tried to kidnap me."

"I am," Rorant said and tossed his coat into the luggage compartment. The train jostled but he was steady on his feet, preparing the sleeping car for the night and working around Dorian. "We knew Bart would try to step in, but we thought Winslow was Untalented now. Imagine our surprise when Winslow took chase."

"Our surprise? Where were you?"

Rorant grinned at him. "I was driving."

"Fates alive! You nearly got us all killed!"

"Well," his father paused as though remembering something, then shook his head, "that was not my most brilliant move. But the horses became unaccountably terrified when Winslow hopped on board."

Rorant reached down and tugged on the seat, pulling it out until the headrest flattened down beside it. When Dorian left, Rorant would do the same with the second seat, creating a flat, semi-comfortable bed to sleep on. But Dorian wasn't leaving, not yet. Not until he found out what the blazes was going on.

Sighing, Rorant sat down again, directly across from him, and leaned forward.

"I suppose I did catch your attention," Rorant said ruefully. "I had only meant to make you put up your guard. There are . . . tensions . . . rising in the Houses."

"There are always tensions rising in the Houses."

"But there has not always been an ark on Delgora soil." Rorant frowned as he said it. "Dorian, I've seen pictures of this . . . this . . . monolith. What is it for?"

Dorian paused. "Pictures?"

He'd thought their security was rather good, but if the Warders had managed to get close enough to photograph the ark, then it was possible others had as well.

"Don't look so troubled. I had Gremor take them," Rorant said. He winked and gave an unapologetic grin. "You didn't think your old manservant had just retired and gone away, did you?"

Surprised, Dorian snorted a laugh. Gremor had visited Delgora a year ago, feigning interest in Elsie's health. At the time, Dorian had thought the old servant was checking up on them for Rorant and it appeared that he'd been right. He just hadn't realized how thorough Gremor had been.

"But really, Dorian, what is it for?"

Dorian debated for a moment. There was no real harm in telling his father the truth. The man held half the secrets of Magnellum in his briefcase and hadn't betrayed a confidence before. Still, Dorian didn't like discussing Elsie's secrets. She tended to get very cross with him when he did.

At the same time, she had kept secrets from him; bringing in Valeda Quinlan, recruiting engineers of every sort just to build the ark. She functioned outside of their marriage and it seemed only fair that Dorian be allowed the same liberty. *And there's the other issue,* he thought, *Winslow's tale of the Wild and where Fate came from.* He knew his father had chased down heretics before, so there was a chance Rorant could disprove the whole story.

"It's a sanctuary for the Untalented," he said at last. "For when the Wards fail."

Rorant was very still for a moment. "And does Lady Elsie know the date when this will happen?"

They stared hard at each other. Dorian knew what he was really asking. The tattoos on Elsie's arm were infamous among the Witch-Born. The last vestiges of life of Magic, the man-god, peppered her skin like gold. If the Council had their way, Elsie would have been locked up years ago. But they were equally afraid of her, so they had left her alone.

"No," Dorian said. "But it is coming, Father."

Frowning, Rorant leaned back in his seat. Dorian was struck for a moment by how old his father looked. Dark brown hair suddenly white at the temples, and there were deep lines around the corners of his eyes and mouth. Rorant Orzebet was not only aging, but getting tired, too. Dorian could hear the exhaustion in his own voice as he spoke next.

"There's something else," Dorian said carefully. "About Winslow."

Rorant raised an eyebrow and gestured for him to continue.

"He says he met with a Wild creature near the tracks," Dorian said, choosing his words carefully. He didn't want Winslow targeted as a heretic, after all. And he didn't want that mother and child hunted down, either. "They told him Magnellum was created by Magic and Fate to protect the Untalented."

Rorant nodded slowly. "That seems confirmed by several nursery rhymes."

"That was my first thought as well," Dorian said. "But the creature also said that we all come from the Wild. They said Fate was a woman suffering from a curse and that Time has ended outside the Pillars."

"And you're relating this to me because you want to know if any of the heretics followed such a teaching?"

Dorian nodded.

"No," Rorant said. "The heretics we chase are . . . violent. Most claim that, through killing, they can become Fate. There is no real doctrine they follow."

Dorian frowned. He wasn't certain if he was relieved or dismayed by the news. It was difficult to think of those outside the Pillars as having been wronged by Fate. It was even more difficult to think of how close they were to failing their primary task. If Winslow was right, then the Witch-Born were literally made as guardians.

"Dorian," Rorant asked with a frown. "What has happened to Winslow?"

Dorian sighed. This trip was going to take longer than he'd planned. But he told his father everything he knew, every detail of Winslow's story, including the exact wording of Fayree's explanation of the Wild. He figured his father would have told him immediately if anyone was going to get burned as a heretic for it. And he felt better when he was done. Rorant always knew what to do, so he sat back and waited for advice.

"Well that's new," Rorant said after a long moment. "It makes my warning seem silly, actually."

"Warning?"

"Saldorian, son, I know I cannot stop you from whatever you choose to do, but I must warn you." Rorant looked him full in the face before continuing. "You and Elsie must stay away from Winter Tournament."

It was Dorian's turn to frown. "Fate might not be a Deity and you're worried about Winter Tournament?"

"Listen, please. Your stepmother has been watching me very carefully. She and Lady Lorant have spent countless hours in private conference. They are planning something. Something that you don't want to happen."

"Why don't you stop them?"

"Dorian, I have no proof. I think Minne stole the Remora stones from me, but I can't be certain.

And even if I were, there are no societal laws for me, the husband, to stand against a Witch."

His father truly was in a pickle. No wonder he'd let Victor stave him off with a gun. The abduction had been a ruse to get him in private without his stepmother knowing. Lifting his fist to his mouth, Dorian closed his eyes and tried to think. He couldn't send a telegram to warn Elsie, they were too easily intercepted. He couldn't get back to her in time to stop her from coming, either. The only thing he could do was tighten the security around Delgora Manor in Lorant.

Maybe we could relocate after she arrived, he thought.

Sighing, Dorian opened his eyes to look at his father again. "How many stones are missing?"

"Two."

Of course, he thought. *One for me, and one for Elsie.*

***

Elsie sat cross-legged on an old picnic blanket, frowning at Witch-Eater Lake. Just beside her, Mirabella munched contentedly on a honeyed biscuit, cooing her appreciation of the treat. Elsie was pleased the girl was enjoying herself, but was too wrapped up in what Fayree was explaining that she couldn't eat herself. In fact, Elsie was glad she was sitting down. With what Fayree told her about the Wild, she had a sinking suspicion she might have fallen over if she'd been standing. This was why Winslow had sent them here, to get her this information.

She felt suddenly sick under the weight of it all.

Why? she wondered. *Why hadn't Magic told me? What else is he hiding from me? Is he running from this Host tree that Fayree described?*

It was possible that Magic wouldn't want to return, not after tasting the freedom of a corporeal form. She glanced at her gloved arm, hoping he would speak, but he didn't.

"Where did the Pillars come from? Why was Magnellum created at all?" she asked.

"People do not always react well in times of strife," Fayree said. She lowered her eyes and began picking at the hem of her gown. She looked altogether remorseful, as though the tale itself was too great a burden to bear. "You must understand that as long as Median was there, time kept moving. Several of our young lost their Talent completely. There was a . . . rebellion of sorts. It was led by a man named Voruke who believed the Untalented were a blight on society. He claimed that Median's sickness would continue to spread and suggested the only way to free us all was to kill her.

"In his fervor he convinced many of us to attack the Untalented. We were to 'set them free' by murdering them. And we had to kill Magic's body, too. It was to be a purging . . . and he believed it would fix the Host tree. I imagine he still believes it."

But Voruke had forgotten one thing: Median could walk through the future now. She went to Magic and told him what was coming. By then there were several hundred Untalented and Magic refused to allow a slaughter. He and Median drew the boundaries of Magnellum and planted the

Warding Pillars. But they knew the Wild would continue to fight and Magic's bodily form was limited in where it could be at any given moment. So, Magic selected thirteen women to act as guardians over the Untalented. He gave them each a portion of himself and commanded that they maintain the Pillars at all costs.

"How can you know that?" Elsie asked. "If the Pillars were up, how could you know of the Witch-Born?"

"Inside the Host tree is still a remnant of Magic," Fayree explained. "It sometimes allows visions of Magnellum . . . mostly in times of extreme strife, when a single Witch expends a large amount of power."

"And the moment the Pillars went up, that's when Time ended for you. Because Fate . . . I mean Median . . . was cut off from you."

Fayree nodded.

Elsie looked at Witch-Eater Lake and took a deep breath. A breeze rippled across the surface of the water, colliding with the natural waves caused by several waterfalls. The lake felt more ominous than ever, churning and waiting for some hapless fellow to fall in. She could imagine thick kelp snagging ankles, dragging anyone into its depths.

She shuddered and forced herself to focus on Fayree again.

"Why are you here in Magnellum?" she asked.

Fayree sighed and leaned back against the tree. "The last great vision was eight years ago. The day Magic's body was killed here in Delgora," she said. "Since his death didn't fix anything, I suggested to Voruke that the whole plan was nonsense. Some agreed with me but the majority have been following Voruke for so long, they don't have a concept of individual thought anymore. I was branded a traitor and sentenced to death."

"But you got away."

Fayree grinned at her. "Yes, I did."

"How did you get into Magnellum?"

"There are some places where the Wards are weak. I imagine that's how the Dellidus got through. But in the end, I didn't have to fight to get in." She smiled again. "Magic has always been fair. That is his one constant. The Pillars were built only to keep your enemies out. As I harbored no ill-will for you, they let me pass. It was almost funny, actually. I ran straight through and they all got stopped at the border."

Elsie could picture Fayree's run very well. Biting her lower lip, she looked over at Mirabella, who was still happily picking at her lunch. As troubling as this story was, as overwhelmed as Elsie felt at the coming war, the little girl and mother gave her hope. *Maybe there could be peace*, she thought. *These two have managed to settle in Magnellum, after all.*

CHAPTER TWENTY

Valeda was more than ready to be off the train. Lord Agoston's taciturn nature had become unbearable. He sat brooding in the corner across from her, only speaking to answer direct questions. His fair hair was tousled from sleep and his fine features were hidden behind a fist as he gazed out the window.

She wanted to scream at him. How was any civilized person supposed to manage twelve hours in a clanky, jostling train with no conversation? Especially when she had so many unanswered questions.

How had she become Talented? Did he believe Fayree's story about the Wild? If he did, what did that mean for Magnellum? How did Fayree's story correlate with Lady Delgora's premonition that the Wild was coming?

Were they all going to die?

Valeda thought of Chuckabee and the children at the Walter's School for Unfortunates and flinched. Wasn't there anything that could be done?

Outside the window the sun was rising. Her heart swelled at the pink and orange hues that swept over the snow-capped peaks. *It's the Wildness of the view that's so captivating*, she thought. The Warding Pillars only covered the length of the tracks and everything beyond was Wild.

"It's just another couple of hours," Lord Agoston said. "Lord Delgora will meet us at the station."

Valeda looked at him and frowned. He seemed tense, his shoulders coiled as though preparing for movement. It took her a moment but she finally recognized his anxiety. She felt like a complete fool. The poor man had been in a wreck recently. No doubt he was uncomfortable, waiting for a similar situation to occur.

"It's very kind of him to come meet us himself," she said, trying to take his mind off the train.

"He's just afraid I might go skipping off on him. Dorian's a strange fellow sometimes. He can be quite overprotective."

"Protecting friends seems more admirable than strange to me."

"Yes, well, you haven't lived through several years of his acquaintance. He did force himself into a private little exile for over ten years while the Bedim assassins were after him. Out of fear for our lives, he severed all contact. That was horrible of him."

"Would the Bedim have tried to hurt you in order to draw him out?"

"A clever Bedim might have, yes."

"Then his fear was justified, don't you think?"

Winslow met her eyes then, something sharp flashing in his blue-gray depths. "Justified, but horrible. We Witch-Born are strongest side by side. Barty and I might have been able to help."

Since this was more conversation than she'd had in twelve hours, Valeda decided to argue. He already thought the worst of her; it was doubtful his further irritation could be any harm.

"And what would you have done in his situation? Would you have risked harm to your friends or gone into hiding?"

"I would have at least sent word to my friends that I was alive," he said and glared.

"So you're admitting that you would have gone into hiding as well?"

"I would have hidden from society, but not from my friends. I would have trusted them with the truth."

"And yet, you did not feel compelled to tell Lord Feverrette why you did not wish him to heal you," Valeda said. "You were afraid for his safety, but could not trust him with the truth."

Winslow glanced at the closed compartment door before replying. "It was not just my secret."

"Ah yes, the infamous woman and child you rescued." Valeda strummed her knee, thinking how best to draw him out. She could not question his loyalty to his friends or the faith he had in them, that would only make him angry. She reached for the only thing she could think of: "Lord Agoston, how did you get your Talent back?"

He appeared startled by the new question but answered anyway. "Damned if I know," he said with a shrug. "How did you turn into a Witch-Born?"

She felt her cheeks flush and smiled. "Well, I've been properly pinned," she said. "I thought you would know better than I."

Winslow smiled, his earlier irritation seeming to melt away as he leaned forward to rest his elbows on his knees. "I've a theory, but you won't like it."

"About me?"

He nodded.

Valeda leaned forward too. This she desperately wanted to know.

"Magic wants you to do something," he said.

"But . . . why not just tell me? Why throw Talent into me without asking first?"

"Fayree said the first Witches were chosen," Winslow said. "They weren't asked."

"Yes, but at least they were told what their duty was."

"Yes, but Magic—" he stopped himself and scowled.

"Magic what?"

"Never mind. Things are just different now."

"Different how?" she asked.

"There's more," Winslow said, ignoring her question. "You're . . . we're . . . not just Talented. We have a little Wild in us, too."

Shocked, Valeda sat back. "What?"

Her heart skittered in her chest as she stared at him. She could feel her magic, coiled and ready, settled just at her center. It seemed to know her distress and a strange warmth spread through her, as though to comfort her as she digested his words.

Wild, she thought.

And she knew, somehow she just knew, that it was true.

"How?" she asked.

"For me it was the verue plant, but I think yours is because of me," he said with a sigh. "My Talent and the Wild fought, but in the end, when I needed it the most, the two fused together somehow."

"So then . . ." Valeda blinked back tears and fought her emotions down. "What are we?"

Winslow shrugged. "Something else, I guess."

"I find it hard to believe that Magic wants a half-Wild, half-Witch to do anything," Valeda said.

"If we trust your friend Fayree, then most of the Wild wants nothing more than to kill us all."

"If we trust Fayree, then all of us . . . Witch or Untalented . . . are Wild. We just don't remember it."

"And why would we choose to forget something so important?"

"Did we forget or did we just move on?" Winslow shrugged. "The first Witches are centuries dead. Society has grown and changed. Fear isn't a driving factor anymore because the Pillars have worked for so long we can't imagine them *not* working."

Valeda frowned. He had a very good point. Society had been warned not only by Lady Delgora, but by Fate Herself, that the Pillars would fall, and no one was listening. It was unthinkable that they would fail.

"So what does that leave us?" Valeda asked.

She wanted him to tell her why she of all people had been chosen. Maybe he had some internal link to Magic. Maybe that was how it worked. But if that were so, then she should be able to talk to Magic too. And that idea frightened her more than she wanted to admit.

"I really don't know, Vee," Winslow said. "I wish I did."

"Wonderful," Valeda muttered, sitting back in her seat.

Closing her eyes, she tried to determine what her father would do in this situation. She'd sent word to her family that they needed to go to Delgora as soon as possible and she prayed they had listened to her. But if she knew her father, and she did, then his immediate reaction would be to hunt for answers. He'd go to her home and discover it ransacked, which in retrospect made her feel guilty. He'd be worried.

But if he were sitting in my shoes right now, she thought, *what would he do?*

The answer was very simple. Whenever a story wasn't making sense, whenever the witnesses said contradictory things, then his main rule of thumb was to shut up and listen. Just listen to everyone and focus. Eventually, the truth came out.

She just had to be patient.

Valeda exhaled her annoyance. She hated being patient.

***

Winslow watched Valeda sleep, her head nestled between the seat and the train window. He wanted to wake her up, to kiss the frown that kept tugging at her mouth, but forced himself to stay where he was. This attraction was insane. He barely knew the woman.

Frowning, he tried to consult his Talent for answers. Or his Wildness. Fates! Everything was so confusing.

At least Valeda had handled the revelation with some grace. She'd been upset, he could sense that through his magic, but she'd held it together. It was possible that the verue plant had made the transfer of his Talent to the woman. It had managed to leak the Wild into his form, after all. But then, why didn't his power spread when he'd touched other

Untalented? He'd tested it on a boy in Tormey, but nothing had happened.

There was one other problem with that line of thought, too. However Valeda had gotten her Talent, it was unmistakably her own. He could feel it in her, as identifiable as her reddish-brown hair. Perhaps the verue had opened her to magic, but something had to have been there to begin with, something that could spark the flame.

Something Fate or Magic had placed in her.

She shifted and Winslow sighed. It was better that she sleep. He didn't want to answer any more of her questions.

Closing his eyes, he tried to think of Bryva. He summoned her image to his mind; soft, round features and blonde hair. Her eyes were hazel leaning on the olive-green side, but if she wore different colors she could pull out the blue in them. Fates alive, how he missed her!

They'd only shared a few short weeks together, but Bryva Gelgova lived every minute with a contagious passion. *She danced and laughed and fought her way through life,* he thought.

She and Elsie were raised together and called themselves sisters. Bryva had told him once about her fear for Elsie. She'd said that Elsie was one of those people who would sacrifice her life for the nation she was meant to protect. That was part of the reason Bryva lived as she had; to give Elsie a lighter view of life.

Winslow caught a memory of her. They were sparring in his private room in Lorant, laughing through a game of some sort. She'd smacked his thigh with the flat of her blade and give him that open, honest grin of hers. He'd cheated then, using his magic to get in close and disarm her. A moment later, they were kissing. Not the heated, fierce passion that normally infused them, but a gentle kiss; tender.

She had loved him just as much, he knew.

His memory switched to another night, a colder night. Standing in the shadows of an alley with Dorian and Lord Rorant Orzebet close by, he'd watched as Bryva conducted a black market trading deal. It hadn't mattered to him then and it didn't matter now that she had been dealing illegal weapons. When the issue was resolved, it had been decidedly not treason. Bryva was working under the soon-to-be House Witch of Delgora, which made the weapons in question quasi-legal.

He could remember Lord Rorant's voice that night, strained and unhappy, demanding to know if Dorian had anything to do with it. Something changed in Winslow at that moment. Bryva, unaware of their observation, looked calm and confident in the soft light. Snow-covered copper and brick shone through the alley, and Bryva in her martial gear, hair pinned up, stood transposed against it.

There should have been a sound, he thought. If someone like Bryva was to die, there should have been something louder than the whoosh of frigid air. Two darts struck Bryva in the chest without so much as a thump signifying they'd met their mark.

Winslow remembered running to her, but the rest of the night was a blur. He'd held her, tried to heal her, but the poison had worked too quickly. It was a poison meant for a Witch-Born, meant for Elsie, and Bryva stood no chance.

He could still feel her, limp and heavy in his arms. Her face was too quiet, her open, warm features bereft of the joy, the verve, that Bryva lived by.

Winslow fought himself out of his slumber. He hadn't wanted to remember that part. He'd just wanted her laugh again. Blinking, he shifted to settle more into the corner of his seat.

Valeda was still asleep. He couldn't determine whether or not he was pleased with the continued silence or afraid of the tight knot of grief in his chest.

CHAPTER TWENTY-ONE

Valeda was still groping with the idea that she was not only Talented—she couldn't get herself to say Witch-Born since her parents were decidedly not Witches—but also part Wild. It was difficult to imagine the two powers living in harmony, let alone residing in one person. Lord Agoston had little to no idea how it was possible, and even if he did, it couldn't help her accept the fact that she was now magically inclined.

Whatever their origins, Magic, the man-god, and Fate had led Magnellum for centuries. As a youth she had trusted them. As an adult she held some skepticism but always remained respectful. Winslow's story about Median and the Host tree actually made a lot of sense to her. It fit. It explained the Pillars and the rhymes and the insatiable anger of the Wild. Not only that, but as a journalist she was trained to weed out truth from rumor and this felt like the truth.

Fear gnawed at her gut. If Magic and Fate knew the Pillars were going to fall, they would act against it. She imagined Lady Delgora's ark was part of their plan. And she had a horrible feeling that she, too, was to play some part. It was the only explanation for her newfound Talent that made any sense.

They needed her to do something.

The train jostled to a stop and she had to brace herself against the doorframe. She shook off her worries and waited for the doors to open. As she disembarked the train, she spotted a familiar face in the crowd. Not two feet from her position

Ambassador Taven stood, wiping his brow with a swatch of blue cloth. He was bundled in furs and wore a navy blue top hat that was dusted with snowflakes. Valeda couldn't help but smile when she saw him, remembering how clearly annoyed he'd been with Lady Delgora at their first meeting.

Things had been a good deal simpler back then, she thought. *Can it have only been three months since my visit to Delgora?*

Lord Agoston broke away from her and moved to collect their luggage. Deciding it best to be polite—and somewhat nostalgic for a time when she'd just been little Valeda Quinlan in a borrowed set of clothes—she stepped up to the Ambassador with a smile.

"Ambassador Taven, how good to see you again."

Monty's eyes widened slightly. He coughed into his handkerchief, but Valeda spotted the way he scanned the crowd. Her Talent rose in warning, stretching through her center, and she had the unexpected sensation of seeing everything around her with unnatural clarity.

She could see in his face that he recognized her, and that he was afraid. For an agonizing moment, Valeda wondered if he'd been the one to order her home ransacked. But then, why was he furtively searching the crowd?

"I beg your pardon, Madam," Monty said as he lowered his handkerchief. "But have we met?"

He's being watched, Valeda realized. And then—*No,* we're *being watched.*

She brought up the first lie she could think of. "I did an interview with you a year or so back. I beg your forgiveness; I should have known you would not remember something so trivial."

The tension in his face eased just slightly. "Not at all, Miss. Not at all. A common mistake."

With that, he turned and left. *Fleeing, more like,* she thought with a frown. She watched him go, simultaneously afraid of who might be observing her and annoyed that Winslow had not taken the time to teach her. If he'd just taught her, she might have been able to locate whoever was spying on poor Montgomery Taven.

"Everything all right, Miss Quinlan?" Lord Agoston asked.

He was carrying their two small cases, both of which were new, along with their contents. He'd been adamant that they not return to her home, so he had purchased all of their necessities. She'd protested, of course, but Lord Winslow Agoston knew how to take the upper hand. He'd simply paid the seamstress in advance. And by the woman's delighted countenance, Valeda was certain the amount was substantial.

"Yes," she said belatedly.

Winslow looked past her and out at the crowd. He frowned and asked, "Are you certain?"

"Yes, I'm quite certain. Is Lord Delgora here?"

Winslow eyed her so intensely that she almost squirmed. She stared up at him with a frown of her own and prayed her Talent could yell at his Talent about his obstinacies. No matter how hard he pushed, Valeda was not going to explain what had occurred with Monty. Not at the moment, anyway. Not while they might still be under watch.

"If you two frown any harder at each other I'll think you've fallen in love," Lord Delgora said at her left.

Valeda jumped a little, startled at his sudden appearance, and then felt her cheeks burn as she realized his words. She turned away from both of them and tried to collect herself.

"Don't be rude, Dorian." She recognized Lord Feverrette's voice and nearly groaned in misery. Was the whole of Magnellum to be privy to her indiscretion? It was one kiss—blast them all—and it certainly didn't mean they were in love.

"What?" Dorian asked, though by his tone she could hear his irritation. "Didn't you see them? I swear, either one of them was going to throw down a challenge or . . ."

"That's enough, Dorian," Winslow said sharply.

"Well," Dorian said with a scoff. "Isn't this a fine day. Winslow Agoston just stood for propriety. Well done, old Winifred. Well done, indeed."

"What in Fates is your problem, Dorian?" Winslow asked.

Valeda took three breaths and turned back before they could argue further. "My Lords," she said and dipped into a curtsy. "Are we to catch a carriage or is our destination close enough to be reached on foot?"

Maybe it was her Talent, but she could no longer think of the three men by their titles. It was remarkably freeing to see Bartholomew, Dorian and Winslow in this light. Her quaint, and now ruined, apartment no longer separated her from them. She was on equal standing and she liked it.

Dorian and Winslow exchanged frowns before looking away from each other. Bartholomew grinned at her and offered his elbow as escort.

"It's walkable if you do not mind the snow," Bart said.

She stepped forward and took the proffered elbow under one hand. "I have been cooped up for twelve hours with an entirely unsociable man," she said, as he turned her away from the train. "Believe me, Lord Feverrette, I would welcome the snow."

"I am sorry to hear your trip was less than engaging," Bart said. "Lord Agoston has been uncommonly anti-social for several years now. I wish you could have known him before. I think you would have liked him then."

"You could try not to discuss my history when I'm still present," Winslow said from behind them.

Valeda smiled at the annoyance she heard in him and continued to walk with Bart. He seemed equally amused because he slanted a wink at her before proceeding to lead them onto Tourney Street.

"Terrible of me, I know, Winifred. But at least it got you to speak."

"Why do you call him that?" Valeda asked.

"Winifred?"

She nodded and heard Winslow hiss behind them.

"It's a tournament thing," Bart said. "Whenever nobles fight in the arena they get . . . well . . . obnoxiously competitive. I think it was Dorian who first called him that. Trying to get a rise out of him, I think."

"Did it work?"

"Only the first time," Dorian said.

"Yes, because it caught me by surprise," Winslow retorted. "And I recall naming you "Sally" and getting jabbed in the gut for it."

"Sally?" Valeda asked.

"Saldorian," Bart murmured to her. "A name he no longer goes by."

By the gravity in his voice, she knew to drop the subject. So she nodded and focused on the late night. Snow fell limp and wet all around them, gathering on the shoulders and hood of her jacket. She could feel the thick, woolen material getting sodden and cold and she pinched it closer to her throat. The walkway had been shoveled, but was still icy, and she found herself relying on Bartholomew's steady arm more than she ought.

"Concentrate, Miss Quinlan," Bart said quietly. "You'll find your Talent can aid you in many things."

Blushing, she almost looked at Winslow.

"I wouldn't know," she muttered at Bart.

"Ah. I take it Winifred did not teach you."

She shook her head.

"Well, I'll thrash him for it later. Right now, just ask your Talent for some help."

Frustrated, Valeda almost retorted that she didn't know how to ask her Talent for anything. But she knew that wouldn't help, so she took a breath and thought of that golden coil again. Immediately she felt a response. Her steps were no longer tentative and she knew instinctively where the ice patches were.

"Better," Bart said. "You're very good at this."

Valeda smiled at this praise and felt more at ease. She was led to a small manor house two spaces from Fortress Lorant's main gate. A man with a large nose and gaunt features met them at the door and stoically ushered them all inside. Bartholomew delivered her to the chair nearest the blazing hearth and promptly abandoned her.

Had she not already been struggling between the sudden warmth after walking through the cold, she might have paid more attention to his absence. Bartholomew was the friendliest of the three Lords and she found herself wanting more of his instruction in regard to magic. Quietly removing her mittens, Valeda held her hands toward the fire and watched the men find separate places in the room.

Winslow flopped into a flowery chair just adjacent to her own and Bartholomew settled on the matching sofa by the draped window. Dorian lingered at the door to the sitting room, handing his jacket to the long-nosed man. Valeda assumed this was the butler or something because he took the garments without complaint.

"Elsie is due to arrive tomorrow," Dorian said. "But after she arrives we may have to relocate."

Valeda perked at this announcement.

"Relocate?" Winslow asked. "Why?"

Dorian scowled and brushed his hair back with one hand. "My father suspects . . ." he paused and glanced in her direction. Shrugging, he continued, "My father suspects that Elsie and I are political targets. Two Remora stones are unaccounted for. Staying here just invites trouble."

"Two stones?" Winslow whistled lowly. "How'd he manage to lose two?"

"They were stolen from his personal stock."

Valeda sensed the undercurrent in the room and stayed quiet. The men glanced at each other, then at her, and she surmised that they knew who the culprit was; they just couldn't say so with her present. Sighing, she looked into the fire.

So many secrets, she thought. *They would never trust me. And why should they? Winslow knows me best of all and that's not saying much.*

"Where are you going to move to?" Winslow asked.

"Feverrette House has already prepared to take us in," Dorian said and smiled at Bartholomew. "We only came here to keep up appearances for the night."

"Won't your stepfather object to that?" Winslow glanced between his two friends.

Bartholomew chuckled. "You've been out of the loop for too long, Winifred. Aubin left Feverrette lands as soon as Caresse became House Witch. He told Lady Jessamine that he wanted his freedom back. He was last seen in Clenci, gambling away his savings."

"And Gaetan?"

"My stepbrother married Lady Ninnette two years ago and resides here in Lorant," Dorian said. "So my mother's home is open to me again."

"It was always open to you," Bart said with a conflicted frown. "It was just . . . contentious."

Valeda tried to turn off the reporter in her, but she just couldn't help it. Dorian Feverrette-Delgora was an enigma in Magnellum society. Scandal seemed to follow him and if she wasn't mistaken, the stepfather and stepbrother just mentioned had been suspected of hiring Bedim assassins to kill Dorian.

That was all speculation, of course, but the animosity behind the rumors appeared to be true.

"At any rate," Dorian said, turning to face her now and giving her a strictly polite bow, "because there is no other lady present in this house, we have made arrangements for Miss Quinlan at the Tawdry Panoply."

"What? Why?" Winslow frowned at Dorian. "She's safest here."

"Perhaps, but her virtue is better served if she stays elsewhere," Bartholomew said. "The Panoply is close enough to Agoston house that we thought you could keep an eye on her."

"I haven't spoken five words with my mother in seven years," Winslow said. "There isn't a chance that I'm staying in that house."

"I told you so," Bart said and turned to Dorian, who sighed.

Seeing the distress in Winslow's face, Valeda frowned. She could sense the anger in him, the bitter distaste he had for his own family, and was at once sorry for his pains, yet at the same time, curious. Unable to sit by and watch him in pain, she cleared her throat until the attention of the room turned to her.

"While I recognize the uncertainty of our situation," she said carefully, "I highly doubt that I'm in any danger. I'm sure Lord Agoston will not need to watch out for me. I'm hardly a target."

"You're Talented now," Dorian said. "If anyone catches wind of that fact, you will be a political target."

"Yes, but no one knows about it," she said. "Nor am I inclined to share the knowledge."

"The fact is," Bartholomew said calmly, "we still don't know how or why you were suddenly gifted with magic, Miss Quinlan. Until we do, we need to be watchful. Your transformation . . . it might not . . . well . . . you could still have . . . um . . . ."

"There might be something more coming," Winslow said.

The way he said it made the hair on her arms stand stiff. Valeda met his blue-green gaze and held it, terrified at the prospect of magic conducting more mischief on her person. *What more could be coming? He'd already said we had some Wild in us and that had been horrifying enough.*

"For that matter, we don't know quite what to make of you, either, Winifred," Dorian said. "Perhaps we should all stay at the Panoply."

"And leave the house unguarded?" Winslow asked.

"Gremor can watch the house," Dorian said. "Father leant him back to me, so I may as well get some use out of him. Besides, this would only be for one night."

"It's agreed," Bart said. "I'm far more comfortable sticking together anyway."

CHAPTER TWENTY-TWO

Elsie double-checked her travelling bag, barely noting the change in clothing and the spare pistol she had stowed in it. The rest of her luggage ought to have arrived already, but on the off chance that she got there before her things, she wanted something suitable to wear. She was already dressed in long velvet material and had a woolen cloak to put on when she got to Winter Tournament, which made her delay here in Delgora insufferably hot.

Still, every time she went to perform the transportation spell, Elsie could not shake the feeling that she was forgetting something. It was maddening.

Lady Leona and her husband, Sir Callen Beroe, stood near the door to her private study, quietly watching. Elsie looked at them and smiled self-consciously. The two were a perfect pair; Leona with her golden hair and Callen with his rough, dark features. The sight of them made her heartsick for Dorian.

“I want you to be ready to move the people into the ark by the time I return,” Elsie said.

Leona and Callen exchanged a look. She’d already been over this and she knew it.

“Of course, my Lady,” Leona said.

“In fact, start sending the orphans and their teachers.” Elsie picked up her travel bag again. “And then gather the poor. Quietly, so as not to start a panic.”

"The organization of the evacuation is already set, my Lady," Callen said. "We can have the people of Delgora inside the ark within five hours."

Not all of them, Elsie thought with a flinch. The evacuation was only set for the capital of Delgora and the closest surrounding villages. Places like Little Delgora Harbor were too far away to benefit.

You can't save them all.

She tugged on her earlobe and scowled.

No, she couldn't save them all, but she could save a few.

"Mirabella and the Cornelius family," Elsie suddenly remembered and faced Leona. "I know it sounds strange but if Mrs. Cornelius . . . if she . . ."

Elsie stopped and wrinkled her nose in displeasure. What was she supposed to say here? *If Fayree turns into a creature, get to the ark immediately.*

No, that would only alarm them further.

"If Mrs. Cornelius says that you should hurry, I want you to listen to her," Elsie said.

"Are you certain?" Callen asked.

Elsie nodded. Another look passed between the couple, but Callen didn't argue. Instead, he nodded back, albeit slowly. Elsie could see the confusion in them both, but she trusted that they would follow her orders. She gave them one last smile and then took a deep breath.

Closing her eyes, she focused on Delgora Manor in Lorant. Or, more specifically, the front vestibule of the manor house. She'd managed to perfect the travelling spell, but it was still dangerous. While she wasn't afraid of ending up someplace unexpected, she ran the risk of transporting herself on top of another person. She'd arranged with Dorian that the front vestibule would be empty during the hours of five and six on this precise day to avoid such a disaster, but she still worried.

"*Yetakupo,*" she said, quickly commanding her Talent into the spell.

As always, there was no pain involved, no sensation of movement. One moment she was in her private office in Delgora and the next, she opened her eyes to the warmth of the vestibule's fireplace. She lowered her luggage and sighed, pleased to find the room empty.

The drapes were closed, shielding her arrival from any passerby, and all of the electrical lights were shut off. Elsie smiled at the many candles shining through the room. Dorian knew how much she preferred candlelight and had taken the time to prepare for her.

A notecard lay prominent on the table beside the front door. She recognized Dorian's stilted, noble handwriting and moved to pick it up. It had only been a few short weeks since they'd parted company, but her heart pinched at the idea that he was here. They were stronger together and she knew it.

"Welcome to Lorant, my wife," the card read. "We eagerly await you in the library."

She smiled again, picked up her luggage and walked briskly into the house. Gremor, Dorian's former servant, met her in the corridor. He stood stiff as ever, his large nose held proudly upward, even when he bent a quick bow at her arrival.

"My Lady," Gremor said by way of greeting and reached for her luggage. "His Lordship is entertaining several guests in the library."

"Yes, thank you, Gremor," she said, handing over her cloak as well. "Are there any nasty surprises I should be aware of?"

"House Witch Caresse Feverrette and Miss Valeda Quinlan are among the guests."

She paused and glanced at the library door. "House Witch Feverrette?"

She'd been expecting Valeda, but certainly not Dorian's sister. There was no question among noble society where Caresse placed her loyalty and support, but Elsie hadn't met with the woman in at least three years. They had mutually decided that they should not stir up the Council while the ark was still under construction. During the interim, Caresse had all but emptied Feverrette lands of its poor and destitute, sending them on the long voyage to Delgora, where they waited to board the ark.

It's ironic that we had to start with the unfortunates of society, Elsie thought. But those better off had more reasons to cling to the way of the Magnellum Council. They might balk at leaving everything behind unless the threat was literally upon them. And they might gossip until all of Elsie's secrets were revealed. So Elsie had chosen to focus on the poor, the lost, or the abandoned. Those would be the first to enter the ark, and she prayed that guaranteed their survival.

"Well then," Elsie said turning to face the library door, "I will not keep them waiting further."

She opened the door to find another welcoming fire and a comfortably crowded room. Dorian stood and walked around the desk at the northeast corner of the room. His smile was full of relief as he crossed the room to greet her. Elsie barely had time to register the positions of the rest of the party before Dorian took her hand and kissed it.

Bartholomew and Caresse sat on the sofa closest to the fire, a commanding and central presence in the room. They looked completely at ease, both smiling in her direction. Winslow and Valeda stood on opposite sides of the room from each other; Winslow at the fire and Valeda at a wall of books.

"We have some news," Dorian murmured to her, "which we could not relay through a telegram."

Winslow and Valeda were both studiously ignoring each other. And they were both shining in that peculiar glow of the Fated. As pleased as she was to see Winslow alive, Elsie could not shake a sense of foreboding when she looked at him.

"*Opowa Ayate,*" she whispered the spell and looked deeper into the room.

"You see we have additional guests . . ." Dorian was saying, but stopped when she suddenly grabbed his forearm.

She could see the magic in Winslow, the golden glow that identified him as a Witch-Born, but there was something else in him. The deep green of the Wild curled around his person, looping in and through him as intricately as his magic.

"How is this possible?" She breathed the question and walked to Winslow.

Winslow squirmed under her scrutiny and cast his gaze to the floor. "I was sincerely hoping you would know," he said.

"Know what?" Dorian asked from behind her.

Elsie took Winslow's hand and lifted it, running her fingers over his tanned skin, but seeing only the woven patterns of green and gold in him.

"Part Wild?" she said aloud, too shocked to hold it in.

"What?" Bartholomew exclaimed. She heard him get to his feet, but she kept her focus on Winslow. "You said the verue plant subdued your Talent for a time. You didn't say it had become a part of you!"

"Why do you think I didn't want you to heal me?" Winslow shot back. "I had no idea what was going to happen. For all I knew, it could have spread to you."

Elsie looked to Bartholomew and checked, but there was no green in Lord Feverrette. "It didn't," she said.

Winslow relaxed and she let go of his hand. "Fates be praised," he said.

"But it didn't because it wasn't meant for him." Elsie turned to frown at Winslow. "Magic would not have allowed this combination unless it was meant for something. You're Fated, Winslow. You weren't when you left us, but you are now."

Winslow tensed again at this news and she immediately pitied the conflict in his face. For a long minute he just stared at her, pain and panic in his eyes. She wanted to comfort him, but didn't know how. It wasn't like she knew Magic's plans; she just knew the part she had to play. And then he looked past her, in Valeda's direction.

Elsie turned again and was surprised to find that Valeda Quinlan had identical markings to

Winslow in her. She blinked twice and looked at Dorian, who shrugged.

"I suppose," Valeda said awkwardly, "that means I am meant for something as well."

"No," Winslow said. "She doesn't know how to use her Talent. She can't help."

"And whose fault is that?" Valeda asked heatedly. "You were the one who was supposed to train me."

"Elsie." Winslow grabbed Elsie by the shoulder and squeezed hard. "I won't let her near a battlefield. Please."

Elsie glanced between Winslow and Valeda. She didn't know what to do. Winslow was pleading with her, asking her in his silence to forbid Valeda from fighting. Valeda was just as confused and angry of her current situation—and who wouldn't be? To be thrust from her calm life and into an end-of-the-world scenario where no one could tell her what was going on? Elsie would have hurt someone by now.

Carefully, Elsie covered Winslow's hand with her own. "When all of it comes down, there will be no place she can hide. The battlefield will be everywhere."

"Send her to the ark," he said.

"Very well," Elsie said. "She will accompany us to the ark, then."

She felt her tattoos needle in her skin and knew Magic did not approve. But Magic did not speak to her, which was a relief, and she honestly didn't know what else to say to poor Winslow.

"Hold on just a minute," Valeda said. "I'm not going anywhere until I have some answers."

"I would expect nothing less from you, Miss Quinlan," Elsie said and turned away from Winslow. "With that in mind, I have news from an unexpected source."

There's no helping it, she thought. *They have to know what they're up against and they have to know now.* So she told them Fayree's story. She knew Winslow was privy to most of it, but when she spoke of Voruke and the origins of the Pillars, even he showed surprise.

"So the Wild is angry about Magic. They want him back," Bartholomew said.

"And they think the only way to get him back is by killing all of us?" Caresse asked.

"For the most part, yes," Elsie said. "But . . . they do seem to be led by a single man. Perhaps they are Timeless, but that doesn't mean they can't think on their own. It's possible some could be persuaded toward peace."

"That hardly seems to matter at this point," Winslow said. "Even if there were people who wanted peace, those who don't, would overrun them. Look at where Fayree is."

"He's right," Valeda said. "The peace lovers are not the ones who will invade Magnellum when the Pillars fall."

"However," Bartholomew said before Valeda could speak again. "As we have a limited amount of time today, I suggest we relocate as quickly as possible."

"Relocate?" Elsie asked.

"Yes." Dorian moved to her side again. "It's too dangerous for us to stay here. I received a pointed warning and we must heed it."

Dorian would only take a warning from his father, Elsie knew. So she nodded. "Where shall we stay, then?" she asked.

"Feverrette House has opened its hospitality to us."

Ah, she thought. *That explains Caresse's presence.*

"Let's be off, then," Elsie said. She nodded her appreciation to Caresse.

The younger Witch smiled and nodded back.

***

They left Delgora House in pairs. Bartholomew and Caresse left through the front door, Dorian and Elsie through the back, and Winslow kept Valeda waiting to leave for at least a quarter of an hour after the others. It was, he had said sensibly, a tactic to keep people from realizing where they were going.

He took her on a seemingly aimless walk, weaving through merchant vendors and the tournament grounds, but his focus was always on the people. The mess of tournament swarmed around them, people chatting and laughing as they passed by. Several heated braziers peppered the streets—a gift from the House Witch of Lorant. Engineers could make pot-bellied stoves and warm a house, but out on the street there was little to prevent people from freezing while the tournament went on.

She wondered if Winslow saw something other than a gaggle of people. Perhaps they were being followed.

She remembered how she'd known that Monty was being watched at the train station. If she asked her Talent it might tell her if there was danger. She glanced up at Winslow, who smiled vaguely at her. His eyes reflected more worry than good humor.

Valeda wondered whose idea it was to move in broad daylight. She would have thought the shadows of nightfall would have been better.

"Winslow!" a voice squealed suddenly.

They both tensed, scanning the crowd again for danger. A moment later, a scrawny, blonde-haired girl fairly tackled Winslow. Valeda was forced to release his elbow and step back, but there didn't appear to be any immediate danger. Winslow huffed a surprised laugh.

"Jemima," he chuckled, embracing the girl. "You gave me a fright."

"I gave you a fright?" Jemima pushed back from him and socked him in the arm. "I'm not the one getting into train accidents, you sod!"

"Jemima!" A new, more refined voice scolded the girl. Valeda looked up as this newest interruption emerged from the crowd, her oval face scrunched into a severe frown. "You are a gentle lady of noble birth. You do not strike people on the street and you most certainly do not call them a 'sod'."

Valeda recognized at once the family resemblance. These, she knew, were Winslow's sisters. The elder was due to become House Witch of Agoston next year. The younger, Jemima, was second born and destined only for a political marriage in her lifetime. Of the two, Valeda found that she preferred the exuberant Jemima over her elder.

"Collata," Winslow greeted. He cleared his throat and looked supremely uncomfortable for a moment.

This might have amused Valeda, but Collata's attention swerved to her and she immediately wanted to hide. Collata Agoston portrayed an icy sort of beauty. She had round features that could have been charming if she permitted herself to smile, and a nose that looked too small for her face. Her lips set into a thin, unhappy line as her dark eyes inspected Valeda from head to toe.

When Collata's attention lingered on her riding pants and boots, Valeda saw a flash of contempt in the woman's gaze. It wasn't unnatural for select women to wear pants, but even Valeda knew that most Witch-Born females did not. Except, of course, for Elsie Delgora. But Elsie had lived half her life in the guise of an Untalented, and her sense of what was proper might be skewed.

"Mother wants to see you," Collata said, turning back to Winslow. "Now."

"What?" Winslow asked, clearly startled. "You mean she's here?"

"Yes, of course she's here. She's been trying to reach you since you lost your Talent." Collata gave them both an ugly smile. "I'm sure she'll welcome your commoner friend, considering the circumstances."

"Will she?" Winslow said flatly.

Valeda couldn't decide what bothered her more: the snarky comment on commoners from Collata, the idea of visiting House Witch Agoston, or the very feral look on Winslow's face as he stared his sister down. She wasn't the only one nervous, either. Jemima shifted from foot to foot, creeping closer to her brother as the seconds ticked by.

Finally, Collata looked away, feigning boredom. "Come along then, little brother. I'm sure this will liven the day," she said. She made several disparaging remarks about the commoners crowding the street and began to lead them away.

"We could always run for it," Valeda said under her breath.

Winslow chuckled and proffered his elbow. When she'd taken it, he crooked the opposite elbow for Jemima, who beamed up at him. They took up pace behind Collata, who led them toward Agoston House. There were no side trips, no pauses to chat with another passing noble, and Valeda found herself suddenly climbing the steps of a tall manor house.

The door opened for them and Winslow drew her inside. Jemima and Collata dumped their coats with the front doorman and proceeded into the drawing room. Valeda almost reached for the buttons on her coat, but Winslow stopped her.

"We won't be here long enough to warrant that," he whispered to her. "Keep silent if you can and follow my lead."

His words immediately alarmed her. She nodded, which seemed to please him because he smiled and winked at her. She smiled back, albeit tremulously, and allowed him to escort her into the front drawing room.

Agoston House was very different from Delgora House. Where Delgora had many flowery patterns gracing the walls and furniture, Agoston was clean white. The only colors in the room were the deep mahogany of the furniture and the flickering red of the fireplace. The House Witch herself wore a creamy white gown with lacey sleeves. Her blonde hair did little to dispel the image of frost in the room, and her eyes were so dark a blue that they bordered on black.

Collata and Jemima wore gold and blue, which made their every movement more pronounced against the plain backdrop. Valeda tried to shrink behind Winslow and out of view, but his grip was steadfast and she couldn't.

"So," Lady Morgana Agoston said from her seat beside the fire, "my son is still alive."

"It would seem so, my Lady," Winslow replied.

What sort of family required the mother to be addressed so formally? What sort of childhood would that bring? Valeda felt her heart break for the man beside her.

Morgana did not smile. She did not appear relieved or happy that Winslow was alive. In fact, Valeda thought as she watched the two, the House Witch seemed more annoyed than anything else.

Without warning, Valeda felt her magic react to the situation. *It's quite angry at the way Winslow is being treated,* she surmised. *And in his own home, too! Any mother would have worried for their son's health and safety, but this one can't be bothered so much as to embrace him.*

Winslow's hand covered her own, squeezing until she looked at him instead. His focus remained on his mother, but Valeda felt his magic calm her down, reassuring her that all was well. Though how all could be well, she didn't know. Someone needed to smack Morgana Agoston into a reaction.

His mouth twitched into a faint smile and Valeda had the horrible idea that he could read her thoughts.

"I've heard two conflicting rumors about you," Morgana said at last. "They say you strained yourself out of Talent rescuing some commoners. But then they say you rescued Lord Delgora from his would-be abductors. A feat that required considerable magical aid."

"Are those the only two rumors about me, my Lady? I've done so many other things that I would have thought the rumor mill would be overflowing by now."

"Do not be impertinent."

"But we get along so much better this way."

Morgana stood suddenly and her face twisted into a scowl. Valeda swallowed her fear, suppressing the urge to run far, far away from this domestic dispute. Winslow remained calm beside her, smirking over at his mother with all the reverence of a toad to a fly.

"You are my son and you will answer me," Morgana said. "Have you lost your Talent?"

Winslow tilted his head to the side and considered her for a moment. "Yes," he said smoothly. "I have lost my Talent."

For a fraction of a moment, Valeda thought she read dismay in the House Witch's face. But then Morgana collected herself and sat back down, smoothing her skirts as she did so.

"Lord Feverrette is the one who rescued Delgora that night. Not me. I was . . ." Winslow turned to Valeda now. With a cheeky smile, he lifted her hand to kiss her knuckles before finishing his sentence. ". . . otherwise engaged."

Collata made an unladylike snort of disgust. "Yes," she said. "You must be so happy. We all know your tastes run toward the Untalented."

Valeda glanced at Collata, distracted by this news. What exactly did that mean?

"Oh, I'm afraid it's true," Collata said with a taunting smile. "Or did you think you were the first Untalented he's ever brought home?"

Valeda felt Winslow's reaction before she saw it. His anger pulsed through his magic, which in turn fed her own. She met his blue-green gaze and held it, ignoring the rest of the room. *He's mourning someone,* she realized. But who or why were too complicated for her magic to answer.

"You are quite mistaken, dear sister, if you think this is my home," Winslow said. "A home denotes a place of warmth and charm. Where someone might feel accepted and loved. Agoston House has never given me such an impression."

"Winslow Fagen Agoston!" Morgana gasped. "One more word out of you and I shall banish you from House lands."

"Do it." He turned to face his mother, his body vibrating with fury under Valeda's fingers. "I don't go there anyway. The only person remotely of interest to me is Jem, and she's always at school. Father is too busy hiding away in the liquor cabinet and Collata's just as frigid as you are, Mother. So please do it. Banish me and make my avoidance of your presence legally binding."

Morgana leaned forward in her seat, gripping the armrests so tightly that Valeda swore she could hear them cracking under the strain. When the Witch spoke next, her voice was changed, deep and reverberating, echoing the rage of the woman.

"You come into my house and speak thus to me?"

"You knew when you summoned me here that this would be unpleasant," Winslow said. "Now banish me and make it official."

Wind gusted through the room, swirling around Morgana in a sudden, malevolent tempest. Valeda felt the danger. Her Talent rose in warning as whatever spell had just been cast whipped toward them. Without thinking, she lifted her free hand and muttered a word she was quite certain she'd never heard before.

"*Tateuote,*" she said.

A purple mist shielded them from the gust, dissipating as soon as the danger had passed. Valeda lowered her hand, every bit as startled as the rest of the room. Morgana's eyes widened in surprise and Collata made a choked sound. Jemima, on the other hand, whooped her joy and rushed over to stand beside her brother.

"Who are you?" Morgana asked Valeda, her voice betraying just how shaken she was.

"She's no one to you," Winslow said curtly. "Just like me."

Then he turned and led her out of the drawing room. Jemima followed on his heels, giggling at the display she'd just seen. None of them actually spoke until they were out of the house and at least three blocks away.

"Did you see her face?" Jemima asked with a laugh. "You'd have thought the Crone herself had spit one of her teeth on the carpet!"

"Jem, don't be crass," Winslow said, but he was grinning.

"Oh, Winslow, I am so sorry!" Valeda said. "I don't know what happened . . . I just . . ."

"Sorry?" Winslow stopped walking to stare down at her. "She was about to douse me with frost bite. You saved me from a whole lot of pain, Vee. Don't ever be sorry for that."

"Frost bite? On her own son?"

"Motherly affection is foreign to Lady Morgana," Winslow said with a rueful laugh. "It wouldn't be the first time she's done it."

Valeda gaped at him and looked back down the street. Anger flinted deep inside her and she felt her magic urge her to go back, to challenge the horrible woman, or something. She couldn't really think past the intense desire to hit Morgana Agoston several times with a blunt object.

Winslow cupped her face with a gloved hand and turned her to look at him. He was smiling at her, almost laughing. Then he bent down and kissed her. Some part of her protested that they were standing in broad daylight on the corner of the street with Fates knew how many people watching. But the bigger part of her just leaned into him, focused only on the warm press of his mouth to hers.

Jemima cleared her throat. “I admit it was fairly amazing, brother, but could you leave the snogging for indoors?”

He jerked away so fast, Valeda staggered on her feet. She was dizzy from the moment, but still caught the look of pained confusion in his face. Then he turned and left her, walking toward the house at the far end of the street.

“Come along,” he called brusquely over his shoulder.

Jemima shot her a look of compassion and then ran to catch up with her brother. Valeda felt tears burn the backs of her eyes as she watched them go. She couldn’t follow. She felt ashamed and exposed and vulnerable, and she would be damned if she let that man see her cry. So she turned down the closest alley and ran.

No news report was worth this.

***

Winslow had just stepped into Feverrette House and hadn’t even managed to get his gloves off when he was accosted by Dorian.

“What took you so long?” Dorian asked and then looked to Jemima. “And who is this?”

“Hey!” Jemima said with a frown. “You know me! It’s Jem!”

Dorian blinked down at her. “Little Jem?”

She grinned. “Not as little now.”

“Fates preserve me, you’re huge.” Dorian laughed and embraced the girl. “But does this mean what I think it does?”

“I was waylaid by family,” Winslow said, unable to stop smiling at his little sister. It had been far too long since he’d seen her and his heart ached at how much taller she’d gotten in his absence. *Time is so cruel,* he thought. “Not to worry, though. I think I’m properly banished from Agoston lands now.”

“You’re gone an hour and manage to get yourself banished from home?” Bartholomew asked as he came into the vestibule. “Why am I not surprised?”

“Where’s Miss Quinlan?” Dorian asked.

“She’s right behind me,” Winslow said, unbuttoning his jacket. “And you of all people should know, Barty, that this banishment has been a lifetime in the making.”

“Um . . . Winslow . . . Miss Quinlan’s not coming,” Jemima said.

“What?” He frowned at his sister.

“I saw her dash the other direction as we climbed the steps,” she said. “I can’t say as I blame her, either. What with you snogging her in the middle of the street and then shoving her away like some gnat in your face. I thought you had better manners than that.”

Winslow felt the pit of his stomach knot in fear. He turned back to the door and yanked it open. He scanned the street for signs of Valeda, calling on his Talent for aid. He saw every distinct face as though they were right next to him, but Jem was right, Valeda wasn’t there. He’d known she wouldn’t be. He couldn’t sense her anywhere, not even the lingering flint of her anger tinged the air around him.

He pushed a hand through his hair and cursed his own stubborn pride.

"You snogged her in the street?" Dorian asked from behind him.

"I kissed her. I didn't mean to," Winslow growled in frustration. "I never know what I'm doing with that blasted woman. My magic keeps pushing me toward her. Like . . . almost like . . ."

"You're drawn to each other," Dorian said. "You can sense when she's nearby. You can read her emotions as though they were your own."

Winslow frowned at the busy street, still searching. "Yes," he said. "What the hell is this?"

"I don't know," Dorian said and clapped a hand on his shoulder. "But it's the same with Elsie and me, if that's any consolation."

Winslow forced himself to look at his friend. "Really?"

"Yes, really," Dorian said. "Elsie said Fate had preordained us together. It was a battle to get her to marry me because of it. She said she couldn't be certain if this was real love or just a manifestation of our Talents."

"But, you love her," Winslow said. "I know you do. I can see it on your face."

"Yes I do," Dorian said with a sigh. He looked at the closed door beside them and shook his head. "But as long as we're both Talented, Elsie will always have a lingering doubt in her mind."

Winslow looked back into the street. Half of him wanted to rejoice with the news. After all, if this was just a byproduct of their Talents, then he was not betraying Bryva's memory in his attraction. The other half of him mourned. Whether he wanted to admit it or not, Valeda Quinlan had represented redemption for him. Or at least the hope of redemption.

Bryva would not have wanted him to torture himself for the rest of his life.

The idea that his growing fascination with Valeda could be nothing more than the machinations of Fate filled him with a sense of betrayal. He was not some puppet to be yanked about and neither was Valeda.

"You should go find her," Dorian said. "People might not know about her yet, but she's still in danger. Her association with us alone makes her a political target."

Winslow thought of the way she'd rescued him from his mother's spell and a renewed sense of urgency hit him. At least one House Witch was aware of Valeda's Talent now. Knowing his mother, word was going to spread very quickly.

He nodded to Dorian and bound down the steps, making a brisk pace back the way he'd come.

CHAPTER TWENTY-THREE

"You're sure you'll be all right?" Caresse asked with a worried frown.

They stood in the vestibule of Feverrette House again, with Caresse bundled to her ears in fur and Bartholomew hovering by the front door. Dorian smiled at his sister, grateful for her concern. Under normal circumstances, he would have insisted on accompanying them to the train station, but everyone had agreed that Elsie should remain hidden for now. And he wasn't leaving Elsie's side, not even to greet his mother.

"You won't be gone more than an hour, sister," he said. "I'm sure we will be just fine until your return."

"I would prefer if Lord Agoston were here," she said.

"So would I," Bartholomew muttered.

Dorian agreed with them, but he understood the danger to Miss Quinlan as well. Winslow needed to find Valeda before anyone else did. And if Elsie was right in her interpretation of Magic's will, then the sooner they had the girl back in their custody the better. Fated or not, Dorian still didn't understand how the woman had suddenly become Talented or what ramifications would come of it. At first he'd been afraid that Winslow would somehow suffer, as if she had somehow stolen part of him, but after careful observation Dorian couldn't believe that. Winslow was every bit as healthy, and every bit as Talented, as the day he was born. So whatever Miss Quinlan had, it was either in her system all along and waiting for the opportunity to emerge, or Fate was sitting somewhere in the corner laughing at them all.

The look on Caresse's face told him that she was thinking along the same lines. *She looks like our mother when she frowns like that,* he thought. All statuesque and prim, with her light eyebrows pinched together in severe thought and her fine nose wrinkled in displeasure, she might have been mistaken for Jessamine Feverrette. Dorian smiled and took his sister by the shoulders, meeting her blue gaze straight on before he spoke.

"It will be all right," he said. "Gremor is here. I lived through many years on the run with that man and I'm certain he won't fail me now."

"Very well," Caresse said, but he could hear the hesitance in her voice.

"The carriage is here," Bart said, opening the door.

Caresse embraced him one last time before turning to take Bart's elbow. They exited together, looking every bit the nobles that they were. Dorian closed the door and sighed, pushing back his own worry.

Elsie was supposed to make her speech at the opening ceremony of Winter Tournament, which would be tomorrow at twilight. She was not scheduled to speak. She would just interrupt. As she'd pointed out earlier, none of the Council cared much for her as it was, so she needn't worry about making anyone angry.

It still felt reckless and impertinent to him, but Dorian couldn't shake the underlying fear that they were already too late. In the back of his mind he could still see the vision Magic had given him while he was wounded. If it was to be believed, then the Pillars would not fail until they were both safely in Delgora. What happened between now and then, however, was still a matter for debate.

Dorian turned back into the house and began checking the rooms. He started with the study, then the drawing room, making certain every window was secured.

It is possible for future events to alter, he mused. Magic Himself had said so on the day of Elsie's ascension. Every person's decisions affected Fate, or at least Time. He tried to imagine what it would be like to be cursed as Median. Stuck, Winslow had said, between Past, Present and Future. It would have to be disorienting, not knowing if you're seeing the present or the past. There could be no peace for her, only the constant struggle to understand how events unfold.

Elsie had been told to come to Winter Tournament, he thought. *Something had to happen here. Something that couldn't happen anywhere else.*

He returned to the hallway and headed for the kitchens.

Eight years ago, Magic had known the most likely course of events when he came to Delgora. He had known as he walked into the manor house that Vicaress Reonne—may she be cursed for eternity—had planted a Dellidus creature in the room. Which meant he had known his physical form would die that day.

Why? What did that gain him? What benefit was there for anyone that Magic had died?

Elsie couldn't imbue anyone with Talent, not even using the tattooed arm. Those among the Witch-Born still had their Talents, but it would be nothing against the oncoming Wild. Magic had to have known that would happen. Why leave them defenseless? Did Magic want them all to die?

Dorian stepped into the kitchen and paused. Gremor lay draped limply over the table, face down in a plate of food. It took several seconds for Dorian to process what he was seeing. Then he rushed forward and touched the old man's throat, feeling for a pulse. He got one, steady and strong, and breathed a curse.

"Elsie!" he shouted and ran for the door.

He'd left her in the guestroom upstairs. Panic squeezed his chest tight as he took the stairs, bending time and pushing himself forward with his magic. He burst into their room and stopped.

Elsie lay unconscious on the bed, but there was no sign of an intruder. He could sense that she was alive, but her Talent felt distant to him. He hurried to the bed and began searching frantically. Only a Remora stone could render her powerless.

He felt under the sheets, checked beneath the bed, but couldn't find it. He knew it was there, though. He could feel his own magic recede into his core from its presence. He finally found it squashed between the mattresses; a hard lump of rock no bigger than an egg.

Yanking it out, he turned to throw it through the window when a dart struck him in the chest. An instant later, his vision smeared and he fell to his knees. The stone dropped from his nerveless fingers. Even if the stone had rolled far enough away for him to access his magic, Dorian knew the poison that had hit him.

Pain flared at the dart's entry point and every muscle in his body contracted. He slumped to the side and struggled to breathe. There was supposed to be a second dart, the one to finish him off, but none came.

Instead he heard a very familiar, very hateful chuckle originate from the far corner of the room. Dazed and incapable of movement, Dorian watched as Alois Orzebet, his half-brother, walked toward him.

"All those years on the run didn't teach you a thing did they, big brother?" Alois said.

A moment later, Alois's fist slammed into his jaw and Dorian fell to the side.

***

Elsie woke slowly. Her head hurt and she had the disorienting feeling that she was somehow sitting up. Her neck was strained and cramped, lolling her head heavily as she began to take control of her body. She finally lifted her head and opened her eyes, fighting off a wave of dizziness as the room came into focus.

She was tied to a wooden chair with one large Remora stone strapped to her lap. She stared at the ugly green stone for a moment, seeing the sharp angles and irregular shape, and understood her predicament. She'd known an attack was coming. She'd felt it every day for the last eight years; a creeping, quiet sensation that told her every breath she breathed in freedom was a gift.

Magic had warned her that there were many plots against her. Magic had said she would be forced to confront them someday. Somehow she'd imagined the Wild would break through before any real harm could come to her. Surely then the Council would see how right she was and desist in this violent spectacle.

But she had been wrong. Someday was suddenly right now.

Cold moonlight pierced the room from a barred window high up on the western wall. The corners were in shadow and there was one very sturdy looking door in the eastern wall. Directly in front of her Dorian sat in a similar chair. He was tied as heavily as she was and his head hung limp to one side. Even in the dark she could see that he was sweating. His fingers twitched at odd intervals and every now and then his muscles strained, though she got the feeling this was not against the bindings.

Dorian was unconscious, feverish and in a great deal of pain.

Poison, she surmised. She'd know those effects anywhere; Fervarium, a poison that Elsie herself had concocted during her time as a Bedim assassin.

The plan had been to use the poison to kill the Dellidus creature that used to lurk in Delgora. That hadn't worked, though. So she'd sold the recipe on the black market instead to raise money for weapons and armor. She thought when Bryva died that she'd paid the price for that mistake, but here it was again. Elsie wanted to look away from Dorian, but couldn't.

"Mother said you'd wake up first," a familiar voice said from the corner.

Elsie glanced up as Alois Orzebet stepped into the moonlight. He was a tall, powerfully built man with a shock of tousled brown hair and his mother's gaunt features. His boots crunched over the pebbly floor until he stopped just beside her chair. Then he crouched down, bringing himself face to face with her.

"We weren't certain how much good a stone would do against you," Alois said, reaching out to touch her gloved arm. "But mother was insistent. At least in regard to you."

"What does your mother want?" Elsie asked.

She tried to muster some sound of nobility to her voice, but she heard only the rough rasp of someone recently choked. Then she remembered how she'd gotten here. She'd gone in to prepare for bed when someone had garroted her from behind. Ironic, really, considering the garrote had been her weapon of choice for many years.

"My mother? She just wants to level the playing field a bit," Alois said with a chuckle. "Lady Lorant? Now she just wants to kill you."

Another time, another place, Elsie might have been alarmed by his proclamation. But she'd spent the better half of her life under the constant threat of death, so instead of alarm, Elsie only felt a prick of sadness. She looked at Dorian, trying to shove away the thoughts of him in mourning. If they didn't kill him too, Dorian would spend the rest of his life fighting to avenge her. She knew this in the deepest part of her soul. His grief would be unbearable.

Lady Lorant, Elsie thought. *Of course.* Eight years ago, Elsie had uncovered Lord Ivan Lorant's plot to overthrow Delgora House, incriminating him in the assassination of Elsie's parents. He was executed by order of the Council just six months after Elsie's ascension to House Witch. Lady Loreena Lorant, on the other hand, was exonerated. The Council proclaimed her ignorant of her husband's political machinations and allowed her to retire from her position as Lorant's House Witch.

Elsie should have known that Orzebet would make an alliance with the Lady. Minne and Loreena were two spiteful women on their own—combined they would be deadly.

"You really don't care, do you?" Alois asked. "Death inches closer to you and you don't even blink."

"Death presses close to all of us right now, Alois," she said. "If I don't die at your hands today, the Wild will kill me tomorrow. Forgive me if I can't work up any excitement for you."

Alois laughed. "You're trying to frighten me with talk of the Wild! How long have you been preaching about its coming? I haven't seen so much as a flicker from any of the Pillars."

"Because you haven't been paying attention!" Elsie snapped. "Every House Witch has had to order the abandoning of at least one town boarding the Wild."

"One town in three hundred," he scoffed.

"One town every year for the last six years," Elsie said. "That's eighteen towns in three hundred. The Council keeps it quiet out of fear of the Untalented, but our borders are slowly shrinking."

"Right, so I'll start worrying in another twenty years."

"There won't be another twenty years, Alois. We're lucky if we have even one left."

"The Pillars have stood for millennia. They won't fall."

"The Pillars stand with the strength of the Witches. We haven't had a new witch in eight years, Alois. Pay attention! When we fall, so will the Pillars."

Alois sneered at her. He touched her cheek with a knuckle and rubbed her skin lightly. "Like I said, my mother wants to even the playing field. The great Elsie Delgora might fall, but Orzebet House will stand."

He stood and left her, opening the door just long enough to exit. She heard a lock slide into place and released her breath. She'd known it was no use talking to him, but she had to try. Alois was vindictive and mean and he hated Dorian, but that didn't mean he had to be stupid, too.

Taking a deep breath, Elsie closed her eyes and tried to search for her Talent. The stone rendered most Talented useless, but she was different. She had Magic inked into her arm. After years of letting the deity drive her insane, it was time to see some benefits from it.

CHAPTER TWENTY-FOUR

Valeda waited until evening before making her way to the Panoply. If she'd had a choice she would have stayed away completely, but her personal effects were stored in the room Lord Delgora rented for her. She was cold, hungry and out of money, so she walked quickly across the street and toward the establishment doors.

She hoped someone else would come for her—Dorian or Bartholomew—but she could sense Winslow's nearness. Her Talent whispered the knowledge to her, but it could not locate his exact position. *It's just as well,* she thought. He would likely find her first anyway. He had spent the better part of a month trailing her in Tormey; he was a practiced hand at it now.

"Another hour and I would have been forced to send Warders out to find you," Winslow said from behind her.

Though she'd been expecting him, the sound of his voice still surprised her. Valeda paused mid-step, but continued on without speaking to him. He had made enough of a fool out of her, she was not going to argue in the middle of the street. Besides which, she had lost feeling in her little toes about an hour ago. The prospect of a warm bath pulled her through the Panoply doors and to the back staircase. He didn't try speaking to her again until they were out of earshot and past the second floor.

"I behaved poorly," he said at last. "I do beg your forgiveness."

They were almost to the third floor. Seven more steps and she could be in the hallway. Four doors down to the left was her room. *Safety,* she thought, *warmth and quiet and food.* But she stopped on the landing between floors. Staring up into the gloom of the hallway, she debated what to say.

All day long Valeda had practiced scathing things for Lord Agoston, but all of them failed her now. She hadn't expected him to apologize, much less feel the sincerity of it coursing through his Talent. Her anger evaporated, leaving her with nothing but an empty exhaustion. Her feet ached from walking all day and her stomach rumbled in protest, so she closed her eyes and sighed.

"It doesn't matter, my Lord," she said. Opening her eyes again, Valeda turned to face him. He looked surprised and wary, but didn't seem to move. "None of it really matters anymore."

"Your virtue suddenly doesn't matter?" He sounded incredulous. She couldn't blame him for that. A week ago she would have agreed with him.

"Do you think my virtue can save me?" she asked. "When they find out about us they won't stop at ransacking my room. I'm smart enough to work that bit out for myself."

She didn't clarify who "they" were. He knew she meant the Council. Winslow looked away, turning to grip the wooden railing. She heard it creak and groan under his hands, felt a powerful emotion pass through him, but couldn't identify it. He couldn't deny her assertion. The Council would come after them when they discovered two half-Wild Witches in their borders. And if the way they treated Lady Elsie was any indication, Valeda doubted they would survive the winter.

She watched him for a moment, fighting the desire to wrap her arms around him and hold on tight. He was so brave and so strong. He'd fought to keep Mirabella and her mother alive. He'd fought for his independence from his own mother. And he would fight and die for his friends, she knew it. But he would never, ever, let her into his life.

He was cradling some distant pain, mourning someone lost, and refused to live fully. To let her in would require that he release that pain, and she could sense that he wasn't ready.

She turned back to the steps. She wasn't a fanciful person, but for a blip of a moment she'd actually hoped there was something real between them.

"I'm tired, Lord Agoston. Good night."

He didn't respond and he didn't try to stop her, so she left. She practically shuffled to her room, she was so exhausted. Emotionally and physically spent, Valeda unlocked her rented room and stepped inside. Reaching blindly for the switch on the wall, she fumbled until the lights flickered on and then she froze.

It was a standard room—Lord Delgora hadn't wanted to draw too much attention to her. One table and one chair were both capsized. But the room was not ransacked like her home.

Montgomery Taven lay sprawled across her bed, his head craned over the edge at an awkward angle. His mouth was open, his eyes wide and empty, and a big knife was buried in his chest.

Valeda screamed. She staggered until she hit the wall, her legs suddenly unable to work.

Covering her mouth, she stared at Monty's body, her mind devoid of rational thought.

Winslow burst through the door, took one look at the body on her bed, and then pulled her into an embrace. She closed her eyes and hid her face in his shoulder, trying hard to forget what was just behind her. She heard a new voice enter the room, but didn't move, clinging to Winslow's solid strength like a lifeline.

"What the blazes?" someone said. "Is that . . . that can't be . . . Ambassador Taven?"

"I believe we should section off this room and call for the Warders," Winslow said.

"Mother, Maiden and Crone!"

"Sir!" Winslow said, forcefully. "What is your name, sir?"

"Milance. Frederick Milance. I'm with room service . . . I just heard the scream . . ."

"Mister Milance, I recognize that this is a shocking scenario, but before the whole floor erupts with gossip, I suggest you section off this room, inform your manager, and send for the Warders."

"Right. The Warders. They'll know what to do."

A moment later she heard the door close and Winslow slowly pulled away from her. Valeda felt her body tremble, felt her head suddenly light as he wiped the tears from her face. He was the only thing safe to look at, so she did. He appeared grim and serious as he quietly took stock of her.

"It's all right," he said. "You are all right, Vee. Just breathe."

"Monty . . ."

His eyes flashed and his jaw clenched, but he shook his head. "I'm going to go check if they left anything behind. I need you to keep facing the door. Do not turn around."

"Won't the Warders do that?"

He smiled at her and she thought she read real affection in his voice. "Here you are in complete shock and you still manage to think clearly," he said. "Yes, the Warders will do that, but I want to make sure Dorian didn't leave anything behind. The last thing we need is his name connected with a murder."

She nodded, mostly understanding. He moved quickly, abandoning her for his investigation. Valeda hugged herself and tried to stop shaking. In all her investigations, she'd never seen a dead body, much less a murdered one in her bed. The sight was jarring, painful, and she felt ill.

Without meaning to, she accessed her magic. The shaking subsided and the aches of the day disappeared. She still felt ill, but as long as she faced the door she was in no immediate danger of disgracing herself. A moment later Winslow returned to her. He rubbed her arms and frowned at the room behind her.

"I think we're safe," he said.

Her mind flashed to the train station and she remembered the fear in Monty's eyes. She'd known he was being followed. *Why didn't I warn someone? I might have prevented his death if I'd just said something to Lady Elsie.*

"I tried to talk to him at the train station," she said quietly. "He pretended not to know me. I knew . . . I knew there was something wrong, I just . . ."

"You couldn't have known this was coming," Winslow said. "Although it is gratifying to know I was right."

"Right about what?" she asked, confused.

"Something really was wrong at the station. You just refused to say what."

"We were being watched. I thought someone could be listening as well."

"A fair summation. Someone probably was. But why did you want to talk to him?"

"I was being polite," she said with a frown. She could still see the way Monty had gallantly escorted her into the Delgora gardens. "He'd been so charming and kind to me before, it only seemed right to return the favor."

The door opened and a dark, stalwart man strode into the room. He brusquely made his way to the bed, ignoring her and Winslow. Valeda turned partway, but kept her face averted from the scene. Winslow shifted beside her, one hand resting on the small of her back. A moment later two more people entered, ignoring them just as much as the first and moving into the room. They were all Warders; she knew by the white tabards they wore. And she could sense something on them, something that called to both the Wild and the magic in her.

"Miss Quinlan, I presume?" the dark man asked, moving to stand before her.

"Yes."

"Miss Quinlan, there is a dead man in your bed. I would like to know how he got there and why."

She blinked up at his stern, unhappy features. "I . . . don't know," she said. "I only just arrived to find him here."

"Convenient," he said. "And where were you prior to finding him?"

"I don't know. Everywhere. I've been walking through Lorant all day."

"All day, you say? How wonderful. No alibi, then," he said and squinted down at her. "What makes a lady walk through Lorant all day on her own?"

"I was upset," Valeda said and frowned. She'd distinctly heard the word 'alibi'. He talked too fast, but she heard it.

"Upset by what?"

"Why does that matter? Poor Ambassador Taven certainly didn't upset me, if that's what you're driving at. I had no idea the man wanted to see me." She felt Winslow stiffen beside her, but she didn't care. This Warder was treading on her very fragile nerves.

"And why would Ambassador Taven want to see you?"

Valeda realized then the blunder she had made. It would have been better if she said she didn't know the dead man. That would have given them time to visit Lady Elsie and explain the matter before the Warders had her arrested under suspicion of murder. The reporter in her connected the dots quickly enough that she could respond without stammering. Valeda lifted her chin and gave the Warder her best angry face.

"Ambassador Taven did a kindness for me several months ago," she said curtly. "I told him then that if he ever needed something within my power that I would see it done. As we haven't spoken since, I can only imagine he came to collect."

"In your bedroom?"

Valeda gasped at the suggestive tone in the Warders voice and nearly slapped him. Winslow, Fates be praised, anticipated her. With a quick move he grabbed her by the wrist and shoved her behind him, successfully blocking her from the rest of the room.

"You will remember that she is a lady above reproach, sir," Winslow said. "Or you will answer to me."

"Relax, Lord Agoston," a new voice said from the doorway. "Victor is trained to upset suspects in order to draw out the truth."

This new man was not wearing a tabard. Instead, he was festooned in cream and black colors, all of the fabrics too rich for an ordinary Warder. His face was familiar to her, but she could not rightly bring his name to mind. He was older, with greying sepia hair and care-worn features.

He took his time removing his gloves before making his way into the room.

"Lord Orzebet," Winslow said after a moment.

Valeda blushed and kicked herself for not realizing it sooner. This was Lord Rorant Orzebet, Dorian's father. That was why he looked so familiar. His son was very near to identical, minus several years, of course.

"Have you called for the surgeon yet?" Orzebet asked.

"I sent a runner," Victor reported.

"Good. I doubt there's much light he'll be able to shed on this case, but make him do a thorough investigation anyway," Orzebet said.

Valeda peeked around Winslow's shoulder. Victor remained in front of Winslow, but Lord Orzebet stood over the bed, staring down at Monty's body. She spied Monty's face in her peripheral vision and shuddered. Mercifully, Orzebet's body blocked out the sight of the knife and blood.

"Search the room, Victor. Monty was a clever man. He'll have left us something." Lord Orzebet turned from the bed to face them. "Lord Agoston, Miss Quinlan, you will accompany me to my office."

Valeda knew better than to argue.

***

"We have some serious problems," Lord Orzebet said as he closed his office door.

Winslow sat in the wooden chair beside Valeda and watched Rorant move to sit behind his desk. In all his years frequenting the building, Winslow had never once been forced to sit in Rorant's private office. It felt wrong to be in there, as though he were trespassing in spite of Rorant being right there. Everything was clean and polished, gleaming under the many electrical lights that lined the walls. Even the arm of his chair showed the deep glow of healthy wood, matching the desk and floor almost perfectly. This was the office of a man who took pride in everything he did.

Something else was wrong; Winslow could feel it.

"You mean other than Ambassador Taven's death?" Valeda asked, though by her tone he knew she sensed the same problem.

"Indeed," Rorant said. "Lord and Lady Delgora went missing from Feverrette House tonight."

"What?" The word was out of Winslow's mouth before he could stop himself. His stomach knotted with grief. "How long?"

"Lord and Lady Feverrette informed me more than an hour ago. They left the house to meet Lady Jessamine at the station and returned to find the servants drugged and their two charges missing," Rorant said and folded his arms over his desk.

He looked lost for a moment, gazing blankly at several sheets of paper stacked neatly on the desk. Winslow's heart broke at the sight of him. Lord Rorant Orzebet always knew what to do. He held most of Magnellum's secrets, had battled two Dellidus creatures in his lifetime and now, at the prospect of his son's death, he was finally broken.

Winslow couldn't bear to look at him. This was his fault. If he hadn't kissed Valeda in the middle of the street she wouldn't have run off. He would have been there to protect them. Defeat lodged in his chest and he slumped in his chair.

"Who would have taken them?" Valeda asked. "And why?"

"Any number of nobles hate them," Winslow said. "Because Elsie is . . . special."

"Lady Elsie is five steps away from going crackers, even I can see that, but she hasn't done anything wrong," Valeda said.

"She married Dorian."

"Many nobles have married outside the Council's wishes. None of them were abducted. This makes no sense, my Lord."

Winslow looked at her and wished he could explain everything. He wanted to tell her that Elsie was their last link to Magic, that it was through Elsie that all of Magnellum might be saved from the Wild, but he couldn't. He'd given an oath to the Council never to speak about the events that transpired in Delgora eight years ago. For the Witch-Born, oaths were hard to break.

When the silence stretched on, Valeda broke, glaring at them both with real heat.

"Now you listen to me," she said angrily, "I may have been a reporter for several years, but I am not always on the prowl for a story. I am not the sort who preys on the suffering of others for my reporting. Now I may not have many things to bring to the table, but I do understand how to investigate. Either let me help or lock me up somewhere. I'm quite done with being molly-coddled and held in suspect."

"We don't suspect you of anything," Rorant said with surprise.

"Then tell me what is going on, so I can help."

Winslow shifted uncomfortably in his chair. He glanced at Rorant, who looked monumentally confused, and realized that Dorian hadn't had the chance to tell his father about Valeda's condition. He didn't like having another person know about her—the more who knew, the more danger she would be in—but she had dispelled frost bite before it could hit him and that rumor was going to surface eventually.

He took a deep breath and sat forward.

"I think we should all lay our cards on the table," he said, mostly to Valeda. "Trust must come from both sides, right?"

She frowned, but nodded at him.

"Valeda is Talented now," Winslow said, turning to Rorant. "She's the first new Witch in eight years, I think. I don't know how it happened, but it did. So the Witch-Born plight is now, at least in part, her plight. Wouldn't you say?"

Rorant knew what he was asking. Leaning back in his chair, the older man folded his hands and surveyed Valeda for a moment. With a deep, unhappy sigh, he conceded with a nod.

Winslow turned back to Valeda. "Eight years ago a Dellidus attacked Magic, the man-god, in Delgora."

Her eyes widened in shock.

"You know how the Dellidus works. It feeds off Magic," Winslow continued. "Except when it took directly from Magic, the man-god, it drew power from all the Witch-Born in Magnellum. We suspect that is why the Pillars are falling."

"So . . . Magic is dead?" Valeda asked.

"Yes and no," Rorant said. "His physical form died that day, but a remnant was left behind. He exists now in Elsie's right arm."

"And that's why so many in the Council hate Elsie," Valeda said. "They would see this as an end to their power and be threatened."

"Yes," Winslow said. "So you see, there are any number of Witches who might have taken Dorian and Elsie."

"Oh, I have a fairly good idea who took them," Rorant said, scowling. "I just can't prove it."

"Who?" she asked.

Winslow felt his gut knot. He knew the answer before it was given. He'd been suspecting it for a while now.

"My wife, Lady Minne Orzebet."

"Oh," Valeda said in a small, shocked voice. Her brow furrowed as she processed this information. "But . . . Montgomery Taven worked for Orzebet House."

"Yes, he did. And he was a damned fine fellow," Rorant said.

"So . . ." Valeda frowned some more. "So why was he coming to see me?"

"I had assumed you two were in cahoots since your trip to Delgora, actually."

"Well, no," Valeda said defensively. "I hardly knew the man. The last time I saw him was at the train station and he made it plain that he didn't want to talk to me."

"At least right then," Winslow corrected her. "You did say you thought he was being watched."

"So you think he came to my bedroom to talk to me? But why? What could I do to help him?"

"I have no idea," Winslow said.

"Whatever it was," Rorant said, leaning back in his chair, "it was important enough that someone killed him."

Winslow rubbed his forehead and tried not to think of what Dorian might be going through. Lady

Minne had been dying to get her paws on Dorian since he was a baby.

"Minne isn't stable enough to come up with an abduction plan," he said with a frown.

"What?" Valeda asked.

"No offense, my Lord," Winslow said to Rorant. "But your wife is seriously unbalanced. She can't plot a decent meal, let alone something like this."

Rorant smirked. "No offense taken, son. And you're right. I believe Lady Lorant had her hands in it as well."

"Neither of those Ladies know anything about the black market," Winslow said. "You can cross off any back alleys or abandoned districts. They'd take Elsie and Dorian where they were confident they could keep them."

"Surely people would notice a pair of bodies being dragged around," Valeda said. "They'd have to go somewhere they could pay people to stay quiet."

"Or someplace where they already had unquestioned loyalty from the staff," Rorant said.

"They couldn't go to Fortress Lorant, every House has spies somewhere," Winslow said carefully. "How many establishments are actually owned and run by Lorant House?"

"Well, there's Fridgets, the Gentlemen's club," Rorant said. "And the Ladies Tea House, but they wouldn't go there. Too many Witch-Born."

Winslow stood and started pacing. They had to find them. But where? Where would those blasted Witches take them?

He moved to the fireplace and stopped. Several sprigs of lavender hung above the mantle, wafting a pleasant scent into the room. He stared at the mantle for a moment, remembering the day he'd found Dorian at Lorant pier. The man had been in hiding for so many years, Winslow almost forgot what he looked like. They'd gone to Fridgets to catch up, him and Dorian and Barty.

Dorian had told them about living on the run. He'd said he'd gone in as a hired hand to collect herbs that grew between the Pillars. Herbs like the lavender hanging on Rorant's mantle. Lorant House financed the collection of lavender so that their noble establishments would always smell fresh. Winslow pointed at the lavender.

"Is Lorant House the only one that collects herbs between the Pillars?"

"I don't think they're the only house, but they're certainly the largest," Rorant said.

"Where do they take the herbs to be processed?" Winslow asked.

"To a storehouse just behind the fortress," Rorant said, standing up.

"It's close enough to the Fortress that two ladies wouldn't rouse suspicion walking through. They'd be comfortable and out of the way," Winslow said.

Rorant came around the desk and charged for the office door.

"Victor!" Rorant shouted into the hallway. "Get the carriage out front!"

Valeda stood as Winslow walked to her. "This next bit could be dangerous, Vee."

“There was a dead man in my bed earlier today,” she said. “I imagine I can handle it.”

Winslow glanced at Rorant, who was watching them with open curiosity. He gritted his teeth and focused on Valeda’s face. She looked quite determined, which made him sigh.

“Stay close to me,” he said, and waited for her to nod before taking her hand and hurrying out the door.

CHAPTER TWENTY-FIVE

"I'm sorry Elsie," Dorian said quietly.

He hurt like crazy and the blasted Remora stone kept him powerless, but at least they were alone. Alois had left them an hour after having relocated them both into a large, central chamber. Most of the room was in shadow, but he could make out a bulky, draped contraption to the left of their position. Bundles of different herbs hung from beams that ran parallel across the room. He scowled at them, recognizing at once where they were.

"This isn't your fault, Dorian."

"I should have known they'd suspect Feverrette House of harboring us," he said. "We would have been safer on our own."

"No," Elsie murmured. He could sense in her voice that she wasn't really listening to him. "They would have found us anywhere. This was meant to be."

His gaze fell to her gloved arm. "Magic told you this would happen?"

"No."

Dorian frowned and debated arguing further. But she needed her focus right now. She needed to access Magic, if she could. It was their only chance at surviving this. Fates knew no one else could find them. He just hoped Elsie could manage the feat before his stepmother made her big move.

So, he focused on what he could do instead. The effects of the poison were slowly wearing off, but his body felt like it had been dragged through town behind a horse. He shifted in his chair, trying to dislodge the stone or loosen the ropes. Neither worked. He scanned the room for something sharp, but found nothing.

He spotted the corner of a table and thought he might be able to scrape the ropes up and over his shoulder. They were damned tight, but it was worth a try. Dorian scooted his chair to the closest table. It was hard work and far too noisy. Every time his chair clattered against the ground, he checked the door.

Finally, flush against the table's edge, Dorian began rubbing his arm, and subsequently the topmost rope, over the hard surface. Wood scraped into his skin and he couldn't lean forward enough to make the rope move very far.

The door opened and his heart fell. They were out of time. Lady Minne Orzebet led Lady Loreena Lorant and Alois into the room. If she noticed what he'd been trying to do, she didn't comment. In fact, his stepmother looked more than pleased. Her wide cheeks dimpled and her eyes creased into sharp blue slits as she smiled at them.

"Lord and Lady Delgora, how nice to see you," Minne said.

"Hello, stepmother," Dorian said. "You're looking less morose today."

He kept his tone flat and forced himself not to look at Elsie. They needed time, so he'd find a way to get it. He'd avoided Minne most of his life, so he wasn't certain how well he could goad her, but it was worth a try. Shc was known for her dramatics throughout Magnellum and he thought that was a good place to start.

"Charming, Saldorian," Minne said. "But you won't upset me today."

"Oh, I don't know. We just got started. I might have a chance yet."

Minne laughed and twirled across the room, skirts flaring out from her stocky, rotund frame. For a larger woman, Minne Orzebet still managed to look elegant. Dorian thought that might be a blessing of the Talent.

He saw Alois lock the door and lean against it. The move was smugly casual and Dorian had the awful sensation that he was already beaten. *But this is my half-brother,* he thought. He knew this man, right down to the way he preferred his toast. Alois was a bitter, angry, unforgiving man, and that made him dangerous. But he was also arrogant and assuming. Alois probably thought the fight was already over.

Dorian took a deep breath. This was the last mistake his brother would ever make.

"I wonder, Lord Delgora, that you can be so flippant in your current situation," Lady Loreena said.

Dorian focused on the prim, chestnut-haired woman in the corner. *She's as cold as winter,* he thought, *and just as dead.* There was no life in her face, not even a spark of hate in her blue eyes. Dorian felt an intense pity for her. She'd had her husband executed for treason against Magnellum and one of her daughters killed by a Dellidus creature. And both those circumstances could be traced back to Elsie Varene Delgora.

"Yes, well, if I'm to meet my death, I should prefer to go with style," Dorian said.

Minne laughed again. "Don't be so silly," she said. "We don't mean to kill you."

"You don't?"

Minne walked to the contraption and fingered the cloth concealing it. She smiled up at it with something akin to admiration and Dorian felt fear lock in his chest. What else could they mean to do if not kill them?

"We're not stupid," Loreena said. "Killing you would result in the death of the entire Delgora state. The Pillars would collapse and thousands of Untalented would die."

"I find it hard to believe that you care about the Untalented," he said.

"We don't," Alois said. "But the Council does. Some within that antiquated group still believe our charge is to protect the people. They would hardly look on us kindly if we caused the deaths of so many."

"They will hardly look on you kindly for stealing Remora stones and holding two Witch-Born against their will," Dorian said.

"I doubt they will care once Magic has been set free," Minne said.

"Set free?" Dorian asked with a frown. "Set free from what?"

Minne tugged on the fabric, pulling it down in a wide, sweeping motion. Underneath was a disturbing rendition of a guillotine. It was smaller, with an added length of wood set at a ninety-degree angle from the chopping block. The angled blade was already raised, tied off at the side in a hard knot.

Dorian gazed at it in horror and finally looked at Elsie. They meant to take off her arm. Elsie didn't seem to notice the threat. Her eyes stayed focused on something he couldn't see and he knew her mind was far off.

"You can't!" he said. "You'll kill her!"

Minne grasped the contraption and wheeled it over to Elsie, humming some cheerful tune.

"Don't worry," Alois said with a sneer. "We'll free you in time to heal her."

Dorian struggled against the ropes, twisting and turning. He spotted Minne removing Elsie's glove, saw the tattoos glinting in the light. He thought maybe one or two were glowing, but he couldn't be sure. Straining against the ropes, he managed to tilt his chair and the whole thing teetered to the left. Dorian crashed onto the ground on his left and squirmed some more, hoping at least to dislodge the cursed stone from his chest. He heard Loreena call for Alois to do something and then pain exploded in his ribcage.

Alois stood over him, grinning, and kicked him again. Dorian gasped and wheezed. He coughed into the cold, dirty floor and tried to find some sense of coherency. He had to do something.

"Help me here," Minne said.

Alois left him to aid his mother in untying Elsie. They pulled her right arm free and slid it into the device. A wooden slat clamped down against Elsie's shoulder, pinning her there. Elsie closed her eyes, either from defeat or for better focus, Dorian couldn't tell. But if she was communing with Magic, then Magic had better make his move soon.

Someone pounded on the door, startling them all. Loreena detached from the corner, her eyes riveted on the door.

"How did they find us?" she asked. Her voice was panicked—the first sign of emotion he'd seen from her.

"It doesn't matter. They can't get through," Alois said. "Hurry up and do it, Mother."

"Minne Orzebet! I order you to open this door!" Rorant's voice roared from the other side.

"They're Witch-Born," Loreena said. "They *can* get through. Quickly, Minne!"

"No!" Dorian shouted.

Minne pulled a dagger from her belt and started sawing through the rope. The door rattled as something hit it. Dorian glanced between the door and the guillotine rope, still struggling to get free and praying his father managed to break in before it was too late. And then, impossibly, he felt his Talent flare to life.

Confused, he glanced at the Remora stone, but it had fallen off in the middle of his struggle. He spotted its roll away from him and toward Alois's feet.

Dorian snapped the ropes off and leapt to his feet. Alois blinked at him in surprise and opened his mouth as though to shout. Dorian didn't give him the chance. Bending time and propelling himself with his magic, Dorian punched Alois three times; twice in the ribs and once in the jaw. Alois staggered away and Dorian rushed for Elsie.

The cord to the guillotine broke and the blade started to descend. Dorian focused everything he had on the rope, reaching for it as it zipped through the air. He heard Minne and Loreena screaming, heard Alois cursing just behind him, and the door splintered open. He reached the rope. Its rough strands bit into his palm as he snagged it to a stop.

The blade hovered just above Elsie's arm. Each tattoo was lit in her skin; swirling golden patterns glowing brighter with each passing second. Dorian stared—they all stared—as Elsie unraveled the ropes binding her with a touch of her finger. She unlatched the wooden clamp holding her down and sat up. The Remora stone tumbled off her chest, but Elsie caught it with her free hand.

"This isn't possible," Minne said.

Winslow shoved the door open and the room became suddenly crowded. Rorant, Victor, Winslow and Valeda hurried in, only to stop and stare at Elsie. Or Elsie's arm, at least, and the Remora stone still held in her grasp.

"This isn't possible," Minne said again.

Dorian stayed where he was, close enough to her that he could smell the power in her. Her face was wrong somehow, too calm for their circumstances. Her umber gaze was replaced with sheer, clear blue. *Magic's eyes*, he knew; so deep and pure a blue that it was like staring up into a summer sky. His Talent was quietly in awe. Dorian was so entranced by the sight that he didn't see Loreena move toward Elsie.

"Look out!" Valeda shouted.

Winslow dived forward, blocking Elsie from the Lady. Dorian released the rope and turned, letting the guillotine slam into its base. He spotted movement at the corner of his eye. Minne bent time, grabbed him by the shoulder, and thrust her dagger into his back. He felt it skim against his spine, felt the arch of it pierce his lung, and choked on a surprised gasp.

His father screamed something angry, but Dorian was too focused on the blade to hear it. Minne twisted the knife, ripping through muscle and sinew before yanking it out. She drew back to stab him again when the whole room stopped moving.

Agony pulsed through his wound. Dorian didn't know how much time he had, but he focused his Talent on healing himself anyway. In his mind he mapped out the injury, noting every torn and flayed muscle before accessing his magic to mend it. An injury this large normally required focus and rest, but Dorian had lived through enough assassination attempts that he'd almost perfected the rushed version of healing.

The trick was to take the mortality out of the equation. He could heal the wound until it was no longer a threat to his life and then leave it for later. Of course, this always meant he had to go back and fix it for real, but at least he could move and fight his way out of the situation. Only this time, when he was finished, he discovered that he still couldn't move.

Confused, Dorian refocused on the room.

Someone was bending time.

A time-bend was nothing new for the Witch-Born. But bending time was specific to the person. Everything slowed down for the individual, not for the whole world or even a whole room. This was bizarre and frightening.

He looked to Elsie, who stayed motionless in her chair. Her eyes were still blue, still focused, but he could read in them a question meant only for him. A second later, as though confirming his own thoughts, he heard Magic's voice in his core.

Are you ready, Saldorian?

If he could have, he might have smiled, but in his frozen state he couldn't even move his mouth to do that. Magic was bending time. He really should have suspected as much.

Time released and Dorian quickly moved to evade his stepmother's second attack. Spinning on the ball of his foot, he rolled around Minne's outstretched arm, coming into position just behind her. She swung again, turning with her attack, but Rorant beat her to it. Suddenly his father was there, grabbing Minne's arm and yanking it about until he'd craned it at an awkward angle against her back.

Minne shouted in pain. Dorian felt her start to draw on her Talent. He tried to prepare himself for whatever spell she might cast in her effort to get away, but then, just as suddenly as she'd started to gather her power, it left her. Yellow light burst from her center, snapping across the room until it settled into Elsie's Remora stone. A moment later, two similar lights were yanked from Loreena and Alois, both of them fusing with the glowing green stone.

"No!" Minne shouted. "What have you done?"

Dorian stepped back from his stepmother and cringed. Pain spiked through his partially healed wound and he held his side in an effort to keep balance. The room spun in his vision but he caught the basics of the battle. Winslow had subdued

Loreena, who was face down on the stone floor and looking dazed. Victor had managed to pierce Alois with a Remora stone dagger, which put the man out of the fight as well.

Valeda Quinlan knelt beside Elsie, but looked too frightened to touch her. Not that Dorian could blame Valeda. Elsie still had that fixed blue gaze and Dorian could sense that his wife was not really present in these proceedings.

"I have no heir!" Minne wailed and struggled against Rorant's grasp. "Think of my people!"

Dorian looked down at the stone in Elsie's hands. Remora stones were always green, but this one was lit from the inside. The combined Talents of three Witches lay trapped inside and Dorian couldn't suppress a shudder. Every Witch-Born feared the day their Talents might leave them. And Magic had very quickly, without preamble, taken back the blessing he had given those three.

"Magic!" Minne said, addressing Elsie. "I know you can hear me, my Lord! You must know that I did it for you. It was all for you, my Lord. To free you from her."

Elsie did not look at her. Instead, she very slowly handed the glowing stone to Valeda, who took it with quiet reverence. Dorian watched as Elsie smiled compassionately at Valeda and touched her cheek as a mother might a child. The voice that spoke through his wife was not her own, but that of Magic, reverberating through his core.

"I am where I must be."

"What?" Minne gasped. "No, that can't be true. I can free you! Don't you all see? I can free him!"

The tattoos in Elsie's arm faded. She blinked once and her golden eyes were back, no longer the blue of Magic. Dorian felt a surge of relief and limped to her side. Elsie smiled up at him, exhaustion lining her features.

***

Elsie slumped against Dorian in the private carriage and sighed. Valeda and Winslow sat across from them, looking every bit as exhausted as she felt. *But then,* she thought as the carriage lurched forward, *my exhaustion is unnatural*. This was more than the feeling of too many hours at practice. Her arm felt numb, heavy and dead, and were she not cradling it in her lap, she thought it might slip right off her body.

She'd been aware of the goings on in that little room under the fortress, but she had also been distant from it. The moment Alois had kicked Dorian in the gut, she'd been yanked from her very consciousness and shoved into a corner in her mind. Magic could take her form, could use her body in any way he pleased. As humbling as this revelation was, Elsie couldn't help wondering why he hadn't done it before.

Surely the people would listen to him more than they listened to her.

Brasen has never been put back, she thought. *Magic had become Brasen. Why would Magic remain in him, but only half participate in me? Is it a gender issue? Or had the Dellidus taken so much power that Magic was now unable to come and go as he pleased?* It had taken quite a bit of focus to work around that stone and at first Elsie had only found the faintest pinprick of power. But the moment she accessed it, Magic had burst through.

She hid a yawn behind her hand. Her whole body ached as though she'd been hefting forty pound rocks all day. Her head felt heavy and her mind muddled. Closing her eyes, she let the jostle of the carriage lull her.

Elsie dreamt of the day she'd buried her sister. On an edifice high up in the mountains, far removed from anyone or anything that might disturb her, she had said her final goodbyes. Her heart still ached at the loss.

In the middle of her mourning, Magic had come. All of her being held still in his presence. She could still see him, smiling down at her, his golden tattoos crinkling up with his compassion. He'd spoken then of Fate, of the mysteries that surrounded Bryva's death and the life of Delgora House. But now, in her vision, she heard him say something else to her.

"If I were to speak through you again it might kill you, Elsie Delgora. Can you not feel your strength abandoning you?"

She *could* feel it, seeping out of her bones and into the ether. For a moment she panicked, thinking of the ark and all the people who depended on her. She had to be stronger than this. She had to fight. But try as she might, she could not get her eyes to open. The dream faded and she drifted off, trusting that the crisis had passed and that Magic would somehow wake her if she was needed.

CHAPTER TWENTY-SIX

The stone fit easily in the palm of her hand. Its smooth contours and jagged edges had a sort of chaotic beauty, as though its symmetry could not have formed any other way. It was an echo not only of the Talents now captive inside, but of the constant battle held back by the Warding Pillars. Valeda imagined she could almost hear the growl of the Wild rumbling through the stone, underplayed by deep drums that beat harder and faster until her heart clamored to keep its pace.

War is coming, it told her as she stared at it.

She stood sequestered in a small alcove to the side of the stage. Valeda knew instinctively how to regulate her temperature now. Otherwise she imagined she'd be frozen stiff. Due to the danger of the moment, she'd chosen to wear the riding pants and bodice Elsie had given to her in Delgora. They fit perfectly, but were made of a lighter material better suited to the tropics. She wore a jacket and gloves for appearances, though she had a feeling the rest of Magnellum was about to learn of her newfound Talent.

The opening ceremonies of Winter Tournament were about to begin and Elsie was somewhere in the crowd, prepared to interrupt the revelry. It seemed senseless to Valeda that they were trying this. The people had already been warned about the coming disaster. They hadn't listened then and they likely wouldn't listen now. In fact, if things turned violent, Valeda had strict instructions to run hard and fast for their awaiting dirigible. Winslow was supposed to watch out for her, which gave her some comfort. He hadn't left her side since she'd discovered Monty in her room two days ago.

Could it have been only two days since poor Monty's death?

So much had happened that it felt strange thinking of him now. Rescuing Elsie and Dorian was a hullaballoo she doubted she'd ever forget, and then the arrest of Minne, Loreena and Alois. Winslow had spared her from having to sit through the Council's emergency meeting, but she knew the trio were now sitting, Talentless, in a Warder's holding cell.

The Talentless part of their conundrum was what puzzled Valeda the most. It felt important, almost strategic. Magic had wanted all of them in the same room, had wanted Elsie so focused that he could work on drawing out those three. Which made her wonder why her Talent hadn't been taken. Or Winslow's for that matter. She liked that it had been the antagonists of the encounter who were targeted, but she couldn't help wondering what it was all for.

Something bigger was at play here; she could feel it.

She rubbed a smooth expanse on the stone with her thumb and watched the light within react to her. She could feel the Wild in her stirring. It was equal parts attracted and repulsed by the stone, like watching a fire rage through a forest, seeing both the tragedy and the beauty of the flames. Her Talent, which she assumed she should not be able to sense while holding the Remora stone, had the same feeling about it.

"What are you?" she whispered to it. "And why did Magic give you to me?"

Winslow shifted in the shadows beside her. Valeda blushed. She'd forgotten how close he was.

"I imagine you're concerned for my mental state now," she said with a sheepish laugh. "Talking to stones and such."

"I've always been concerned about you," he said. "Though I admit, talking to a stone does seem slightly more alarming than your other quirks. Let me know if it talks back."

"Other quirks?" Valeda asked, returning the stone to her pocket. "Just how many quirks do I have?"

"Oh, you have several," Winslow said. He moved to the entrance of the alcove and looked out.

Two young lords had taken center stage and the crowd roared to life. They hoisted a large trophy, identifying themselves as last year's tournament winners. Valeda felt her pulse quicken. Any moment now, Elsie would make her move.

"You're far too independent," Winslow said conversationally. "And headstrong. You hold your breath when you're angry. And you hum to yourself when you're reading, but not while you're writing."

"I do not hold my breath when I'm angry!"

"You don't?"

"No, I most certainly do not."

"You're quite certain?"

"Absolutely!"

He hummed and shrugged before looking back to the stage. Valeda glared at him. The nerve of the man to make such a summary of her! What did he mean she was "far too independent"? She was proud of her independence.

"Breathe, Vee," he said, with a chuckle.

Valeda inhaled sharply. She felt her cheeks burn and she stammered for some kind of rebuttal. He was teasing her. They were about to anger the whole of Magnellum society and the arrogant man was teasing her.

"You're also the bravest creature I've ever seen," he said.

"This is no time for teasing, Lord Agoston."

"Call me Winslow," he said and grinned at her. "And I meant every word."

"You're incorrigible."

"So they all say."

Valeda crossed her arms and turned to watch the stage. She felt exposed by his words, and foolishly good. But she knew him well enough now to know that his mood was about to change. *This is his pattern,* she reminded herself. *He shows affection and then he shoves you away.* The sooner this business is done, the sooner she could get away from him.

Out in the courtyard, Elsie and Dorian stepped onto the stage. The crowd went quiet. No one seemed to move, not even to whisper their appall. Valeda bit her lower lip and prayed the Fates would be merciful. Upsetting the Untalented was bad, but prodding the fury of the Witch-Born Council as they were could result in a swift execution for all parties involved.

And she was inextricably involved now.

The thought made her queasy and Valeda scanned the crowd, identifying the nobility.

Magnellum had thirteen Houses, each with a House Witch. As powerful as Elsie and Dorian might be, twelve against one were still bad odds. *Well,* Valeda thought, *eleven against one*. Caresse and Bartholomew Feverrette were already on the dirigible, keeping it ready for their departure.

She spotted Morgana Agoston at the front of the crowd and shuddered. This was going to end badly, she could just feel it.

"People of Magnellum," Elsie shouted above the rustle of feet on snow. "Eight years ago Fate gave us a warning. Fate told us that the time would come when the Pillars would fall."

Valeda felt a surge of pride at how confident Elsie sounded. No matter the odds, Elsie Delgora was going to do as she believed was right. The woman was uncompromising and unabashedly herself. There wasn't another witch in all of Magnellum who could deny her that.

"You've all heard the rumors," Elsie said. "Some of you have even had to evacuate your homes due to the crumbling Pillars. You know that it has already started."

Several of the Witches began to protest, but Elsie overrode them all by removing her glove and lifting her tattooed arm.

"Magic is dead!" she proclaimed.

The Untalented in the crowd rose up at this, silencing the Witch-Born and demanding to know more. The entire courtyard teemed with urgent voices, alarmed families trying to locate each other and a great many Witch-Born simmering in anger. Elsie ignored them all and plunged through her speech.

"The Pillars are falling! One by one they are crumbling. The Wild is coming and we must stand united to face it."

"How?" several voices rang out.

"In Delgora there is an ark. It will keep some of you safe. I beg of you, send your children and your women to safety. Do not delay! The enemy is approaching . . ." Elsie said.

"The enemy has been hammering at the Pillars for years!" Morgana Agoston said and climbed the stairs onto the platform. "Ignore Lady Delgora. She has gone mad."

Whatever else might have meant to follow Morgana's statement was lost. A massive vine shot up from the ground, hurling rocks and dirt through the air. It bent and swiped at the screaming crowd, scattering bodies in its wake. Valeda stepped forward, too stunned to recognize fully what she was seeing.

Five great cats leapt out of the crater in the ground and began to attack. They were striped orange and white, just as magnificent as Winslow had described to her, and just as deadly. Valeda watched as one cat tackled onto the back of a retreating man, its jaws clamped tightly on the juncture of neck and shoulder. It released the man, lifting its blood-stained maw to snarl at the fleeing crowd.

Valeda felt her stomach pitch at the sight.

Winslow grabbed her shoulder and drew her back into the alcove.

"Stay here," he ordered.

"What?"

He turned and ran into the fray, propelling himself forward with his magic to intercept one of the cats. Valeda held onto the alcove wall and watched as Winslow snagged the creature by the tail and swung hard, spinning until its feet lost purchase with the ground. Then he released, sending the cat soaring into the fortress wall several feet away. Valeda felt the shudder through stone as it crashed into the wall.

The cat slumped down, dazed, and struggled to return to its feet. It looked helpless and defeated, but Winslow was suddenly at its side, leveling his pistol at its face. Her heart ached at the sight and she had to look away before he pulled the trigger. The Wild in her lamented the creature's death in spite of the terror in the yard. *Something so beautiful deserves better,* she thought.

At the center of the yard she saw the vine curl itself around the obsidian and gold fountain of the Fates. It ripped the fountain out of the ground, spewing rock and water over those few Untalented still trying to escape. Then it raised the statue high, the three-faced depiction of Fate glinting in the moonlight just before the vine threw it at the stage. Several of the Witch-Born had rallied at the base of the stage, trying to protect the Untalented in their flight. They all scattered, desperate to get out of the way.

"*Susbeni!*" Elsie shouted.

She was still on the stage and had one arm lifted, all of her focus riveted on the falling statue. The fountain stopped, water and rock suspended in the air. For a breathless moment, those beneath the wreckage stared, and then they all scrambled to get out of the way. Elsie fell to her knees under the strain, holding the mass of fountain aloft until she was certain everyone was safe.

The vine had other plans. It whipped across the stage, striking Elsie in the chest and breaking the spell. Dorian, engaged in a fight of his own with one of the cats, shouted something that was lost in the crash. Valeda gasped as Elsie went flying off the stage. She hit the ground several feet away and rolled to a stop near the alcove. Valeda ran to her, sliding to her knees beside the Lady's prone form. Elsie coughed and wheezed as Valeda searched for something she could do to help.

"My Lady!" Valeda said.

Elsie rolled to her side and smiled weakly up at her. "Miss . . . Quinlan."

Valeda looked up at the battle. She needed a male Witch-Born to heal Elsie. Several witches had gathered together and were fighting the vine, each of them chanting and throwing different spells at it. Valeda couldn't recognize any of them, but she could see the effects of fire and ice as they hit the vine in turn. The men were all focused on the cats, most of them too far away to hear her call for help.

"You will need to be brave now, Valeda."

She looked back down at Elsie, frustrated at how helpless she was. But Elsie was not looking at her. Instead, she stared gravely at a point just behind her. Valeda felt the hairs on her neck stand on end. Very slowly, she turned to look.

Another cat stood there, malevolently gazing at them both. It was enormous, its paws twice the size of Winslow's hands. It had one green eye and one blue eye and the fur that should have been white was stained pink from battle. Its ears flattened and it made a sharp, terrible sound that nearly made Valeda's heart stop.

She heard a distinctive click just beside her. Elsie had drawn her pistol. Weak as she was, the woman aimed her weapon at the creature.

"Run now," Elsie said and fired.

The crack of the gun partially deafened Valeda, but she still heard the cat cry out in pain. Or maybe she felt it because the Wild in her seemed to cry out too. But it was the magic in her that got her to her feet. Valeda hoisted Elsie up and flung the taller woman onto her shoulder. Her Talent made lugging the woman easy and she ran for the alcove.

They had almost made it when Elsie was suddenly whipped away. Valeda fell backward with the force, landing half on top of Elsie. A heavy paw struck her shoulder, sharp claws piercing through layers of jacket and skin. Valeda grabbed the paw and shouted in agony. Then its mouth clamped onto her shoulder and it started to shake her, yanking her off Elsie.

Valeda tried to dislodge its grip, but it only shook harder. She tried to get leverage with her feet, but the cat kept dragging her back, pulling her away from Elsie and the alcove. Her head struck the ground several times before she quit struggling. The last thing she saw before darkness took her was Winslow running at them. He didn't look frightened or angry, just determined.

***

He ran harder and faster than he'd ever run before. His legs strained and his lungs burned, but he pushed his magic to keep going. He'd been so embroiled in battle that he hadn't noticed Valeda leave the alcove. His Talent had told him of her pain, alerting him to the danger and he'd immediately began searching for her. What he'd found was a great cat lugging her toward the crater.

He wondered why the cat hadn't killed her already.

They'd just reached the lip of the crater when Winslow caught up. He shouted and threw himself onto the cat, tackling it with all the force of his magic to help. The creature lost its footing and slammed into the ground. Winslow kept hold of it as they slid over ragged stone and overturned dirt. His knee bashed into something sharp and he felt his toes go suddenly numb.

It released Valeda as they came to a stop and immediately lunged for him. Winslow jerked away from its teeth, then had to dodge a paw as it swung at him. He swiveled around the paw and launched himself for its neck. He got his left arm around its throat and threw his leg over its massive back, determined to choke the life out of it.

The beast bucked and shook, but Winslow just held tighter. He felt it struggle to breathe, felt it try to pull its head out of the lock and for a crazy second considered biting it. Then he saw another cat emerge from the hole. It went straight to Valeda, bit her by the ankle and headed back for the crater.

Winslow couldn't release the cat and he couldn't just watch her get taken.

Above him, the vine groaned under pressure. The witches had managed to subdue it and the giant thing was about to fall. He saw it teetering and knew instinctively which way it would collapse. Valeda's head disappeared into the crater. Winslow let go of the cat and ran for her. He didn't know how many more would be in there but he couldn't leave her.

She was brave and intelligent and irrational and, Fates help him, he needed her.

He leapt into the crater just as the vine fell over it. Stone and dirt pushed him down. For a dizzy moment he didn't know which direction was up. Then something grabbed him by the leg and wrenched him out of the debris. Before he could regain his equilibrium, he was pushed flat against rocky ground with something heavy and sharp pressing into his chest.

He tried to call on his Talent to give him clearer vision in the dark, but it wouldn't respond.

Remora stones, he realized. He was lying on top of dozens of Remora stones.

"We must go back!" a heavily accented voice called through the shadows. "Octamin was almost to safety."

"We can't go back." This voice was closer, practically on top of him, and distinctly older. "The vine has fallen. There is no returning. The witches will have the wards up soon and we must leave."

"But Octamin—"

"Was a brave soldier. He brought the abominations to us. Now we must do our part."

Two, Winslow decided. There were only two of them. But without his magic he couldn't hope to fight even one of them. Octamin must have been the cat he'd been fighting. The rest of their party was cut off in Magnellum, now at the mercy of the Witch-Born. He almost felt sorry for them, but his mind caught up with the conversation.

"The abominations" had to be a reference to Valeda and himself.

Winslow chose not to struggle as their captors began dragging them away. He felt every stone scratch into his back, felt the sharp clamp of teeth on his shoulder, but let it happen. They were needed for something. He didn't know what and he didn't care. All he knew was that he had a little time left and only one option at his disposal.

He had to connect with his Wild. It was the only way he would have the strength to get them both out of this alive. Closing his eyes, he thought back to his school days, to those first few lessons with magic. His Wild was connected to him in much the same way as his Talent, it wasn't a far stretch to believe he could access it the same.

"Relax your mind," he could almost hear Mistress Abigailia coaching him again. "Just breathe and relax. Every Talent is particular to the Witch. It will introduce itself to you with an image. Something that you alone can summon to mind when you need to access magic."

His Talent had always been represented as a loom, which he'd thought was bizarre. But he'd learned to access different elements of his magic by focusing on the different strings, which helped him considerably in combat. He imagined those with more complicated visions of their Talent took a good deal longer to master.

But his Wild would be different. It wouldn't be an object. It would be a creature.

Their captors didn't speak further. They just kept dragging them through the tunnel, so Winslow ignored everything else and concentrated.

An image started to form in his mind; snowy terrain and sharp rocks. On a ledge staring back at him, looking agitated and ready to pounce, was a cat with black-spotted white fur. It was different from the striped cats that had attacked Magnellum, slightly smaller, but just as menacing. All slender curves and lean muscle, the creature paced on its ledge and Winslow had to quell a spurt of fear.

This was the Wild in him. This graceful, deadly beast was what dwelt under his skin. He could feel its anticipation, its desperate desire to be free.

It was not friendly, as his magic had been. His Talent had always welcomed him to use it, to work the strings of that loom until he could move them all without having to think about it. His Wild, on the other hand, dared him to access its power.

What now? he wondered.

Mistress Abigailia's voice came back to him: "Now you take control."

With a careful breath, Winslow focused on the creature.

CHAPTER TWENTY-SEVEN

Dorian leapt off the stage and ran for Elsie. Behind him his father had mostly subdued one of the remaining great cats, leaving him free to find his wife. He knew she was still alive, he could sense that much, but she was also severely wounded. He could feel it in his chest, a growing, unified ache pulsing through him.

She lay in a tangled mass of cloak face down in the dirt. Dorian slid to a stop beside her, kneeling and gathering her up as quickly as he could. Her head lolled to the side and her limbs were limp in his grasp.

"Elsie Varene Delgora, you do not die here," he said firmly. "Our last moments are in Delgora by the ark. I've seen it. Now wake up."

He tore his gloves off, somehow managing to keep her close without dropping her, and pressed an open palm to her cheek. Their skin met and he felt her Talent flare in response. She'd exhausted herself when she caught the fountain and he was surprised Magic hadn't helped her. He could sense the deity in her, lying in wait, and had to suppress his outrage. Magic could have stopped her from getting hit, could have stopped the whole blasted attack if he'd wanted to. Why in Fates had Magic allowed this to happen?

Elsie groaned and Dorian focused on healing her. The vine had hit her in the right side with enough force to concave several ribs. She was lucky that there was no internal bleeding. Dorian heard each of her ribs snap back into place and grimaced when she cried out. She had a small concussion, several scrapes and bruises, but beyond the ribs he couldn't find anything serious.

Perhaps Magic had helped her after all, he thought.

"You've seen it, have you?" Elsie asked quietly.

He met her golden gaze and held it. As much as he wanted to deny the vision Magic had shared with him, he couldn't lie to her.

"I've seen where we make our last stand," he said.

"At the ark." Elsie smiled and covered his hand with her own. "Then it will work, won't it?"

Dorian remembered the scene all too clearly. He could still see the way the vines smashed into the ark, bending it and nearly breaking in. *Nearly,* he thought, *but not quite*.

"Something more needs to be done," he said. "I don't know what it is yet, but there's something else we need."

"You did this!" Lady Agoston's shrill voice pierced their conversation.

Dorian helped Elsie sit up and scowled at the woman.

"You did this to us! You let that thing in!" Agoston continued.

The fighting was over and those left standing were tending to the wounded. But they all turned now, focusing on Morgana Agoston's confrontation. Dorian could see some of the Witch-Born agreed with her, but for the most part the people were wary and uncertain. If Morgana was compelling enough, she could turn the remnants of this assembly against them.

"Oh, be quiet," Elsie said and stood up. "I've had it with the lot of you. Destruction beats on your door and you'd still rally for a political move."

Morgana gasped. "How dare you speak to me in such a way!"

"I'd dare a lot more than that if I had the time," Elsie said. Then she faced what few Untalented people were left. "A dirigible waits in the city. In one hour it flies to Delgora. If you want to live, then I suggest you be on it."

Dorian grinned at the stupefied look on Morgana's face. He followed Elsie on her trek to the stage, all too happy to ignore the woman. He wondered where Winslow was. The man wouldn't want to miss this. Dorian searched for his friend, but didn't see Winslow anywhere. He was still looking when Elsie stopped beside Rorant.

"That was a bit more curt than I expected you to be," Rorant said.

"I'm tired," Elsie said. Then her focus shifted to the wounded creature at Rorant's feet and she whispered the spell to see the unseen.

Whatever she saw through the vision spell made her frown. Dorian watched as she crouched beside the cat and tensed. Wounded or not, it still had sharp teeth. Elsie stared at it for a long moment, as though she could determine its character just by looking.

"I know that you can understand me, creature," she said. "Can you speak in this form?"

To Winslow's consternation, the cat answered, "Yes."

"Answer me truthfully and I will allow my husband to heal you."

Dorian raised an eyebrow and shared a look with his father. Aside from the fact that he was still trying to accept a talking beast, neither he nor his father wanted to fight the cat again. Winslow's story hadn't mentioned that the people were sentient in this form. Now that he thought about it, he wondered why he hadn't considered them intelligent before. They fought with cunning. They'd even ambushed Winter Tournament.

No, he thought. He hadn't considered them sentient because he didn't want to. It was far easier to think he'd slain several animals rather than cursed men stuck on the wrong side of the Pillars.

"I do not want healing," the cat said.

"A clean death, then. I can end your suffering," Elsie said and waited for a reply. When none came, she asked, "Does the man known as Voruke still lead you?"

"Still? We have no sense of Time. Voruke leads us."

"Is there no way to parlay with Voruke? Surely you can see there are innocents here," Elsie said.

The cat took several labored breaths before hissing its answer, "You're all a blight . . . You Witches with your stolen Talent . . ."

"Magic gave us our Talent, we didn't steal it. Magic made the Pillars. You must see he was protecting us," Elsie said. "Please, there must be a way for peace."

"Return Magic . . ."

"How?"

But it was too late. The cat's eyes closed and Elsie reached out with her altered arm. She touched its paw and sharp light burst around them. It was so bright Dorian was forced to look away. When he looked back the great cat was gone, replaced by a fur-clad man. Rorant exhaled his surprise. It was one thing to hear the story, it was quite another to see the truth. The man looked like anyone else, dark hair and strong facial features, with rough, strong hands.

"The people of the Wild," Rorant said.

"We have far more similarities than differences," Elsie murmured, closing the man's eyes. "I do wish we could show them that."

Dorian held his tongue. He watched as Elsie inspected the man, her slender fingers passing over the dark fur coat that covered him, moving down the arm and to his exposed hand. Compassion flowed from her, pressing into Dorian's Talent. He wanted to share that compassion, but couldn't.

This creature looked like a man now, but it had fought like an animal. Dorian could still feel several bites and scratches in his own body from the battle and could not find the will to pity the dead thing. He'd always prided himself on being an educated, intelligent man, but even he had his limitations. These were creatures intent on killing them all. They'd rampaged through the assembly, tearing down women and children alike. Elsie couldn't really mean to find peace with the people, could she?

Everything Magic had shown them about the events to come painted a bloody, hopeless future. What peace could be found with such focused hatred?

Elsie rose to her feet again and faced him. Dorian moved closer, cupping her cheek and tilting her head up, but he didn't kiss her. He wanted to. He wanted to make her forget whatever pain had spurred this emotion, but he stopped there and searched her gaze instead. Her eyes burned like molten caramel, begging him to understand.

He didn't, of course. How could he understand? Nothing made sense to him anymore. But he would try. For her, he would try.

"It's true, Dorian. Everything Fayree said is true," she said. "I had hoped it wasn't. For all our sakes. What are we supposed to do against this?"

He glanced down at the dead Wild man. Then he sighed, looked back to Elsie and kissed her hand. "We do what Magic created us for. We protect the Untalented."

She looked away from him. Dorian followed her gaze, noting that they were the only ones left. The overturned fountain lay in quickly chilling mud and only the dead cats littered the ground. None of the council had deigned it necessary to investigate their attackers and none of the Untalented were brave enough to remain. He spotted two Warders at the yard entrance, but they appeared to be standing guard, keeping watch over Rorant.

"We should go," Rorant said. "You did give the people only an hour to get to the dirigible."

"Wait," Dorian said. "Where is Winslow?"

Elsie's brow furrowed and she started to search the ground. "Valeda came to my aid. I remember firing my pistol at one of the cats, but after that . . . I'm sorry, but I don't know what happened."

"Perhaps they're already at the ship?" Rorant suggested.

"No, Winslow wouldn't leave without us," Dorian said.

***

They didn't have time to search. Elsie could feel the threat of the Wild pounding against the borders, cracking down the Pillars. They had to get to the ship and head for Delgora. But the panic on Dorian's face made her wait. She would normally require a salt circle and several candles to perform a summoning spell, but they had neither, so she was determined to go without. Both were meant to enhance the range of her magic anyway and Winslow couldn't have gotten far.

Elsie moved to the center of the stage and took a deep breath. Closing her eyes, she focused inward, touching the core of her Talent and calling it to life. It answered, as it always did, and she felt the wind pick up around her.

"I, Elsie Varene Delgora, call for Magic to my side," she said clearly.

Then she asked Magic to show her where Winslow was.

She opened her eyes to gaze at the whirlwind of snow surrounding her. An image formed in the midst of it, showing Winslow and Valeda being pulled out of what looked to be a cave. Valeda was unconscious, her limp form draped over someone's shoulder. Winslow, however, was awake. His hands were bound and the men around him prodded at him with swords and sticks.

He looked up as the image focused on him.

"Elsie?" Winslow whispered.

She knew he could sense her observation. But she also knew he couldn't converse with her. To do that would require him managing a summoning spell of his own and, at present, he couldn't stop. He was being led somewhere and she could sense he was in the Wild.

"Why?" she asked quietly. "Why would they take them?"

"Who took them?" Dorian asked from outside her circle.

"Who is 'them'?" Rorant asked.

"Valeda and Winslow," Elsie said. "They've been taken into the Wild."

"What?" Anguish filled Dorian's voice. "How?"

She dropped the circle and turned to face him. "They're still alive, Dorian. Focus on that for now."

"But—"

"We must get to the ark. There are too many lives at stake." Elsie moved to take his hand. "We will find a way to help them, I promise. But there is nothing we can do right now."

CHAPTER TWENTY-EIGHT

Valeda woke to the sensation of falling. Her body was pitched off the shoulders of some giant of a man and she opened her eyes just in time to see the ground rushing up at her. She tried to pull her hands forward to catch herself, but discovered they were bound at her back. She hit chest first, her chin knocking against the pebbly ground hard enough that she felt the impact through her jaw. She craned her head to the side in defense and her cheek scraped through dirt.

When her body finally slid to a stop, she groaned. Her shoulder flared to agonizing life, piercing her consciousness with pain. She was lying half on top of the wound and squirmed in a desperate attempt to turn over. Flopping onto her back crushed her bound hands, but some of the pain lessened. She lay there, dizzily gazing up at a leafy canopy, and tried to coach herself into thinking properly.

"Vee?" Winslow leaned over her, peering down in concern. "Vee, are you all right?"

It was a truly stupid question to ask. The aching throb in her shoulder had her hissing and the fact that her hands were bound told her of their predicament. They were prisoners. Of whom or what she didn't know yet, but given the unfamiliar landscape and equally unfamiliar men huddled in a circle nearby, Valeda had a sinking suspicion they weren't in Magnellum anymore.

"No," she whispered up at him. "No, I am *not* all right."

Winslow frowned and glanced at their captors.

"Why haven't they killed us?" she asked.

He looked back down at her. His hands were bound as well and his face was bruised from battle. He couldn't hide the fear in his hazel-green eyes and Valeda felt an icy knot form in her gut. They stared at each other for a long moment and Valeda could sense his painful recognition of the situation. Something inside her echoed the warning she felt from him.

Death was too easy for them. They weren't just Talented, they were also Wild. They were something different, something new, and if there was one thing that frightened all people, it was change.

Movement among their captors forced her attention away from Winslow. A new man had joined the group. He wore dark furs and heavy necklaces laden with many claws and teeth. He stood a good head taller than the rest of the men and had the stance and build of a fighter. Valeda was at once impressed and intimidated by the cold black gaze the man sent their way. He was bald and scarred and his features were dramatically angled, like some potter had allowed the clay to partially dry before shaping his face.

"Who is that?" Valeda whispered.

"I imagine that would be Voruke," Winslow said flatly.

"Who?"

"Voruke," Winslow repeated. "Remember? Hates all Untalented. Wants to see us dead."

"And how do you know it's him?" she asked.

"Just a wild guess," Winslow said and smiled wryly at her.

Exhaustion threatened to take her but Valeda forced her muddled brain to concentrate. If they were on the outside of the Pillars, did that mean they were outside of Time, too?

"That's strange," she said quietly. "I don't feel any different out here."

Winslow bent down and she drew a surprised breath, thinking he meant to kiss her again. But he didn't. He pressed his forehead to hers and closed his eyes. She felt her Talent surge to life at the contact, felt her wound quickly begin to mend.

"Try not to cry out," he whispered to her. "They'll notice."

Valeda bit back a whimper and grit her teeth. Her flesh pulled back together, her muscles rebinding themselves where they had been torn. Pulsing between them was the force of their magic, invisible and constant, reveling in the mere fact that they were together. She focused on that instead, remembering their stolen kiss on her balcony in Three Points.

He withdrew a moment later. "Hide it until we can run," he said quietly.

A foot shot out and kicked him in the chest. Valeda shouted in protest as Winslow fell away from her. She tried to move, to turn and see him, but strong arms yanked her up. She was flung over a fur-clad shoulder and had to crane her neck to see Winslow again. She watched as he was kicked in the stomach and growled in fury. She wiggled and squirmed, kicking her feet in an effort to break free, but nothing she did seemed to faze her captor.

She was marched into a large clearing full of people. At the center stood a massive, gnarled tree that seemed to twist around itself. Its leafless limbs looked distorted and sick, clawing up at the sky in an abnormal and disturbing way. Valeda ceased her struggle and stared, stupefied, at both its size and malevolent bearing.

The Host tree, she thought.

She was still staring when she was tossed into the middle of the assembly. This time she was prepared and curled her body, hitting the ground on her side instead of her face. Winslow was shoved to his knees beside her. He spit blood off to the side and muttered a curse, grimacing in anger and pain.

"Behold! Behold my people! The abominations!" the man, Voruke, said from the front of the crowd. His arms spread wide in his proclamation and the great diseased tree stood stark black behind him.

Valeda was shocked by the title, but knew Voruke meant them. Voruke pointed at Winslow, vehemently continuing his speech, "Long have we suffered the plague of Magnellum, but now they seek to harness the Wild itself. Can you smell it on them? Hiding under their skin, twisted by their magic!"

The crowd seemed to snarl at them. They looked very similar to Magnellum denizens, if slightly better in build and height. These people had the lithe, trim grace of the creatures she knew dwelt inside them. All of them had long braided hair stretching down to their thighs and they wore furs of varying color. They were all quite beautiful in a sharp, exotic way and Valeda was almost saddened by the unified hatred they sent her direction.

Her general terror overcame that emotion very quickly.

"But we will suffer no longer!" Voruke shouted. "Tomorrow the Pillars will fall! Tomorrow we will tear Magnellum to the ground and erase its people from the world!"

The crowd cheered at this, rallying to the battle cry. Valeda pushed herself to her knees and glanced at Winslow's grim expression. He was staring at something beside Voruke and she forced herself to look. A strange woven basket lay just steps from the Wild man's feet. It looked innocuous enough, but even she could sense the danger emanating from it.

Somewhere close by, drums began to beat. She could feel their deep rhythm reverberate through the ground and into her chest. It was slow at first, punctuating Voruke's words as he continued to shout at the people, building them all up to something.

"Whatever happens . . ." Winslow started quietly. He stopped himself and she turned to look at him. He met her gaze and held it before continuing. "Whatever happens now, I need you to know . . ."

"What?"

She ignored the drums and the frenzied crowd and focused wholly on Winslow. He smiled faintly at her, but didn't look away.

"I tried to fight it. I thought that somehow . . . loving you would insult Bryva's memory." He swallowed then and his next words came out hoarse and quiet. "I loved her so much, Vee. I planned to mourn her my whole life until you showed up. You with your short hair and independent spirit driving me mad."

"But . . ."

He glanced at Voruke and then back at her. The speech was reaching its climax and they both knew their time was short.

"I pushed you away because I thought it was the only way to preserve Bryva's memory. And I hurt you," he said. "Fates preserve me, but I can't die without letting you know that I love you."

Valeda stared at him, speechless. Simultaneously frustrated by his timing and ebullient at his proclamation, she leaned closer to him. His mouth found hers, kissing her fiercely. She wanted to throw her arms around him, but her wrists were still bound. So she kissed him back, tasting sweat and the faint traces of blood, and prayed he could hear her answer in that.

He was wrenched away from her, dragged by two men and tossed at Voruke's feet. Valeda watched, stunned by too many emotions and the sudden loss of his proximity. They forced Winslow to his knees again, but he was facing her, facing the crowd. A sick feeling gnawed at her center and she couldn't look away.

The drums beat faster now as the basket was brought forward. Even before they lifted the lid, Valeda knew what was inside. Her magic told her, whispered the creature's cursed name into her awareness: *Dellidus*.

Until recently, the creature was nothing more than a myth, but she saw it now. Voruke lifted the long serpent from the basket, holding it at the base of its grotesquely large head. Its mouth opened, revealing curved and dangerous fangs as thick as her forefinger. Reddish-brown scales glistened in the dim light and its muscled tail curled in displeasure as Voruke displayed it to the people.

"No," Valeda whispered, turning her attention back to Winslow.

Someone had lashed a rope around his neck and was pulling him down, forcing his face toward the dirt. Seeing him in that position of forced supplication broke something inside her. She shoved herself to her feet, not certain what she intended to do yet. She just knew she couldn't allow this to happen.

The Dellidus wouldn't kill Winslow, it would take over. It was a living death, a daily torture, to be bound to one. He would have no control over his own body. The creature would feed off his Talent and the man she knew would be gone forever.

"Stop!" she screamed. "You can't!"

She'd gotten no more than three steps before someone knocked her down. Bound as she was, Valeda couldn't find the balance to stay upright and fell sidelong into the ground again. She tried to get back up, but a foot pressed against her cheek and its owner put enough weight behind it that she felt her head might pop. Winslow shouted her name as several hands grabbed the rest of her body, holding her down. It was no use fighting further.

Her assailant's fat, dirty toes obscured part of her view, but she could still see Winslow's face. He strained against the ropes when Voruke bent to speak something in his ear. They weren't that far from her and she could hear him clearly.

"Do not worry, Witch," Voruke said. "Soon, the only thing you'll see when you look at her is food."

Winslow's eyes widened in horror and Voruke let go of the Dellidus. The creature slithered around Winslow's torso, curling its long length about his chest. She saw its head appear just behind Winslow's neck and choked on a sob. Its mouth opened wide and it struck, sinking fangs deep into the muscles at the nape of Winslow's neck.

He let out a tortured cry as the ropes were released and fell to his side. He jerked against the ground, trying to dislodge it, but Valeda knew it was already over. She could sense his magic as it was drawn out of him and pulled into the Dellidus, and stared in despair.

CHAPTER TWENTY-NINE

Using the combined Talents of several witches, Elsie was able to lead one very full dirigible from Lorant lands to Delgora in just over twenty hours. It wasn't as efficient as a transportation spell, but it was a good deal safer. As good as she was at zapping herself from place to place, she wasn't certain she could do the same with another person. Even if she could, the time and energy she would have expended would leave her weak for the encroaching battle.

She was already strained from producing the wind necessary to push the dirigible, but a moment with Dorian should fix that. She searched for him in the crowds disembarking the ship. Just prior to docking, Elsie had given instructions that everyone was to head for the ark. Those Witch-Born who had chosen to accompany them were to help direct the Untalented through the jungle and then take up a position for whatever was coming.

Dorian wasn't on the ship.

She had to lean over the railing to see him, but she spotted his unruly hair at the stables below. He was loading several small children onto the back of a horse. She recognized Forvant and Sir Callen doing the same just beside him. Her heart swelled at the sight. They'd discussed this part. A carriage wouldn't make it up the steep, awkward slopes of the mountain, but a single horse could. The fact that Dorian had to retrieve the horses told her that the Delgora denizens had already fled for the ark.

Elsie prayed Fayree had been the cause of that. She hated to think that Delgora might have suffered the same kind of attack in her absence as what had happened in Lorant. But then, she couldn't see any damage to the town or the Manor. From her perch near the rear of the ship she could see the chaotic sprawl of Delgora Proper weaving through massive banyan and mangrove trees. Just beside the dirigible's dock, the Manor stood proud and unscathed, its grey walls looking formidable in the evening light.

"Lady Elsie," Caresse said, walking up to her, "this is the last group to disembark. I've urged the Captain and crew to be among them."

"Good," Elsie said. She looked back to the crowd and was pleased to find it dwindling.

"Jemima Agoston has insisted she wait for you."

Elsie paused, startled. "Winslow's sister?"

She'd only met the girl briefly at Feverrette House before her own abduction and was ashamed to say she'd completely forgotten about her. Bartholomew had taken to caring for Jemima just after Winslow was discovered in the Wild. She had no idea if Jemima was aware of her brother's whereabouts.

"Yes," Caresse said, glancing to the sword at Elsie's hip. "I fear she is quite adamant and refuses to leave without you."

Elsie touched her hilt and frowned. She'd chosen to wear her Bedim gear and knew many of the Witch-Born recognized it. She'd worried at first that they would balk at her, angered by the trademark assassins' gear, but if she was heading to battle, then she needed what she could fight in.

No one had said anything. Those few Witches who had joined them included Dorian's parents, Lady Jessamine and Lord Rorant, as well as Bart and Caresse, Lord Sasson Clenci, and Gaetan Feverrette—Dorian's half-brother on his mother's side.

And, of course, Jemima Agoston.

"Tell her I'm leaving now," Elsie said. "When we get to the ark, we'll have to throw her in. I don't want her fighting. Winslow would kill us all if anything happened to her."

Caresse nodded and left. Elsie watched her go, noting the riding pants and boots the lady wore. She was unarmed. Elsie wondered if there was time to visit the armory, but knew there wasn't. Caresse would have to depend solely on her Talent when the time came.

Elsie turned to grip the railing and prayed Caresse had been trained well. *Eight witches against the oncoming storm,* she thought; *eight out of a hundred or more populating Magnellum.*

It would have to be enough. Magic probably meant for more Witches to be here, but society had long since forgotten its roots. They were all political creatures now, their servant-hood long abandoned to great halls and wealth.

"Now you listen to me," a small voice said from behind her.

Elsie turned to find Jemima, bony arms crossed against her flat chest, glaring with hazel-green eyes up at her. She was wearing men's trousers that were too big and a shirt that she'd ripped the sleeves from. She had also sawed off the bulk of her hair, which left her with frizzy blonde curls bouncing around the top of her head as she spoke.

"I mean to fight in my brother's stead," Jemima announced stubbornly. "If he were here, he would be fighting beside you. I'm not Untalented and I don't belong in the ark."

Elsie prayed for guidance, but Magic was insufferably silent in this regard. She looked up at Caresse, who was staring in horror at the girl's butchered hair. Bartholomew stood beside his wife, his normally passive expression replaced by pity and compassion. As Winslow's closest friend, Bart would feel obligated to protect the girl, but Elsie could read the pain in him, too. Jemima was a physical reminder of Winslow's absence. It would be difficult for him to separate the two in his mind.

"If Winslow were here . . ." Elsie said, returning her focus to the young girl. "Where would he want you to be?"

Jemima's face flushed. "That doesn't matter."

"I think it does."

"He isn't here." She stomped one foot. "That's what matters."

"No, Jemima," Elsie said, leaning forward to meet the girl's gaze. "Winslow isn't here. And as his friends, we must honor him. So I ask again, if your brother were here, where would he want you to be?"

Her shoulders slumped and the mulish expression fell from her face. Without another word, Jemima turned and trudged toward the last remnants of the crowd. Elsie straightened and watched her go.

“That was far too easy,” Bart said. “She’ll try something before we reach the ark.”

“We’ll just have to keep an eye on her,” Elsie said.

“Keep an eye on who?” Dorian asked, striding forward from the gangplank.

A handful of people were still disembarking, but most of them were wearing the uniforms of the crew. She spotted one or two Warders in the mix. Those were Rorant’s personal men, but they were mostly directing things and likely wouldn’t leave until everyone else.

“Jemima,” Bart answered Dorian.

Dorian frowned. “Why? What’s she done?”

Elsie reached out to clasp his hand. She felt her Talent spark in response, rejuvenating in the space of three breaths as Bartholomew recounted the situation to him. Dorian stood closer to her, obviously sensing her need, and continued to frown in the direction of the people.

“I’ll tell my father,” Dorian said. “He’ll set the Warders to watching her too.”

“Where is Lord Rorant?” Bart asked. “I haven’t seen him since we boarded in Lorant.”

Dorian’s face turned a funny shade of pink and he cleared his throat awkwardly. “My father is giving his regards to my mother.”

“Oh, my!” Caresse gasped and covered her mouth. “Do you mean—?”

“Please, sister,” Dorian said, “let’s not speculate.”

Elsie smiled in spite of his discomfort. For one happy second, she forgot about the Wild and just enjoyed his company. *Everything will be all right,* she thought as she watched him. Somehow, everything was going to be all right. They just had to stay close to each other.

***

The ark had three doors set into its circumference. They were large and curved with the iron of the outer hull bolted down and reinforced in such a way that they hoped the Wild couldn't break through. But even with the three entryways into the monolith, people had to wait in line to get in. Dorian watched them as they breathed their surprise, murmuring about how big and wide the ark was. He could imagine their awe once they stepped inside and were escorted to one of the many housing sectors held within.

Elsie had thought of everything. Gardens, food, clothing, bedding, artificial light—though he had to admit the engineers hadn't done so well with the lighting. But then again, nothing could replace the daylight. He looked up at the descending sun. It hovered on the edge of a distant ridgeline, blazing orange and red across the horizon. The darker hues of twilight seemed to cover its glory, slowing creeping in to invade where the brightness of day once shone.

He felt a chill even in the tropical heat and tried hard not to compare the sunset to Magnellum. But his mind would not let the image go. Big, magnificent Magnellum was on the eve of battle. The Wild was seeping in, leaking through the borders, like the twilight took the day. And just like the sun, Magnellum would disappear from view.

"They really should move faster," his mother said.

Dorian glanced at where she stood, just to his left and half hidden in shadow. Her thick brown hair was draped in a braid over her shoulder, and the glint of her grey eyes shone in the dark. They were far enough away from the crowd that he knew no one else had heard.

"You sound like Elsie now," he said.

Jessamine laughed softly and moved to stand beside him. "A compliment, I think. Your wife has shown remarkable resilience and foresight. She withstood the Council where I failed, and managed to build . . . this."

"You never failed, Mother. You were already married when you met my father. There was nothing you could do."

"There were several things I could have done, Saldorian," she said frankly. "I could have pretended not to love Rorant. I could have pushed him away and avoided the scandal. Or I could have sent your stepfather away. He would have gone, at my request. Aubin is a good man, no matter what you think."

"Why didn't you?" Dorian asked.

He wouldn't normally have braved such a question, but after thirty years of pretending not to be curious, he had to ask. They could all be dead shortly, so he couldn't see the harm in knowing the truth. Several in noble society had called him an abomination, a strange mix between first born and second born that they couldn't understand; first born of his father, second born of his mother, and nowhere to fit inside the normal rules of Magnellum society.

"Because he's a good man," Jessamine said and sighed. "I may not have loved him as I do your father, but I cared for him, nonetheless. I could not cast him out like baggage, merely on account of my heart."

Dorian watched her for a moment, silent. She looked sad and he wondered if she was worried about Aubin. The man had not come at the urgings of Delgora and was somewhere on the mainland. What he remembered of his stepfather was a cold aloofness, a distance that he'd only understood when he'd grown older and learned the truth of his parentage. There hadn't been any cruelty, not from Aubin anyway. Dorian wasn't certain when he'd come to sympathize with the man, but he did. If Elsie's heart ever strayed, he would be devastated.

"No, Mother," Dorian said quietly. "No, you couldn't have."

She reached over and clasped his hand in her own. She had slender hands, warm and strong in his grasp. He squeezed her fingers lightly and turned to look back at the crowd.

A scream pierced the calm procession. Dorian scanned the people, hunting for the source. All at once the crowd surged forward, pushing for the entrances as several more cries rang out. Three creatures leapt from the edges of the jungle, running fast for the people.

These were different from the cats in Lorant. They were more canine in shape, but far larger than a typical dog. Dorian recognized them at once as the creatures from Elsie's vision. He saw them separate and move to each of the different entrance lines.

"Go!" Jessamine said, releasing his hand.

Dorian drew his sword and bent time, pushing his body across the distance to intercept the nearest beast. He made it there just as it started to jump, intent on an old man who was scrambling to get away. Dorian released time and raked his sword in a horizontal slash that hit the creature at its exposed chest. It yelped and crashed to its side, safely away from the old man.

Dorian watched it as it struggled to its feet, backing away in the process. Its left foreleg was useless, curled up and dangling in the quick retreat. As big as the creature was, Dorian felt a pang of regret at having injured it. The move was so natural, so dog-like, that his compassion swelled.

"There doesn't have to be further bloodshed," he told it. "Please, I know you can understand me."

The creature snarled in response.

Dorian ignored the sounds of people running away and prayed someone else had managed the other two beasts. The creature before him hobbled on three legs, its hackles raised, and continued to growl at him. He had the sense it was debating the next move, glancing between him and the quickly fleeing crowd.

"Magnellum means you no harm," Dorian tried again. "Please. Don't do this."

"Magnellum is a scar upon the land," the creature said in reply. "The Wild will sunder it to oblivion."

"There can be peace," Dorian said, keeping his sword pointed at the creature.

"Return Magic, then."

"How?" Elsie asked, coming up from behind it.

The beast growled at them. "Just die."

"Killing us won't return Magic to you," Elsie said. "We didn't pull him out of the Host tree. Sure you can see this."

"It's worth a try."

Dorian scowled. "This is getting us nowhere."

"Agreed," Elsie said, and stretched her arm toward the beast. "*Susbeni temporum.*"

The creature froze, tongue lolling out of its mouth and half crouched as though to pounce.

"What was that one?" Dorian asked.

"Suspension without a time limit," she said. "Basically, he can't move."

"You're certain?"

"Mostly. I've never actually performed that one before. It could last a day or a few moments."

Dorian lowered his sword and eyed the dog-like animal with distrust. "Why were there only three of them?"

"Advanced party," Elsie said. Dorian could hear in her voice that she was repeating this news and glanced at her arm. "The Pillars are cracked and only a few could cross. But the rest will be here very soon."

"Lady Elsie!" Sir Callen ran up to them. He glanced at the wolf with a frown, but refocused quickly. "Everyone's inside."

Dorian looked back at the ark, surprised to find the people gone. *Nothing like a little motivation to spur things along,* he thought. He wondered if their frozen prisoner would howl at the news that his appearance had only hastened the retreat. He certainly hoped so.

"Seal the ark," Elsie said.

CHAPTER THIRTY

Dawn broke on an empty camp. Footprints littered the ground, both human and animal alike, stirring the morning snow into a mix of frenzied, muddy patterns. Campfires were black now, their charred remains hissing smoke as the snow continued to fall. Just an hour before, the place had been a raging, teeming mass of various creatures. From her spot, tied to a tree, Valeda had seen great cats of every size and color, wolves and bears, all restless with impending violence.

They had ignored her for the most part. Surrounded as she was by Remora stones, they must have assumed that she wasn't a threat. They were right, of course. Even if the stones hadn't been there, she still had the morphed one in her pocket. It bit into her thigh where she leaned against the tree, calling her to some kind of action. But she couldn't feel her magic anymore.

She wondered if it had been severed from her when Winslow was taken. Perhaps she'd only had it because of him, and now that he was mutated by the Dellidus, it was gone. That made a little sense. After all, she hadn't been Talented until that incident on his balcony.

Her eyes strayed to the pit into which they had thrown Winslow. It was several feet away, covered by a wooden grate. She could hear him screaming a berserk, half-man half-wild cry of outrage. Every now and then, the grate would rattle, giving evidence to his continued struggle for freedom. Her heart broke at the sound. She wished they'd just killed him.

She wished they'd kill her, too.

Why, she wondered. *Why not kill us? If they hated us enough to call us abominations, then why keep us alive?*

She looked away from the pit. Voruke stood by the massive, sick tree at the center of the clearing. He alone had stayed behind when the others had run off for Magnellum. He faced the tree and fell to his knees, raising his arms in something akin to worship. Valeda watched him. Twisted limbs began to move, curling and swaying as though in response to his prayers.

Valeda felt the stone in her pocket begin to heat. Confused, she shifted against the ropes holding her down and managed to cover the pocket with her hand. Warmth pulsed out, thawing her numb and frozen body. She could sense the Wild in her. She'd never attempted to communicate with it as she had her Talent. She didn't know how and, frankly, it scared her.

She could feel it now. It was angry. Frighteningly angry. At first there was no real form for it. The anger was just present, boiling in her center with no purpose behind it. Then Voruke began to speak, sibilant whispers urging that anger toward Magnellum, and her Wild started to respond.

"No peace," he said, "no mercy."

Valeda closed her eyes and shook her head, trying to dislodge the words from her mind. But shutting her eyes only seemed to connect her to the Wild. She was suddenly a part of a larger whole, no longer just little Valeda Quinlan, but a member of a community. *A community,* she realized, *whose singular purpose is to destroy everything I've ever known or loved.*

For one aching moment, she wanted the Pillars to fall. But that was not her voice raging against Magnellum. She opened her eyes and forced the voices from her mind, cutting them off from her consciousness. She saw the tree again. It was still swaying with Voruke's chanting prayer of hatred.

The Wild was everywhere, imbued in all living things, but that tree was the source. She knew this like she knew her own soul. And she knew that there was something very, very wrong with it. It was a brackish gray color, festering with some kind of moss that drooped and hung off its branches. It creaked and moaned, straining to move, and she could sense that deep anger thundering through it.

But the anger was not for Magnellum. Not originally, anyway. Voruke was the one pointing the fury at their borders, not the Wild.

She gasped at the implications.

If the Wild was being directed by a man, then it could be stopped by a man, too. All they had to do was shut him up.

Valeda struggled to get her hand into her pocket. Voruke was alone. He'd sent everyone off to the war, believing himself safe from the "abominations." Whatever plan he had for them when this was over was most likely violent and painful and she would be damned if she just sat by and waited for it. This was her best chance at taking him down and she knew it.

Her fingers closed on the rough stone and she pulled it from her pocket. It had several sharp edges. She picked one and started sawing at the ropes, periodically glancing to where Voruke continued to pray. Her fingers warmed under the stone where she gripped it, but her knuckles froze in the winter air. The contrasting sensations reminded her of her Talent, its reaction to the Wildness in her.

There has to be a balancing point, she thought; *like scalding water left to cool to the right temperature for tea.*

Fates preserve her, she was comparing herself to a cup of tea. Magnellum was falling, people were dying, Winslow was screaming in pain and she was looking for an appropriate analogy.

"Mother, Maiden and Crone!" she hissed, annoyed with herself.

The rope snapped free and Valeda paused. That had been far too easy. Her toes and body were no longer numb from the cold, either. Somehow she had called on her Talent, and it had answered. She glanced at the Remora stones surrounding her.

"Half Wild, Half Talented," she murmured to herself.

"And still doomed," Voruke said from above her.

Valeda looked up, surprised at his sudden nearness. He sneered down at her, his pitted face wrinkling into the most sinister expression she'd ever seen. He had crooked, yellow teeth, with two prominent canines on either side of his mouth. She could see scars running over his bald skull, crisscrossing in small white lines as though he'd fallen headlong into a bramble patch and never healed.

"Magnellum means you no harm," Valeda said.

She didn't know why she said it. She knew he didn't care. But she wanted to buy time. It was one thing to attack him while he was vulnerable and chanting, it was another thing to try fighting him straight on. She didn't even have a sword.

"What harm are mice to a cat?" Voruke asked.

"They why kill us?"

He crouched down and grabbed her chin, bringing his face intimately close. His black eyes bore into hers, seething and hateful in their intensity. "Because you are mice," he said.

Valeda felt her Talent coil at her center, prepared for action. Without really knowing what she was doing, she shoved him back with one hand. He soared away from her, propelled by the force of her magic. Valeda blinked in mingled surprise and horror.

Before he hit the ground Voruke changed form, his body morphing and elongating into a giant cat. He landed on all fours and immediately sprang for her.

Valeda screamed and rolled out of the way. He came at her again, rocketing himself off the tree. Scrambling to her feet, she turned in time to strike him with the stone. It hit him in the head and Voruke let out a startled cry, falling back into the shape of a man. A great, purplish mark covered the left side of his bald head.

The tree suddenly let out a groan, bending toward them. Several of the branches looked to be reaching for her, clawing in desperation at the air.

"No!" Voruke shouted.

She looked back at him, but he was already up and moving. His fist caught her in the jaw with blinding accuracy. Her open mouth clattered shut, pain blooming through her teeth and straight into her temples. She staggered backward, holding tight to the stone.

He kicked her in the stomach and she fell back. Agonizing nausea churned in her gut. Her body hit something wooden and dizzy lights swirled in her vision, but she still had the stone.

She tried to call on her Talent to subdue the pain, but remembered at the last moment that only male Witch-Born could do that.

Such a stupid rule, she thought, and rolled onto her side.

She was half on top of the wooden grate. In the gloomy shadows of the pit she could see Winslow's blond hair. He wasn't screaming anymore. Winslow leapt at her, far too fast for a normal man. He looked like a streak of blond blur and before she could react, he snagged her wrist and began to fall.

Valeda's arm slipped through a slat in the grate and she crashed back into the wooden surface. Winslow's descent jerked to a stop, anchored by her body. She felt her shoulder pop out of its joint and she screamed in pain. The stone tumbled from her numb fingers, landing somewhere in the pit below.

She called to her Talent—asking for strength, for a spell, for anything—as she tried levering herself up. But the movement only brought Winslow closer. His other arm snaked through the grates and he grabbed her neck. She fell forward again, choking. His fingers dug hard into her throat. She tried to dislodge him with her other hand, but he was too strong.

"Winslow . . ." she wheezed. ". . . please!"

The grate began to crack under their combined weight. She felt his nails pierce the skin at the side of her neck and saw him smile in triumph. The Dellidus had changed his teeth, giving him two curved and horrifying fangs. Darkness clouded her vision and her chest squeezed tight with grief.

Oh, Winslow, she thought.

"This was meant to be done at our victory feast tonight," Voruke said from somewhere nearby. The grate splintered again and her body tilted forward. "But no matter. I'll just hang your empty carcass to the Host tree. The people can spit on you in passing."

Valeda couldn't reply. Where Winslow's fingers had pierced her, she felt a sudden wrenching. It tugged insistently through her, locating the core of her Talent, and began to pull the unseen substance from her. Her scream came out as a high-pitched, half-choked wheeze. The grate finally broke, but Winslow's grip was too strong. She felt him feeding on her Talent even as they fell into the pit.

***

Winslow landed in a crouch, releasing Valeda at the last moment. They couldn't risk her neck snapping on impact, after all. They needed her alive. Her Talent would return to its original form if she died and that would force them to hunt for another Witch to feed from. And they had their doubts there would be any Witches left after today.

Valeda crumpled to the ground, coughing and dragging in ragged breaths. Her beautifully angular face was dirty. He saw smudges of black on her forehead and cheeks and realized she'd been crying.

No, she is *crying.*

The little thing has given up hope.

That's for the best, the Dellidus told him.

He took a step toward her and stopped. He was fully aware of every move he made and simultaneously incapable of stopping himself. At every sign of rebellion, the creature attached to him would draw more Talent out, weakening his resolve. He felt its fangs buried deep inside him. They were a constant, burning torment on either side of his spine. The tail of the serpent clung to his torso, tightening every time he tried to move on his own.

But the worst of it was the invasion of his mind. The Dellidus crept into every memory, every thought. It did not wish to join with him like his Talent or the Wild, it wanted absolute mastery over him. And it had it, mostly.

Valeda struggled to her knees. He could see that her left hand searched the ground frantically for something, but her gaze remained on him. He took another step and stopped.

Winslow knew the creature's will. It would feed on her Talent until she was nearly depleted, then stop. After an hour or so, she would be regenerated enough to feed from again. Hour by hour, day by day, it would keep her until she finally died. And he could not—would not—willingly let that happen.

It drew on his Talent again, tearing the magic out of him until he shouted and staggered. The tail squeezed so tight he couldn't breathe. Winslow stumbled back until he hit the wall of the pit. He clawed at the coils wrapped around his chest, desperate for air and release.

"Winslow?" Valeda asked.

Her voice was a balm. She'd found whatever she'd been looking for and stood with her back against the opposite wall. Her dove-grey eyes were full of remorse and terror.

"Run!" he pleaded. "Vee, you have to run!"

The Dellidus redoubled its assault and Winslow collapsed, screaming in mingled fury and agony. Out of the corner of his eye, he saw her take a step toward him. He threw up one hand to stave her off.

"No!" he said, panting. "Just . . . run."

"Run where?" she asked, but had the good sense to back away.

He arched against the ground as the Dellidus bit down more forcefully. It was getting insistent now. He could read the annoyance and frustration in its mind. It couldn't understand how he had regained control, couldn't fathom why they weren't feasting on Valeda's Talent yet. What terrified him was that he was beginning to wonder why he was fighting it. Feeding on Vee's magic had been more than satisfying—it had been euphoric.

He felt the unnatural bulge of the Dellidus's head press into him as he lay prone, barely able to pull in air. *Was feeding on her worse than suffocating to death? She wouldn't die, after all. He could keep her safe. They could find a quiet place somewhere, far removed from the tribes of the Wild, and they would protect her from everyone else.*

Winslow struggled to refocus his mind. That was the Dellidus talking.

But she would be safe. The tribes would undoubtedly want her dead after today. What did it matter if they fed on her now and again? At least she would still be alive.

"No."

His voice was no more than a whisper, but he heard it for what it was. He heard the sibilant, changed tones, the evidence of just how far the Dellidus had invaded him.

How could he fight something that had taken hold of him at such a primal level? He was saturated in the creature's essence, a captive in his own body. No amount of magic could aid him. Not that the Dellidus had left him much to use.

He thought suddenly of snowy terrain and sharp rocks; a granite cliff face with a ledge, and on it sat a black-spotted great cat, watching him with large, blue eyes.

His Wild.

It still wasn't friendly, but it also wasn't hostile.

Winslow shut his eyes and reached for it. He didn't have any idea what he was doing, but anything was better than giving in to the Dellidus. Heat pulsed in the center of his chest, ebbing outward with a strange surge of strength. He rolled onto his hands and knees. It was an effort to maintain control of his body. Whatever power his Wild had lent him strained under the might of the Dellidus.

With one hand he reached back and gripped the head of the snake. With another shout Winslow summoned all of his strength and ripped the creature off his neck. He felt its fangs tear out of him, felt his mind suddenly freed from its influence, and immediately had to tighten his grip as the Dellidus snapped at him again. His ribs cracked under the squeeze of the creature's tail, but he knew better than to let go.

Winslow rolled onto his side, wrestling the serpent's head around until he could grab hold with both hands. Its mouth opened wide, curved teeth stained with his blood, and it hissed up at him. He felt his magic sputter to life and recognized when it had fused with the Wild in him. In an instant he was rejuvenated and dug his thumbs into the creature's throat. He slammed its head into the ground over and over again until he was certain it was dead.

Panting, Winslow released the limp Dellidus and began to squirm out of its coils. He shucked off the serpent's tail and staggered to his feet. The fusion of Wild and Magic made him giddy and he had to brace himself against the dirt wall.

He'd done it. He'd broken free from a Dellidus. It was impossible, but there it was.

He stood there, staring at the smooth, curved scales of his former captor, and almost forgot where he was. Then Valeda rushed over to him, wrapping herself around him one-handedly with near as much strength as the animal. He cringed as several of his ribs protested, but held her anyway.

"Fates alive!" Valeda whispered against his chest.

"Indeed," Winslow said. He kissed the top of her head. "Let's never do that again."

She huffed a laugh and held him tighter.

The grate overhead flew open, thrusting more light into the pit. They both looked up as Voruke leapt down. The man changed on the drop. There was nothing fantastical or violent about it, he simply changed, landing on all fours in the pit. Winslow recognized the great cat at once. Its jaw was askew and it had a familiar presence that drew him back to the train wreck.

"You?" he asked, altogether surprised. He hadn't thought Voruke would be so bold as to attack inside Magnellum while the Pillars were still up. Then again, from what he knew of Voruke—which was next to nothing—the Wild man's hatred probably drove him to it.

Winslow read the violence in the creature and very carefully pushed Valeda behind himself. He had no weapons, just magic. He would need something more than that to fight Voruke in this form.

Form, he thought, remembering his own spotted cat.

It was time to give his Wild a little more freedom.

CHAPTER THIRTY-ONE

Elsie felt it when the Pillars fell. Like the reverberation of a thousand drums all struck at once, it hit her and she collapsed to her knees. The incantations that had gone into securing the Pillars dispelled, rushing back to her, back to her arm, with a flood of power that left her dizzy. Her tattoos flashed in sudden golden color, too bright to look at. She heard several people exclaim their surprise, and then the light faded to its normal glitter in her skin. A moment later, Dorian was at her side.

"Elsie?" he asked, kneeling down.

"It's starting," she said.

"Is she all right?" Rorant asked, rushing up to them.

"Yes," Dorian said, and looked up at his father. "Tell them all to man the lines. We won't be alone for long."

Rorant nodded once and ran off. Elsie watched him go. Their meager number made a perimeter twenty feet away from the ark and lined by torches. Ten feet behind the Witches stood the Warders and what few Hemic knights they'd managed to find. Elsie felt guilty about not promoting Hemics in Delgora. She'd left the faction of Untalented fighters alone ever since her sister died. Bryva would have slapped her upside the head for such a gross oversight.

Forty men in all, she thought. *And every one of them is doomed. Every person outside of the ark, Witch and Untalented alike, would be dead by morning.*

Elsie had led them all to their deaths.

"Elsie," Dorian said, forcing her to look at him. She expected to see fear in his face, or regret or pity, but was greeted instead by firm resolve. He cupped her cheek, his steel-grey eyes echoing what his magic was already telling her.

We're as ready as we can be and I won't leave you.

It was the second thought that gave her the most comfort.

"Dorian!" Bartholomew's voice tore into their silent conversation.

They both stood as he approached. On either side of him, Bartholomew towed two smaller figures. Even in the shadow of night, Elsie recognized Jemima. Jemima looked defiant and surly, glaring up at Bart as he stopped in front of Dorian.

"I'm sorry. I'm so sorry," Bartholomew said. "I swear I watched her go in."

"I did go in," Jemima said. "And then I snuck out."

"Why would you do such a thing?" Dorian asked, his voice barely holding onto a civil tone.

"Because I can fight!" Jemima said.

Something grabbed hold of Elsie's leg and yanked her downward. She caught herself with her hands before her face could slam into the ground and hissed in surprise. An instant later, several massive vines exploded out of the dirt and battle began. She looked down to find a smaller vine wrapped around her leg. A dozen more of the little vines thrust up at her, capturing her arms, her waist, her neck. Before she could think to escape, Dorian's sword flashed, slicing through the vine anchoring her neck. The vine flopped frantically about and then snapped back into the dirt.

"Get her out of here!" Dorian shouted to Bartholomew as he continued to attack the vines holding her.

He freed her right arm and she immediately grabbed her dagger hilt. She felt the pressure at her waist release, knew Dorian had cut another vine off, and set her own dagger to the vine on her left arm. She cut herself in the process of sawing through the tough green thing, but ignored the sting of pain. It too went flopping to the ground before sinking back into the dirt.

Dorian helped her up as the last of the vines were cut. They shared a brief look before a bright blue light drew their attention to the Witches' line. Caresse stood out front, her hands stretched forward. A dozen yards ahead of her, several wolves crashed into a barrier of ice too thick to break and too high to jump.

Two of the larger vines curled around the icy wall, crushing it down until the wolves could pass. Elsie glanced at Dorian, who nodded at her. She drew her sword and ran for the front line. The jungle ground was soft and uneven, but she'd trained here all her life and knew how best to keep from falling. Propelling herself with her Talent, she reached Caresse's side just as three hounds leapt for the woman.

"Susbeni!" Elsie shouted at the closest beast. It stopped mid-jump and she turned, dragging her sword in a diagonal slash that cut through the creature from its chest to its midsection. Only then did she release the spell and the wolf toppled to the ground.

Caresse set one wolf on fire and Dorian skewered the third. Ascertaining that Caresse and Dorian were safe, Elsie scanned the battlefield. Rorant and Jessamine fought side by side, their combined magic spurring every stroke and spell with terrifying accuracy. She watched as Jessamine made a powerful push that knocked back two wolves and sent them flying several feet away.

"Elsie!" Dorian shouted.

She turned in time to catch another wolf by its throat, summoning as much strength as she could under the surprise. It yelped and snarled as she threw it at her feet. The wolf tried to roll back onto all fours, but she stabbed it with her sword, equal parts relieved and horrified by the sight.

We shouldn't have to do this, she thought.

There should be peace.

Wave after wave, the beasts came, pouring out of the jungle with staggering speed and bloodlust. Elsie lost track of time. Every moment she had to breathe was cut short by another series of attacks. When she wasn't fending off a hoard of wolves, she had to focus on what vines were closest to them. The blasted things didn't seem to care how thcy swung, knocking down or smashing both Wild creatures and Witches alike. She tried suspending one as she had in Lorant and was rewarded by a dozen smaller vines trapping her legs. Her Talent strained from overexertion. Dorian was too far away to touch, so she reached for Magic, but the deity was mournfully silent.

Why do this? she thought furiously. *Why stand by and watch us all die? He'd made the Pillars to protect us and now he was content to see us all slaughtered?*

"We can't hold them here," Caresse said from behind her.

Elsie could hear the exhaustion in the woman's voice, but focused first on tearing away from the finger-sized vines holding her legs. Caresse was right. They could manage to hold off the wolves on their own, but the vines posed a greater threat. But falling back to the Warders would almost certainly mean the Untalented warriors' deaths. And then the larger plant-life would be in reach of the ark.

She saw one such vine crash into the ground near Lord Clenci. It swept the young lord off his feet and threw him toward the ark. Elsie prayed the man would survive the fall.

She tore her foot away from the last little root and glanced back at the iron and steel monolith.

"There's something more we have to do," Dorian said.

She was terrified that the ark wouldn't hold up against a direct assault.

Because it won't.

"Oh, so now you come back?" Elsie growled at her arm. But the bigger part of her despaired at Magic's words.

Why had he made her build the cursed thing in the first place? It was all for nothing. Everyone was going to die and she never stood a chance at stopping it.

Ward it.

Elsie stiffened and gaped at the ark.

Of course! The Warding Pillars had failed because they'd been spread too thin. The ark, however, was small by comparison to all Magnellum. Warding it would protect the people inside.

She looked to Dorian. He had blood on his face and was panting, eyeing all sides for the next attack.

"I know what I have to do," she said.

"What?" Caresse asked.

"Get everyone to fall back to the Warders. Hold them off for as long as you can," Elsie said. "Dorian, I'm going to need your help."

Elsie dug into her Talent and forced her body to move faster than she'd ever done before. She sprinted past the Warders' line, narrowly avoiding Sir Callen on her mission to the ark. It was difficult, but she tried to ignore the sound of battle close on her heels. She stopped directly in front of the ark's outer wall and fell to her knees.

Pressing her palms to the cold, metal surface she began the Warding incantation. Dorian slid to a stop beside her and gripped her shoulder, allowing their Talents to fuse for the spell. He seemed to know instinctively what she would need. She blessed him for that.

The spell—or, rather, set of spells—was a familiar one. Every House Witch was required to Ward their lands with the Pillars and maintain those boundaries throughout their rule. The only difference here was that she was warding a full, visible structure and not a Pillar.

"*Evioxuote,*" Elsie said—the clear command to strengthen.

Her tattoos started to glow. She felt power pulse out from her, transferring to the ark. Her skin tingled and then burned. It felt like she'd plunged her whole arm into the heart of a fire and couldn't get it out. She ground her teeth together and concentrated.

"*Enioquen,*" she growled the spell for strength.

Dorian grunted and fell to one knee beside her. His sword tumbled to the ground. He was sharing her agony, maybe even trying to heal her, but she couldn't tell him to stop. It was all she could do to focus on the last portion of the spell.

"*Tateuote,*" she whispered.

The command to protect barely made it out of her mouth before a vine struck at the ark. She felt the tremor shock through its iron surface and pleaded for Magic to do something. *This has to work. It has to.*

The glow in her arm spread, pouring out into the ark itself. The light became so intense that Elsie had to close her eyes. She sensed her Talent waning, but knew the work wasn't done. Elsie resigned herself to what she had to do and pushed every ounce of her Talent into the spell.

The burning sensation flared through her shoulder, ran down her chest and into her core. She screamed—more in determination than in pain—and let Magic, the man-god, her constant tormentor and companion of eight years, filter out of her.

This is why Magic hadn't told me everything, she thought, and battled to keep the spell focused. Because he knew the level of sacrifice she would have to pay in order to succeed. She wasn't certain if she was hurt that he hadn't trusted her, or flattered that he'd believed in her at all.

***

Dorian held on with everything he had. It felt like fire had ignited in his very skin, but he just held tighter. Light leaked through his eyelids—the cursed ark was still sharp and white enough that he couldn't open them. Elsie's scream rent him to the core.

She was in pain.

Fates preserve me, so much pain!

And yet, she couldn't stop.

She slumped suddenly, falling back against him. Dorian nearly collapsed himself, but managed to hold her up. A moment later, the light died down and he opened his eyes. Elsie lay unconscious in his lap, still breathing, but somehow different. He spotted that the tattoos were gone. He looked to the ark, shocked to see swirling golden patterns set into the iron structure. They were larger on the ark and easier to see, but still that unmistakable golden hue of Magic.

He watched as a vine tried to strike the roof several yards away. It stopped a foot above the monolith's wall, bouncing off the newly established warded barrier.

"You've done it," he said hoarsely. "Elsie, you've done it."

"Dorian!" Bartholomew suddenly sped to his side, dragging Jemima by one arm.

His heart sank at the sight of the girl. He'd actually allowed himself to believe she'd made it inside the ark safely. Jemima looked terrified, but she was doing her best to stay brave. Bartholomew had been through the rough of it. Dorian could see several scratches running down his friend's left arm, and another set had torn into his pants just above the thigh.

"Dorian, we can't risk opening the doors," Bart said, panting for air.

"I know," Dorian said and turned to focus on Elsie.

He would need to heal her before she could help in the fight. He reached for his Talent and faltered.

His magic was gone.

Stunned, he looked up at Bart. He hadn't thought about how much magic they'd used to seal the ark. He remembered it straining, remembered sensing Elsie's magic waning as well, but they'd kept at it anyway. Normally their Talents burgeoned against one another, growing with intensity when they reached the threshold, but this, he realized, had gone far past that.

"What is it?" Bart asked.

"I—I can't heal her," he said.

"What?" Bart had to duck as a severed vine flew past them.

They both glanced out at the raging battle. The Warders were falling back, heading for the ark. He saw his father decapitate a wolf before seizing Jessamine's arm and running.

Dorian searched inside himself again. *I can't be Talentless! I just can't be! Not when my family and friends need me the most.* But he felt hollow—empty—and the loss of his magic crashed into him.

Still clutching Elsie's limp body, he looked up into Bart's face.

"It's gone," he said quietly.

He knew the battle around them swallowed his words, but Bartholomew heard him anyway. For a heartbeat, they both remained perfectly still.

"My magic is gone," Dorian said again.

Jemima gasped and covered her mouth. She looked more heartbroken than afraid and, for reasons he could not fathom, her expression gave him strength. Gently setting Elsie aside, he stood up and faced the battle. He picked up his sword from the ground and pulled the pistol from his belt. He would fight as a man. There were still Warders standing, he could see them as they engaged the enemy.

I can do this, he thought, taking aim at a wolf charging after his mother.

"No, I will do this," he said aloud and pulled the trigger.

The shot struck the wolf. He saw the creature stagger away and he tossed the pistol away. He didn't have time to reload, and even if he did, he wasn't certain he had any more powder. Three more wolves charged him from the right. He saw Elsie's limp, booted foot in his peripheral vision and clenched his jaw. Every ounce of him ached for his magic, for some chance against the creatures snarling at them.

Bartholomew and Jemima pushed past him to intercept the wolves. Dorian shouted for Jemima, but it was too late. The scrawny, stubborn girl bent time and went blurring through his vision. The aspects of the fight that he could see proved that little Jemima had a strong mastery over her Talent. She took the first beast down by diving at its feet. It jaws snapped at her, but Jemima had magic behind her movements and it missed by inches. Jemima grabbed the creature by one paw and forced it to do a somersault over its own body, crashing heavily onto its back.

Jemima was up an instant later, skewering the wolf's exposed belly with her toothpick of a sword.

Dorian stood in dazed shock and wonder, staring at Winslow's baby sister in action.

A thin vine lashed around his neck. Dorian grabbed at it and tried to turn, but the vine yanked him off his feet. He smacked hard into the ground and dropped his sword. The vine pulled tightly, cutting off his air and garroting him against the ground. He clawed at the vine and dug his heels into the ground, twisting in the effort to get free. His lungs strained for air. Darkness throbbed into his vision, echoing his panicked heartbeat.

A blade flashed above him, snapping the vine and burying into the ground just above his head. Dorian blinked up at Rorant, who stood there panting with Jessamine just beside. Dorian choked on air, coughing and wheezing as he rolled onto his hands and knees.

"Get to the ark!" Jessamine yelled.

Rorant helped him up. He spotted Caresse squashed up against the curving hull of the ark with wolves clawing at her. But the creatures could not tear past the new Wards.

Dorian grabbed his wife and shoved her against the hull, holding her up with one arm. His parents pressed up beside Elsie and an instant later he saw

Jemima, followed closely by Bartholomew, as the two made it to safety. Still struggling to breathe, he flinched as a large vine crashed just above him. He saw magic spark as it absorbed the impact inches away from his face. The vine slid away and reared back for another strike.

"Great," Jemima said. "Now we're trapped."

She was right. He knew she was right. But for the moment he really didn't care.

CHAPTER THIRTY-TWO

Valeda huddled behind Winslow, clutching the stone in her good hand. She could see Voruke's cat form around Winslow's shoulder. He was hunched in the clear indication that he was about to attack and her heart picked up speed. The stone felt suddenly rough and heavy, reminding her of the unnatural bruise it had left on Voruke's head. She glanced down at it, feeling that same sense of fascinated revulsion it had always given her.

Half Wild, Half Talented, she thought. It called out to both parts of her in a compulsory way and for half a breath she couldn't stop staring at it.

Voruke launched forward, yanking her attention from the stone. Winslow moved to intercept, somehow changing in the process. She saw him push off with his feet, saw the way his head bent and his hair transformed from blond to white. By the time he reached Voruke, Winslow was no longer a man, but a massive, spotted cat.

The two cats crashed into each other, each of them making a terrible, ferocious sound that made her hair stand stiff. Valeda watched in dazed horror as Winslow swiped a mighty paw at Voruke, catching the other cat at the jaw and shoving him away. But Voruke twisted, his sinewy body curling around to attack Winslow on the left side. They locked together, rolling toward her in a writhing mass of claws and teeth.

She finally had the presence of mind to step back, but encountered the pit wall. She leapt to the right, narrowly avoiding the oncoming fight. Her foot caught on an uneven bit of ground and she pitched forward, stumbling to her knees and she dropped the stone.

She looked back just as Voruke bit down on Winslow's shoulder. Winslow twisted around, scratching Voruke's side, but the older cat wouldn't let go. She had a sudden, sick feeling that Winslow wouldn't be able to win this fight.

Valeda grabbed the stone again and struggled to her feet. She thought about trying to hit Voruke with it, but was afraid she might accidentally hit Winslow.

Then her mind flipped back to the tree.

When she'd hit Voruke, it had been leaning toward her, trying to reach her. The Host tree seemed somehow connected to all of the Wild. Even she had felt its power when Voruke had prayed to it.

She looked up at the mouth of the pit. Voruke had tossed the grate off and she had a clear view of the tree's topmost branches. Drums beat through her mind again, distant at first and then growing louder, more insistent.

The stone, she realized. She had to get the stone to the tree.

Magic had infused the stone on purpose. He had taken the Talents of three Witches and shoved them inside because he knew she would be here, by the Host tree.

Winslow's voice pierced through her thoughts and she looked back to the fight. He'd returned to the form of a man and Voruke, still in cat form, had his jaws clamped tight on Winslow's collarbone. A heartbeat later and Winslow went limp.

The great cat released him and turned to her. Valeda ran for the closest wall, mustering all the Talent she could find to go faster than she'd ever run in her life. But Voruke anticipated her move. He tackled her, slamming full force into her right side and sending them both to the pit floor. She swung the stone at him, but he rolled on top of her, pinning her to the ground.

His mouth curled into a snarl, revealing thick, blunt fangs still stained with Winslow's blood. Her heart ached for Winslow, who was probably dead or dying just a few feet away. That above all else beat her fear into submission.

Her magic coiled in her center.

Voruke snapped at her face, but she caught him by the throat. She kept him suspended there for a long minute, her fingers constricting around his throat as she tried to think of what to do next. His paw was on her good arm, the one holding the stone, and she could feel his claws sink into her skin as he began to writhe, trying to get away.

An arm snaked around Voruke's neck and Winslow's face popped up on the other side of the cat. With a sudden, angry shout Winslow dragged Voruke off her and threw him across the pit. The cat struck the far wall and fell.

"Go, Vee," Winslow said, moving to stand directly between her and the dazed Voruke. "I've got this."

Valeda hurried to her feet, cringing as her bruised body protested. By the time she was standing, she had to catch her breath again. Winslow wouldn't look at her. All of his being was focused on Voruke, who had gotten to all fours again and was preparing for another charge.

She looked at Winslow's strong, capable stance and knew he was telling the truth. He really did have this fight.

She turned, snagged her magic into functioning, and leapt to the top of the pit. Voruke roared behind her, but the sound was cut off. She didn't pause to look back. Once at ground level, Valeda launched herself toward the Host tree. She thought Voruke might have left someone behind as a guard, but no one stopped her. She reached the giant, sick tree and thrust the stone at its trunk.

Green light burst from the stone and a thin branch captured Valeda's wrist. Several more branches peeled away from the tree, wrapping around her arms, legs and waist. She fell against the trunk and craned her neck away, trying to get free, but the branches pulled her forward, pulled her into the suddenly pliant surface of the tree. She closed her eyes and held her breath as her face passed through a soft, moss-like substance.

She heard a million voices all at once, saw a million indistinguishable things and ceased struggling under the sheer magnitude of what was being shared. She saw the ark in Delgora. Dorian and Elsie and several others lay flat against the ark's outer hull as vines rammed against a barrier of magic too thick to cross. Valeda immediately recognized the golden symbols protecting the ark.

Magic Himself, she thought.

She'd never fully understood the synergism between the man-god and his Witch-Born, but she could feel his affection for them. *Not just for the witches,* she realized, *but for every sentient being on the battlefield.* He was just as pained at the loss of the Wild men as he was for the Untalented scattered through Magnellum.

The fighting had to stop.

The tree groaned around her and she sensed its agreement. The stone suddenly burned her hand. She tried to look down at it, but still couldn't move. She couldn't even open her eyes. She was breathing, somehow, but her chest wasn't moving. Her rational mind began to panic, but then an image replaced the ark in her mind; the golden rope that represented her Talent. It was unraveling, slowing pulling away from her center. She could feel it leaking out of her, through the stone and into the tree.

"She was almost too late," an aged voice said.

"No, she was right on time."

She thought it should hurt more. Her Talent continued to pour into the tree, but instead of the pain she'd felt with the Dellidus, Valeda could only sense a growing warmth around her. *The tree,* she realized, *is coming back to life.* She thought of the way Median had become stuck in Time and began to panic again.

They wouldn't have sent me here to have history repeat itself, would they?

Valeda struggled to break free, but still couldn't move. The warmth spread, curling around and through her with a sense of vitality that she'd never experienced before. It was almost tempting to let it take her, just to remain inside the tree and keep the healthy feeling alive. But she thought of Winslow fighting Voruke and knew she couldn't stay. She needed to get out. She had to help him somehow.

She shouted, but the noise was muffled in her ears.

Valeda stopped as several more images flashed through her mind. They went so fast she felt sick, but she managed to recognize them. The tattoos on Elsie's arm, a train wreck that made her think of Winslow, and the balcony at Three Points.

It was strange to see the balcony from an outsider's perspective. From this new vantage she could see Bartholomew and Winslow's Talents fighting, churning about in elemental battle. And there on the ground beneath Winslow's body was herself, with a clear golden glitter seeping into her skin from all sides.

"Do you see?" Magic asked.

She knew his voice now. Somehow, she'd always known it. And she knew what he was telling her, too. They'd needed Magic's body to die. They'd needed him outside corporeal form, capable of fusing with someone else at will. But that fusing had needed a powerful explosion to initiate it, which explained the elemental battle between Bartholomew and Winslow.

The stone in her hand was acting as a conduit. And the core of who Magic was, or is, now slipped out of her and back into the Host tree.

What she had thought to be her Talent was really Magic Himself. But then, what was Elsie carrying in her arm?

"I am a part of every Witch, Valeda. Elsie just had more of me than most."

But why her? Why had they chosen to use her? Valeda was nothing, just a nosy reporter from Tormey.

"Because you sought me out."

The vines released her and she pulled out of the tree. Valeda took a long, deep breath before staggering away from the Host tree. It was no longer sick, but full and vibrant. She watched as the trunk began to close the hole she'd been sucked into. The stone was gone and she was in one piece and, for some reason, that took its time registering. Then she heard Winslow's voice shouting from the pit and turned away.

They'd returned Magic. Surely the Wild would cease its assault now.

Valeda hurried to the edge of the pit. Below Voruke was screaming, writhing on the ground and alternating between human and cat form. Winslow stood a few feet off, panting and watching the spectacle, but otherwise unharmed. Valeda breathed in relief, too happy to see Winslow in one piece to appreciate fully what she was seeing.

Voruke emitted a tortured sound that cut into her core and she remembered that the people hadn't changed until after Magic left the Host tree. Voruke's form finally settled on his human body, but then Time started in, rapidly aging him. His skin wrinkled, sank into him, and finally he stopped screaming. But then he started to decay, muscle and sinew melting off him so fast that Valeda fought the urge to be sick. When it was over, his bones steamed and an unpleasant sizzling sound filled the air.

Valeda tried hard not to think of how many Wild creatures had undergone the same fate. *Fayree and Mirabella,* she wondered. *Would they be all right?* They'd lived in Magnellum for a while, so there was a chance that Time's reinstatement wouldn't hurt them.

Winslow leapt out of the pit and moved to stand beside her. He looked horrible, all blood-soaked and sweaty, but he was alive. She smiled and hugged him, burying her face in his chest. The Pillars had fallen, Magnellum was sacked, but at least they were alive.

EPILOGUE

For the first day after the fighting ended, Elsie didn't know if she wanted to laugh or cry. She had awoken inside the ark with Dorian sleeping in a chair beside her bunk. Disoriented was a mild word to describe her emotional state. She was simultaneously overjoyed that they had managed to survive, and grieved at the loss of her Talent. She even missed Magic's intrusive voice popping in at unexpected moments.

They had placed her in the ark because it was the only habitable structure left in Delgora. The manor and village were gone, torn down as the Wild had rampaged through. What had been meant as a safe haven was now a base of operations as they began rebuilding.

All of the wolves had disintegrated as Time took its rightful place in their lives. It seemed uncharitable for her to be glad, but at least the fighting was over. Fayree and Mirabella were fine, which relieved her to some degree. She'd almost considered the two as an endangered species or something, but if Magic was back in the Host tree, then they were all of the same race again.

Except that many of the Witch-Born who survived still had a substantial amount of Talent to work with. And Fayree couldn't change form to a cat anymore.

More than a month had gone by and Elsie finally had enough strength to start working. She stood in the middle of her decimated garden, staring down at the remains of her mother's rose bush. She knew Dorian was nearby. The man hadn't left her side since she'd opened her eyes to the new world they were left with. He seemed anxious and uncertain, as though he wasn't sure what he should be doing now.

She couldn't blame him. She didn't know what she should be doing, either. Even if she had her Talent back, there wasn't anything for her to do anymore. It wasn't right to keep the title of "Lady". The people didn't need Witches to protect them.

She was, for the first time in her life, free from obligation.

"You understand now, I think."

Elsie looked up. Valeda Quinlan walked toward her, looking small and powerful all at once. Elsie recognized the stance of a Witch and, for a brief moment, mourned the loss of her Talent again.

"What is it I'm meant to understand?" Elsie asked.

Valeda smiled compassionately at her and Elsie was struck with the irony of the moment. They had completely swapped places. Valeda had come to her seeking answers and now it was Elsie hunting for clarity. And Valeda seemed to play the part of furtive Witch-Born quite well.

"Magic knew the greatest reward he could offer his most faithful Witch was to set her free," Valeda said gently. "The rest of the Witches will be sought after, put back into places of power, because that's what brings the people the most comfort. But you, Elsie Delgora, can become something more. Or less. You can choose your own destiny."

Elsie frowned and looked down. Several dirty, trampled rose pedals littered the ground with bright pink and white. *Free,* she thought. No more politics or assassination attempts. No more servants jumping every time she entered a room. She tried to imagine a life where the only trouble she might face was arguing with Dorian over cutting his hair.

Maybe there would be children.

The images that that brought to mind made her smile.

"Free?" she asked and looked up at Valeda.

"With Magic's sincerest compliments," Valeda said with a nod. "Though he may look in on you from time to time."

Elsie chuckled. "Oh, I would expect as much."

"Expect what?" Dorian asked as he walked into their conversation.

"Nothing," Elsie smiled and took his hand.

She nodded to Valeda and turned him away, leading them both out of the garden. They passed through the remains of the Manor House, walking in comfortable silence. Several of the villagers were out, picking through what had once been their home. Elsie saw them all, alive and healthy, preparing to start again. With a deep breath, she squeezed Dorian's hand and prepared to do the same.

Milton Keynes UK
Ingram Content Group UK Ltd.
UKHW040817030424
440519UK00001B/15

9 781786 954923